ARCHIVING THE UNDERTOW

ARCHIVING THE UNDERTOW

ALYS MYKELS

PART ONE: THE STIRRING SEA

1

CHAPTER ONE: THE LAST DELIVERY

The rain in Ashcliffe-on-Sea wasn't a gentle drizzle, it was a persistent, insistent wet that clung to everything. It plastered itself to the slate roofs of the cottages, slicked the cobblestones underfoot, and beaded on the branches of the wind-battered trees that bravely lined the cliffs. Today, it was particularly grey – not a cheerful, fluffy grey, but the bruised, heavy grey of impending storms, like the sky had been pressed down by something ancient and weary. The sea itself, normally a restless turquoise, was a sullen pewter, churning with a low, constant growl that vibrated through the foundations of the houses. Ashcliffe-on-Sea wasn't beautiful, not in the conventional sense. It was weathered, worn, like it had seen better days and didn't particularly care to remember them. Generations of fishermen and their families had carved a life out of its unforgiving coast, leaving behind a collection of sturdy, slightly crooked buildings that huddled together for warmth against the elements. There was a certain charm to its bleakness, perhaps, but one that felt more rooted in hardship than happiness.

Eve pulled her worn but still serviceable coat tighter around her, the familiar scent of lavender and beeswax – from the polish she used on her bicycle and her mailbag – offering a small comfort. It was just past eleven in the morning, and she was making her last delivery route of the day, the one that wound its way along the narrow lanes leading to the westernmost houses, closest to the jagged teeth of the cliffs. It was a solitary job, this delivering mail. Most people these days relied on electronic notifications, but old Mrs. Higgins still insisted on receiving her letters by hand, and Mr. Linden needed his daily paper – even if he rarely read it. Eve liked that. The quiet rhythm of the route, the brief exchanges with the residents, was a comforting constant in a life that often felt adrift. It kept her connected, she supposed, though sometimes she wondered how much connection was truly needed.

There was something about Ashcliffe-on-Sea, she thought, that made you feel observed. Not necessarily by people – although there were plenty of watchful eyes peering out from behind curtains and windows – but by something older. A sense settled over the town, particularly on grey days like today, a feeling of weight and memory. It wasn't always frightening, just persistent. Like the sea itself was holding its breath, waiting for something to happen. It felt as if Ashcliffe remembered everything, every storm weathered, every secret whispered, every life lived and lost against the relentless backdrop of the ocean. And sometimes, on a day like this, you could almost hear it sighing with the weight of those memories. The rain intensified as Eve pulled her bicycle up to the cottage, a small, almost swallowed-up building at the very edge of Ashcliffe. Number Seven Cliffside was perpetually damp, even on the best days, and today it seemed to be actively trying to soak through the stone walls. The path leading to the front door was slick with mud, and she had to navigate carefully around a pile of driftwood that had been deposited by the latest wave.

The cottage itself looked as if it were slowly being consumed by the sea – grey slate shingles, climbing ivy that threatened to overwhelm the windows, and a crooked chimney puffing out a thin plume of damp smoke. It was one of those places that felt like it should have crumbled into the ocean years ago, yet stubbornly held onto its existence. "Emily Thornton?" Eve called, her voice swallowed somewhat by the wind. Although she knew Emily fairly well, they'd both lived in Ashcliffe for a long time, Eve still felt that the elder lady's seniority meant a level of respect was owed to her. So Eve always used her full name when she was delivering Emily Thornton's post. The door creaked open almost immediately, revealing a woman who looked as if she'd been formed out of old paper. Emily Thornton was small and birdlike, with a face etched with lines that spoke of long hours spent reading and thinking. Her silver hair was pulled back in a loose bun, and her eyes – a startlingly bright blue – held a remarkable sharpness. She wore a simple woollen cardigan over a floral dress, and the scent of old books and lavender hung about her.

"Yes?" Emily asked, her voice thin but surprisingly clear. "You're late. The wind was really picking up."

"Apologies," Eve replied, handing over the mail bundle. "Just finishing my last route." Emily took the bundle with a delicate hand, almost reverently, and laid it on a small table cluttered with books – volumes of varying sizes and ages, stacked precariously high. Many looked as though they'd been rescued from some forgotten archive. "Thank you," she said, her gaze fixed on Eve for a moment that felt longer than it should have. "You have a pleasant face. A bit rosy for this weather, but pleasant."

"Just the usual," Eve chuckled, adjusting her coat. "Ashcliffe tends to turn people rosy."

"Indeed," Emily agreed, turning her attention back to sorting through the mail. "It has a way of doing that." She paused, examining a particularly worn envelope. "Do you find it... heavy? This town?"

Eve nodded, unsure what prompted the question. "Sometimes. Like there's something pressing down on you." Emily didn't respond immediately. She continued to sort through the mail – bills, junk mail, a postcard from a place Eve couldn't quite place – before her hand paused over the bundle she'd received. "How very intriguing," she said, pulling out a small, brown paper package.

Inside, nestled amongst crumpled tissue paper, was an old photograph. It was slightly faded and creased, depicting two young people standing on a windswept beach. The boy – tall and lean with dark, unruly hair – held the girl's hand, her face tilted up to the sky in a smile that seemed to capture pure joy. They were dressed in what looked like early 20th-century clothing: he wore a tweed jacket, she a simple cotton dress."Louisa and Miles," Emily murmured, her fingers tracing the image. "A long time ago." She didn't elaborate, but Eve noticed a flicker of something – sadness? – in those bright blue eyes. Next, she pulled out a single sheet of cream-coloured paper, folded carefully into a square. On it was written in elegant, slightly faded script: "The tide remembers everything. Don't forget to look beneath." Emily frowned, turning the note over in her hand. "That's odd." Emily studied the note for a long moment, her brow furrowed. "I haven't the faintest idea," she said finally, handing it to Eve. "But I have a feeling... a strong feeling... that you should know."

Emily looked at Eve again, her gaze more intense now, as if she were seeing something beyond her. "You remind me of someone," she whispered, her voice barely audible above the wind. "Someone who knew Ashcliffe very well." Before Eve could respond, a sudden gust of wind rattled the windows and sent a shiver through the cottage. Rain lashed against the glass, and for a moment, the room seemed to grow colder. "You should go," Emily said abruptly, her hand instinctively covering the photograph. "The storm is gathering."

Eve hesitated, feeling as though she'd only scratched the surface of something significant. "Is there anything else?"

Emily nodded towards the photograph. "You keep that. And don't dismiss the note. It might be more important than it seems." She paused, then added with a touch of mystery, "Some things are best left to reveal themselves in their own time." Eve was used to the strange and eccentric ways of Ashcliffe's inhabitants – she'd seen enough things on her postal route, things that she kept close to her chest... mostly.

The next day, the news of Emily Thornton's death settled over Ash-cliffe-on-Sea like one of those persistent grey rains. It wasn't a bois-terous, town-wide celebration, more of a quiet acknowledgement, a gentle ripple in the rhythm of their lives. Everyone knew Emily – or at least, they knew of her. She was the steadfast presence on the corner of Cliffside, the woman with the sharp eyes and the scent of old books, always there. Her death felt less like an ending and more like a slow, inevitable tide coming in. The Town Council meeting, held in the draughty hall above the bakery – its walls lined with portraits of stern-faced fishermen and long-forgotten mayors – was sparsely attended. Most residents relied on each other now, a habit ingrained by gener-ations of living close to the sea's whim. But Councillor Davies, a man whose face seemed permanently etched with the worry of keeping the harbour lights burning, insisted it was important to formalize things. "Miss. Thornton," he announced, his voice echoing slightly in the hall, "was, without doubt, Ashcliffe's most devoted archivist. Her home – her life, really – was the Archive." He gestured towards the room at the back of the hall, a small, cluttered space housing the town's his-torical records. The Archive had been Emily's passion, and indeed, her burden for decades. It contained everything from ship manifests dat-ing back to the 18th century, to handwritten accounts of storms, to faded photographs of families who'd long since vanished.

"We need to decide what to do with it all," Councillor Bellweather, a portly man known for his fondness for strong tea and even stronger opinions, grumbled. "It's gathering dust, that Archive. A waste of space."

The discussion drifted on for nearly an hour, punctuated by the occasional cough or the rustle of papers. Most of the councillors favoured simply selling the records to a historical society in a local city – a safe, predictable solution. But then, Councillor Peterson, a quiet man with a thoughtful gaze and a perpetually ink-stained finger, brought up Emily's will. "She left specific instructions," he announced, unfolding a yellowed document. "She bequeathed her entire Archive...

to Eve." A collective murmur rippled through the room. The choice of 'the postwoman,' as Councillor Bellweather had rather dismissively called her, was unexpected, to say the least.

"To Eve?" Davies sputtered. "But she's just a simple delivery girl!"

"Indeed," Peterson replied calmly. "And according to the will, Miss. Thornton requested that Eve digitize all of the Archive's records – photographs, documents, maps – everything. Furthermore, she specified that this digitization should be completed within five years, and that Eve be paid a modest sum for her time."

A ripple of something akin to smugness passed through the council chamber. They'd chosen 'the right' postwoman. Someone reliable, unassuming – someone who wouldn't splash about in the Archive and ruin everything. "And what guarantees do we have that Eve will actually do it?" Bellweather demanded. "She barely seems to know her own way around town!"

The rain hadn't let up when Eve arrived at the hall. It was a heavier fall now, driven sideways by a brisk wind that tugged at her coat and plastered strands of hair to her face. The draughty steps were slick with mud, mirroring the cobblestones outside, and she pulled her scarf tighter around her neck. Inside, the room smelled faintly of damp wool and lukewarm tea – Councillor Bellweather's particular brand. The council chamber was already buzzing when she entered. A dozen or so residents, mostly older, were clustered near the fireplace, their faces a mixture of curiosity and mild amusement. Councillor Davies, looking flustered as always, spotted her first and gestured for her to take a seat at a small table piled high with papers – the same table where he'd been outlining the plans to sell off the Archive.

"Ah, there you are, Eve," he said, his voice slightly strained. "Just in time to hear the news."

The news, as it turned out, was delivered by Councillor Peterson, who looked remarkably calm considering the circumstances. He stood before them, a thin sheet of paper held aloft like a banner.

"As I announced earlier," he began, his gaze sweeping over the room, "Eve has been bequeathed the Archive by the late Emily Thornton." A murmur rippled through the chamber. Councillor Bellweather let out a sound that was somewhere between a grunt and a sigh. "Well, I'll be," he grumbled, adjusting his spectacles. "The postwoman. Of all people."

"Indeed," Councillor Peterson replied, unfurling another sheet – this one covered in neat, handwritten script. He repeated its contents for the benefit of Eve, whose expression had yet to register what was happening. "Miss. Thornton requested that Eve digitize all of the Archive's records for a moderate, regular payment that will tide her over for five years of work."

There was a collective intake of breath. The idea of the Archive – and its contents – being entrusted to the postwoman felt unexpected. Almost absurd. "And... how much is this 'modest sum'?" Councillor Bellweather pressed, already calculating the cost.

"Miss. Thornton didn't specify," Peterson stated simply. "I'm sure we can arrange some reasonable amount for the care of such a valuable collection."

Councillor Davies cleared his throat nervously. "It's a bit odd, isn't it?"

"And there's one more detail contained within the will." He produced a final sheet – another handwritten note, this one even more faded than the others. "'To ensure the Archive's future, and to connect with its past, I entrust it to someone who, upon discovering its secrets, will know which to keep and which to make publicly known.'"

The room fell silent. The rain hammered against the windows, sounding almost like a question. "'Secrets'?" Councillor Bellweather repeated, frowning. "What secrets? This Archive is just full of old shipping records and dusty portraits."

"Miss. Thornton was rarely one for simple explanations," Peterson replied thoughtfully. "She held her cards close to her chest, as it were." Eve found herself holding her breath. She'd delivered mail to Emily

Thornton for years, a quiet observer of her life and the strange little cottage on Cliffside. She'd always sensed there was more to the woman than met the eye – and now, it seemed, she was right. "And what if... what if she's wrong?" Councillor Bellweather demanded, his voice rising slightly. "What if she doesn't know which secrets to keep? What if she leaves us with a mess?" Before anyone could respond, Councillor Davies stepped forward. "Well," he said, straightening his tie, "it's settled then. Miss. Thornton has chosen wisely. Let's just hope this 'postwoman' is up to the task." He shot Eve a brief, assessing glance – a mixture of scepticism and grudging respect, she thought. As she sat there, feeling the weight of expectation settle upon her, she noticed Councillor Peterson was studying her intently. "You seem... thoughtful, Miss. Thornton," he observed quietly. "Do you have any thoughts on the matter?"

Eve looked around the room, at the faces of the town's residents, each one holding its own little piece of Ashcliffe's history. She glanced down at the photograph Emily had given her – the boy and girl on the windswept beach. "I think," she said finally, a small smile playing on her lips, "that I do. But I'll keep my thoughts to myself for now. Thank you for telling me," she looked at Councillor Peterson especially here, "I accept."

Back at the Post Office, a small, slightly damp room crammed with overflowing shelves, Eve felt like she'd stepped out of a dream. The rain continued its insistent drumming against the slate roof, but it seemed muted, distant – as if Ashcliffe itself were still processing the news. She slumped into her stool behind the counter, the worn wooden surface cool beneath her hand, and stared blankly at the small brass bell in front of her. It felt ridiculously cheerful after everything that had just happened. "Rough day?" asked Krissy, appearing suddenly beside her with a flourish of brightly coloured scarves – crimson, turquoise, and sunshine yellow. She was already sketching in a small notebook, her brow furrowed in concentration, and a smudge of charcoal dusted her cheek. Krissy was a vibrant splash of colour in

Ashcliffe's muted palette – a whirlwind of self-employed illustration, quirky outfits, and infectious enthusiasm.

"You have no idea," Eve mumbled, pushing a stray strand of hair behind her ear.

"Let me guess," Krissy said, tilting her head, "the council decided to give you the Archive? Like it's some sort of prize?"

"They did," Eve confirmed, still reeling. "Emily Thornton bequeathed it to me."

Krissy stopped sketching and let out a small shriek of delight, nearly dropping her notebook. "No way! Emily Thornton?! That's brilliant! And utterly bonkers, of course. She was always a bit...eccentric."

"Eccentric, it turns out, is putting it mildly," Eve replied dryly.

"Oh, she was! Remember when she tried to pay for her groceries with seashells? Or claimed to have tea parties with the seagulls?" Krissy chuckled, shaking her head. "Always a bit mysterious."

"Well," Eve said, feeling a small smile tugging at her lips, "it seems she's left me with plenty of mysteries now."

"It's about time you were haunted," Krissy declared dramatically, snapping her fingers. "Honestly, you'd think after all those years living in that old place, someone would have finally noticed the Archive was a goldmine. And look who got it – the girl who spends most of her days delivering the post! Perfect."

"I don't know about 'haunted'," Eve said, though she wasn't entirely convinced. "It just feels...significant. Like it holds something important."

Krissy snorted. "Of course, it does! It's full of Ashcliffe's history – and probably a few secrets. You know, old Councillor Bellweather always said Emily was hoarding the town's memories."

"He did," Eve agreed. "She kept everything."

"Well," Krissy continued, returning to her sketching, "you'll be busy for ages. Good for you, though! It's a proper honour."

Eve glanced at the bell above the door, expecting Councillor Bellweather any minute, and wondered if Krissy was right. "Do you think it's... daunting?"

"A little," Krissy admitted, squinting at her sketch. "But you're good at noticing things, aren't you? Like that photo she gave you – the one with the boy and girl on the beach. You have a good eye."

Just then, the door opened and in shuffled Albert, looking slightly windswept but carrying a toolbox. He was a study in comfortable chaos – his jacket always had a bit of sawdust clinging to it, and he often wore a pair of mismatched socks. "Morning, Krissy," he greeted cheerfully. "And morning, Eve! What's all the excitement?"

"We're discussing the fate of Ashcliffe's Archive," Krissy announced with a flourish. "Apparently, Emily Thornton has decided to pass it on to... her!" she gestured towards Eve.

Albert raised an eyebrow, peering at her. "Really? That's fantastic! You, of all people. What do you know about dusty old records?"

"Enough to know it's a massive undertaking," Eve replied, feeling the weight of it settle back on her shoulders. "And apparently, Emily left me with some rather cryptic instructions."

"Cryptic was her middle name," Krissy declared. "She used to tell me that everything in the archive held a tale, that hidden messages were the nature of her work."

"Well," Albert said thoughtfully, setting down his toolbox. "Sounds like you've got a bit of a mystery on your hands. Maybe I can help with the digitization – I'm pretty good with computers." "That would be brilliant!" Eve exclaimed, a genuine spark of excitement flickering within her.

"And," Krissy added, grinning at both of them, "you have the rest of the Ashcliffe Afternooners! We can all lend a hand." She paused, studying Eve's face with an insightful gaze. "You know, you remind me of Emily a little bit. Quiet, observant... and shrewd as they come."

Eve hesitated, unsure how to respond. "Maybe," she said finally.

A moment later, the door bell chimed again, this time announcing the arrival of Eloise, trailing a cloud of chamomile and carrying a steaming mug of tea. "Right then!" Eloise announced, settling into a chair with a contented sigh. "Let's hear all about it! Did you find out anything exciting about the stars while you were delivering mail?" Surrounded by her friends, Eve began to discuss the news in greater details. The rain continued its steady rhythm against the roof of the Post Office, although it felt a little less insistent now. It felt as though, in that small, cluttered room, filled with the scent of paper and tea, and the warmth of companionship, Eve had accepted her new calling: to unravel the secrets of Ashcliffe's past whilst protecting those memories in electronic form for future generations.

At the Post Office, the warmth of the room and the chatter of her friends had felt like a welcome shield against the gathering gloom outside. As she stepped out into the rain – which now fell in a more insistent curtain than before – Eve couldn't shake the feeling that something had shifted within Ashcliffe itself. It wasn't dramatic, not yet, but there was a subtle difference, a heightened awareness as if the town were holding its breath, waiting for her to begin. She cycled towards her own cottage, the familiar route now imbued with a sense of anticipation. The rain plastered her hair to her face and slicked the cobblestones, mirroring the feeling in her chest – a mixture of excitement and perhaps, just a touch of apprehension. As she passed the corner of Cliffside, where Emily's cottage stood, she paused for a moment, gazing up at its grey slate shingles and climbing ivy. It looked as if it were silently welcoming her to the task ahead.

Inside Eve's own small cottage, it was exactly as she'd left it – comfortable and slightly cluttered. She ran a hand across her desk, smoothing down the worn wooden surface, and noticed something she hadn't seen before: a single sprig of lavender, perfectly preserved, lay nestled amongst the papers. It was Emily's signature scent, a subtle reminder of the woman who had entrusted her with this unexpected legacy. "That's odd," Eve murmured to herself, picking up the sprig and inhaling its delicate fragrance. As she turned to head upstairs to bed, Eve caught sight of herself in the small mirror above the desk – a rosy-cheeked delivery driver with a thoughtful expression and, she hoped, a touch of determination.

2

CHAPTER TWO: THE ARCHIVE OF ECHOES

The rain in Ashcliffe-on-Sea was relentless, a damp, insistent hand pressing against the Archive's slate roof and clinging to everything like a memory. It wasn't the cheerful, sporadic drizzle that occasionally kissed the town, instead this was a proper, soaking grey – the colour of bruised stone and distant storms. Inside the Archive, though, it was a different story. A comforting one, at first. The air hung thick with the scent of damp paper, beeswax polish from the shelves, and something faintly musty – the accumulated aroma of decades spent gathering dust. In short, it smelled of stories waiting to be told. Eve pulled up a rickety wooden chair, its legs groaning slightly under her rangy weight, and adjusted the headtorch strapped to her forehead. The light cast a warm circle on the small table in front of her, illuminating a chaotic landscape of stacked boxes, overflowing shelves, and scattered documents.

The digitization equipment – a bulky old scanner that had perhaps seen better days, yet had a reassuringly efficient sounding fan – sat patiently waiting, like an expectant child. It was a comforting routine, this: the quiet hum of the scanner, the scratch of the stylus on the digital tablet, the methodical click of each photograph being saved.

A welcome antidote to the usual solitude of her deliveries. Not every person she delivered to was as welcoming as Emily Thornton had been, and Eve had always been happy to endure a little eccentricity when it came alongside true warmth. Eve had been at it for nearly three weeks now, slowly chipping away at Emily Thornton's legacy. The Archive was a sprawling beast, a haphazard collection of Ashcliffe's history crammed into the building next to the butcher. Councillor Davies had called it "a waste of space," but Emily, it seemed, had disagreed vehemently. There were maps rolled tight and tied with faded ribbon, detailing fishing grounds from the eighteenth century, shipping records filled with meticulous handwriting listing cargo and captains, stacks of black-and-white photographs depicting generations of fishermen and their families. Face upon face etched with the salt and wind of the sea. And then there were the folklore notes – handwritten accounts of local legends, whispered tales of smugglers and shipwrecks, and cryptic observations about the "sea's moods."

Today's target was a box labelled 'Cliffside Portraits,' filled with sepia-toned images of Ashcliffe's residents from the early twentieth century. She selected a particularly worn photograph – a stern-looking man in a tweed suit, his gaze direct and unwavering – and carefully placed it on the scanner bed. "Come on, you," she muttered to herself, adjusting the focus. The picture was stubbornly blurry, as if the image itself had been yearning for clarity. "Just like those letters Mrs. Higgins was sure that the Archive needed," she chuckled, remembering the endless struggle to get a decent scan of her handwriting.

It wasn't that Eve minded the work – there was something satisfying about bringing these forgotten pieces of history into the digital age – but it could be frustratingly slow. The paper was brittle in places, threatening to crumble at the slightest touch. And some of the photographs were faded and cracked, their colours muted by time. She adjusted the scanner settings again, experimenting with different resolutions and lighting angles. Suddenly, a small detail caught her eye – a delicate sketch tucked into the corner of the photograph, almost hidden amongst the shadows. It was a simple drawing of a lavender sprig, rendered in fine pencil. A tiny, perfect rendition that evoked Emily's scent – a familiar blend of lavender and beeswax polish. Eve paused, turning the photograph over in her hand. It felt strangely personal. Like Emily had deliberately wanted to draw attention to it. She hadn't noticed it before, lost as she was in the details of the portrait. A small smile touched her lips. Tiny things like this – a shared scent, a hidden sketch – were what connected her to Emily, and to the place that they had both called home for so many years.

Eve continued scanning, the rhythm of the work settling around her. As she moved on to the next photograph – a young woman with bright blue eyes gazing out at the sea – she noticed a handwritten note tucked behind it. It was addressed simply to 'Emily.' Eve carefully unfolded it and read: "The tide remembers everything. Don't forget to look beneath." A shiver ran down her spine. It was the very same words that Emily had gifted her with. Councillor Davies might have called this place "a waste of space", but Eve was becoming ever more confident that he had been sorely mistaken. It wasn't just a collection of musty records of days gone by, it was a repository of secrets waiting to be unearthed.

As Eve scanned photograph after photograph, she felt the weight of the Archive pressing in on her – the weight of generations, of memories, of stories both grand and small. It was a heavy responsibility, this – preserving Ashcliffe's past for future generations. And as she glanced at the rain still hammering against the windows, she couldn't shake the feeling that she wasn't just digitizing records. It felt as if Emily had left more than just the Archive to Eve, she had somehow passed on an inch or two of her dogged enthusiasm for the work ahead of Eve. The rain continued its onslaught, and Eve was especially glad of her headtorch and its powerful beam's ability to illuminate the gloom of the day. Whilst it perhaps didn't have her looking her best, Eve had always been one to favour practicality over fashion. It just didn't make sense to her to focus on aesthetics when the core of the thing – or the person – was what mattered the most. Eve had just finished scanning a particularly striking portrait of a grizzled fisherman, his face etched with the stories of countless storms, when she heard the door open and a new presence enter.

He was tall, with a slightly rumpled air about him – as if he'd spent more time hunched over books than worrying about appearances. His dark coat was dripping puddles over the floor that threatened to merge into one alarming lake. He carried a battered leather satchel slung over his shoulder, bulging ominously. "Morning," he said, his voice carrying a more than a hint of a Welsh lilt. "I'm Geraint, and I was just asking around about Emily Thornton – she seems to have been quite the force of nature." He offered a polite smile, although the gesture looked like it pained him somewhat. Clearly, Eve thought, this is not a man who is used to dealing with other people on a regular basis. Eve straightened up from her chair, adjusting her headtorch. "Oh? Did you know her?"

"Not personally, no," Geraint replied, his eyes already scanning the room with an appraising gaze. "But I'm researching the local folklore here in Ashcliffe – specifically, 'The Storm.' It's a fascinating case study. A prominent local folklorist, Miles Thornton, vanished during a particularly violent storm back in 1938, and there's been a lot of speculation ever since about what happened to him."

"Miles Thornton?" Eve asked, tilting her head. "He was Emily's cousin, wasn't he? She mentioned him occasionally – said he was obsessed with the sea."

"Indeed," Geraint confirmed, pulling out a small notebook and scribbling something down. "A fascinating character. He was known for his meticulous research into local legends, particularly those concerning smugglers and shipwrecks. And of course, the rumours about 'The Siren' – a mythical creature said to lure sailors to their doom off the coast."

Geraint moved further into the room, running a hand along a shelf stacked with ancient maps. "Emily's Archive may just prove to be an invaluable resource," he observed. "I've heard she had quite a knack for collecting obscure details."

"She did," Eve agreed, returning to her desk. "She was very dedicated." Eve wasn't entirely comfortable with his presence – there was something about him, a quiet intensity, that made her instinctively wary. "What exactly are you hoping to find in here?"

"Well, I'm looking for anything that might shed light on Miles Thornton's disappearance," Geraint explained, tapping his pen against his notebook. "Local accounts, old newspaper clippings, even just casual mentions of the sea – anything that might give me a clue." He paused, studying her thoughtfully. "You seem to know quite a lot about Emily and her family."

"I've lived in Ashcliffe for most of my life," Eve replied simply. "Delivered mail around here for years. You get to know people's homes, you know? The things they keep close, the things they distance themselves from."

"Naturally," Geraint agreed. "But did you know much about the Thornton family? Emily doesn't seem to have been particularly forthcoming in answering questions from fellow academics." He paused, clearly hoping that Eve would pick up the conversation with some family lore. When Eve continued to meet his gaze coolly, Geraint continued. "Did she ever mention any particular stories or legends that were important to her?"

Eve hesitated for a moment, considering how much to reveal. "She mentioned 'The Storm' a few times," she said finally. "And that her cousin was searching for something. Something connected to the sea and music."

"Did she say what?" Geraint pressed, his eyes gleaming with interest.

"Not really," Eve replied, feeling slightly defensive. "Just vague things. She always seemed a little reluctant to talk about it."

"That's not surprising," Geraint said, nodding knowingly. "Some families have their secrets. It's interesting – I was just reading one of

Albert Locke's haikus about the family. He writes beautifully. It mentioned Louisa's Cove by name."

Eve frowned. "Louisa's Cove? I've never heard of it."

"Exactly!" Geraint exclaimed, a spark of excitement in his eyes. "That's what makes it so intriguing! Locke's poem seemed to hint that it was connected to Miles Thornton in some way. I'd love to visit it – do you know where it is?"

"No," Eve admitted truthfully. "I live here, I deliver mail around here, but I've never really ventured into the coves past the main drag of the beach. We tell children it's too dangerous to play past a certain point, and I guess I've always respected that boundary."

"Well," Geraint said, a hint of impatience creeping into his voice. "You're the local expert! Surely you've heard something about it over the years? It should be a well-known landmark." He shifted slightly, adopting a more insistent tone. "How can an archivist – someone who has dedicated her life to Ashcliffe's history – not know about a place like Louisa's Cove?"

"You're putting a lot of stock in Albert's poetry – have you asked him about Louisa's Cove?" Eve asked pointedly, feeling his scrutiny. She wasn't sure why she was being so guarded, but she couldn't quite shake the feeling that he was getting to her.

"I have not." Geraint answered stiffly, "But if you could point me in his direction?"

"You'll find him at The Saltwater Siren, most likely," said Eve, silently hoping that Albert was out on an electrical job instead of helping Stella and Eloise with the venue they all had dragged back to life over the past year or so.

"I will try that, thank you." Geraint said, not sounding at all grateful for Eve's suggestion. With more than a touch of determination in his voice, he continued. "Maybe you should find out about Louisa's Cove. It might hold a clue to Miles Thornton's disappearance – or even to something Emily knew about." He paused, studying her face intently. "Don't dismiss it so easily." He flipped open his notebook and began scribbling furiously, as if committing every detail to memory. "You know," he added, looking up with a thoughtful expression, "it's remarkable how little is documented about the western side of Ashcliffe. Emily must have been quite the keeper of secrets."

As Geraint continued to pepper Eve with questions about Emily and the family's history – questions that seemed to grow increasingly specific – Eve realized she had a choice to make. She could either reveal a little more, or continue to guard what limited knowledge she did have. One thing was certain, Eve was starting to suspect that the truth about Ashcliffe, and its secrets, might be far more interesting than she'd initially thought. When Geraint finally left, presumably to ferret out Albert and maraud him with questions about Louisa's Cove, Eve felt a new surge of urgency. When it came to this digitization project, there was so much that she didn't know, and so much that needed finding out. Eve wanted, quite badly she now realised, to be the one to do it.

The rain continued its steady drumming against the Archive's roof, now sounding less like a question and more like a persistent encouragement. Eve found herself lost in the labyrinthine shelves, pulling out box after box filled with Emily Thornton's collected curiosities. Geraint's visit had been a catalyst, pushing her beyond the comfortable routine of digitization and into the deeper currents of Ashcliffe's past. She started with Louisa Thornton – Emily's mother. The initial records were sparse, mostly detailing a rather flamboyant arrival in Ashcliffe in 1920, heralded by whispers of a vanished fortune and a penchant for extravagant dresses. Then came the photographs – portraits depicting a woman of undeniable beauty, with a wildness in her eyes that hinted at a life lived outside the bounds of convention. There were pictures of Louisa strolling along the beach, a parasol shielding her from the sun, and another showing her perched on a rock overlooking the sea, sketching furiously in a notebook.

"She was obsessed with pirates," she murmured to herself, reading from one of Emily's notes. "And smugglers, apparently. Claimed they were 'the true children of Ashcliffe.'" The notes detailed Louisa's fascination with local legends – tales of hidden treasure, secret tunnels, and a legendary pirate captain who had buried his loot somewhere along the coast. There was also a recurring reference to "The Siren," spoken about in hushed tones – a mythical creature said to lure sailors to their doom with her enchanting and endlessly longing song. Digging deeper, both literally and figuratively, Eve unearthed a collection of Louisa's own journals – delicate volumes filled with elegant script and intricate sketches. The entries were a chaotic mix of observations on the local wildlife, philosophical musings, and increasingly fantastical accounts of encounters with "The Siren." One entry, dated just weeks before Miles Thornton's disappearance, read: "She sang to me last night, carried on the wind. A voice both beautiful and haunting... I believe she's calling us back to the sea."

"Interesting," Eve muttered, carefully turning a page. She continued to sift through Louisa's journals – looking for some clue that would connect her to Miles Thornton. Then, tucked between two sketches of seabirds, she found it: a faded map, meticulously drawn in pencil and ink. It depicted the coastline around Ashcliffe, with several locations circled in red. One of those circles was labelled simply: "My Cove."

The name triggered something – a faint memory that Emily had once shared about her own childhood. "She used to tell me stories about Louisa's Cove," Eve recalled, a smile playing on her lips. "Said it was her favourite place to play as a little girl. She described it as a secret haven, hidden away from the world." Louisa's Cove wasn't marked on any modern maps – not that anyone bothered looking beyond the main stretch of Ashcliffe's pretty beach anyway. However, a much older, hand-drawn map showed a small cove located on the westernmost tip of the coastline, tucked between two jagged cliffs and accessible only at low tide. As Eve scanned the map, she noticed something else – a small sketch in the corner, depicting a figure standing on the rocks overlooking the sea – a young girl with bright blue eyes and a wild tangle of hair. It was unmistakeably Emily Thornton. "Well, well," Eve chuckled to herself. "Looks like both Emily and Louise had a penchant for that particular cove."

Just then, she heard the door open and Geraint stepped back into the Archive, his face illuminated by the glow of the rain-streaked windows. He was carrying a steaming mug of tea and a slightly crumpled newspaper. "Any luck?" he asked, setting down the tea and newspaper on her desk. "Did you find anything about Louisa's Cove?"

"Did you find Albert at The Saltwater Siren?" Eve countered, not wanting to give up her information without a little bit of sharing from Geraint himself.

"I did indeed. He was not at all what I expected... seemed more interested in discussing the siren than his own poetry."

Eve nodded. "That sounds like Albert." Well, she thought, if Albert was happy to discuss folklore with this odd gentleman, then perhaps I can do the same. It is, after all, my job. Holding up the map she'd been poring over, Eve said, "I did find some references to Louisa's Cove. And it looks like Emily spent quite a bit of time there as a child." Geraint examined the map with interest, his brow furrowed in concentration. "Interesting," he said, tilting his head. "Did she ever mention anything about pirates or smugglers?"

"Emily did mention the siren fairly often, but then everyone around here does if you give them enough opportunity," Eve replied. "What she never told me was that her mother," Eve paused to point to a passage from one of Louisa's journals, "seems to have been almost as obsessed with the siren as Miles himself was." They both fell silent for a moment, contemplating the connection.

"You know," Geraint said, his eyes widening slightly, "I noticed something in one of Louisa's photos – the one from 1928. She looks remarkably like... well, she looks remarkably like you." Eve picked up the photograph – a stunning image of a young Louisa Thornton, standing on the beach with Miles Thornton, both gazing out at the sea. She studied it carefully, comparing it to her own reflection in the polished surface of the scanner. There was no doubt about it – they shared a striking resemblance: the same bright blue eyes, the same slightly up-turned nose, and even the same hint of wildness in their expressions. "It's incredible," she said, a shiver running down her spine. "Emily never mentioned that I looked like her mother. Although, perhaps that would explain why she left me with this place to set to right – Mummy issues?"

"Perhaps," Geraint replied, "but it certainly adds another layer to the mystery." He paused, then added with a thoughtful expression, "I feel like we're starting to see things clearly now – that there's a distinct link between Emily and her mother, Louisa's Cove, and Miles Thornton himself."

"It's strange," Eve murmured, turning the photograph over in her hand. "Like she was trying to hide something. Like she wanted us to know... but also, somehow, didn't want to let us." As they continued to examine the photograph, a small detail stood out – a tiny sketch tucked into the corner of the image, almost hidden amongst the shadows. It was a drawing of a lavender sprig, rendered in dainty pencil strokes. The same lavender sprig that Eve had seen on her desk at home – and that she'd noticed with the photograph of Louisa Thornton. "That's... odd," Eve said, turning to Geraint. "I hadn't noticed it before." Geraint examined the drawing closely. "It's beautiful. Almost like a signature. Do you think it's a clue?" He adjusted his glasses. "Did Emily ever wear lavender?" For the first time since inheriting the Archive, Eve felt a genuine sense of connection – not just to Emily Thornton, but to the secrets that lay hidden within the walls of the building where Emily had spent such a large portion of her life.

Emily Thornton, much like Eve herself, had never married. She'd never even had a whisper of a lover about her, as far as Eve could remember. Emily, until the last decade of her life, had been the kind of woman whose beauty was such that it defied time. It was impossible to guess how old she was, because she was so striking. Those intense blue eyes, that wild and reckless laugh – they'd dimmed in recent years, it was true, but the same shrewd Emily Thornton remained constant. Emily had always been in Eve's life, she'd been great friends with Eve's parents and would often join their warmly quiet home for celebrations, delighting in bringing Eve gifts of books and trinkets. The scent of lavender had always clung to Emily, and still whenever she saw or smelled that telltale plant, Eve could only think of Emily. A memory surfaced – Emily had once told Eve that she'd found the sprig pressed between the pages of one of Miles's books when she was little. She always said it reminded her of him, Eve recalled.

Geraint gestured once more towards the photograph of Louisa and Miles, snapping Eve back from her thoughts. "Look at them – they look so happy. Like they'd just discovered something wonderful." Eve studied the image. It wasn't simply a posed portrait; there was a palpable warmth in their expressions, a shared secret that seemed to radiate from the picture itself. "They look as if they were deeply in love," she agreed, "but that's not right. She was married to Emily's father – Alexander Thornton."

"I didn't know Miles had a brother," Geraint began.

"He didn't." Eve cut him off, shortly, proud she knew something about the Thornton clan that Geraint did not. "Alexander was Miles's uncle... although through a quirk of Victorian family dynamics, Alexander was the younger of the two."

"Oh indeed?" Geraint replied, before being pulled back in by the photograph. "Look at her eyes – they hold a certain intensity. A hint of something wilder than most. I bet she knew about the smugglers, about the treasures hidden along the coast. You know," Geraint said, after re-examining the hand-drawn map that Eve had found with Louisa's journals, "the location of Louisa's Cove – if this is indeed Louisa's Cove – is remarkably specific." He paused, then added with a touch of excitement, "I think we should visit it, even if it's just to rule out any connection."

"It's quite a trek," Eve pointed out, touching the map reverently. " And the tide comes in pretty quickly."

"Precisely!" Geraint exclaimed. "A perfect spot for smugglers and secrets."

A sense of urgency began to build within them, fuelled by the shared discovery. They started to delve deeper into Emily's notes, searching for any mention of Louisa's Cove or the lavender sprig. They discovered that Emily had written about it frequently – describing it as a place of "hidden secrets". "She believed it was connected to the 'Siren'," Eve read aloud from one of Emily's notes, one of the ones from the same box that had held Louisa's journals, "that the Siren's song could still be heard on the wind if you knew where to listen."

"She thought that her mother had known about all this," Geraint said, his eyes gleaming. "That Louisa was somehow connected to the legend?"

As they were scanning a stack of faded letters – penned in elegant script by Miles Thornton himself – Eve noticed something unusual. One of the letters was addressed to "L," and it contained a drawing – a sketch of a small, secluded cove with a distinctive rock formation, it had the look of a curled dragon about it. "Look at this!" she exclaimed, showing it to Geraint. "This must be Louisa's Cove! At least, that's what it looks like."

"Remarkable!" Geraint said, peering at the sketch. "And look at this – he refers to 'the key' and says he will leave it where she can always find it." He paused, then added with a note of excitement, "Do you think we could find this key?"

Just as they were about to discuss their next move, there was a knock on the door. It was Councillor Davies, looking flustered. "Forgive me for interrupting," he said, wiping his brow with a handkerchief. "But I need to see those letters from Miles Thornton. The ones detailing his research into the 'Storm' and the local legends."

"What do you want them for?" Eve asked, a little suspiciously. "We're just starting to catalogue them."

"Councillor Bellweather insisted," Davies replied, clearly uncomfortable. "He said we needed to ensure that everything is properly documented before... well, before anyone else gets their hands on it."

"And did he say when you're going to start selling off the Archive?" Eve asked, a wry smile playing on her lips.

"Not exactly," Davies replied nervously. "But he's rather keen on getting it done quickly."

As Councillor Davies rummaged through the pile of documents, looking for the specific letters, Geraint turned to Eve with a pointed look. "You seem reluctant to let him see those," he observed. "Why is that?"

"I don't know," Eve replied evasively. "Just a feeling. He's... intense. And I want to make sure we digitize them properly before we hand them over."

"Perhaps it's because you sense there's something hidden within them?" Geraint suggested, his eyes twinkling. "Something that Councillor Bellweather wouldn't want the town to know."

Just then, Councillor Davies emerged from the pile of papers, clutching a stack of letters and looking triumphant. "Here they are! Don't worry, everything is properly documented." He paused, glancing at Geraint with a hint of suspicion. "Though I do think you two are spending far too much time poring over those old records."

"It is my job, though," Eve began.

"It's part of my studies," Geraint spoke too, their words overlapping. They shared a wary smile. As Davies bustled out of the room, leaving behind a lingering scent of cologne and disapproval, Eve couldn't shake the feeling that they were being watched – not just by the residents of Ashcliffe-on-Sea, but by something older, something connected to the Archive's secrets. She glanced at Geraint, who was already studying one of the letters with renewed interest. "I think," she said quietly, "that we should start looking for that key."

3

CHAPTER THREE:
AFTERNOONERS AND
TEAPOTS

The rain hadn't truly stopped, though it had eased to a persistent drizzle by the time Eve arrived at The Saltwater Siren. It smelled of salt, woodsmoke, and something faintly floral – lavender, undoubtedly. Inside, the afternoon light was already softening, casting long shadows across the mismatched furniture and shelves crammed with books and curiosities. The "Ashcliffe Afternooners" were settled in, a comfortable chaos of mugs and knitted blankets. "About time you showed up!" Krissy declared, waving a hand dramatically. "We were starting to think you'd been swallowed by the Archive." There was a genuine note of concern in her voice, layered beneath the usual theatricality. "Albert was muttering about 'lost postwomen' and 'forgotten legacies.'"

"She just looks... drained," Albert observed, meticulously polishing a brass telescope with a soft cloth. "Like she's carrying the weight of all those old papers."

"Exactly!" Eloise said without looking up from her cards, her brow furrowed in thought. "Your heart feels like a tightly wrapped parcel,

27

darling. Let it breathe." Eloise shuffled the tarot deck with a quiet grace as Eve walked, bewildered but not wholly unsurprised, and sat with her. "Let's see what the cards have to say about that..."

Eloise laid out three cards: The Tower (reversed), The Moon, and finally, The Hermit. "Intriguing," she murmured. "The Tower reversed suggests something potentially disruptive or overwhelming has been averted – perhaps a secret revealed was contained just in time. The Moon speaks of intuition, hidden emotions, and the subconscious. And... The Hermit! It shows a reflection of the past, reflecting both lineage and secrets – and a need to look inwards for answers."

"Lineage?" Eve asked, a little bewildered. "What do you mean?"

Krissy, who had been rambling about a local legend involving lost lovers and the sea – "...and they say their voices still echo on foggy nights, calling out for each other!" – suddenly paused, her eyes wide. "Oh! She's right, isn't she? It feels like she's connected to it all."

"Indeed she does," Eloise confirmed, smiling gently at Eve. "It suggests a connection to something older than you might think."

Tom, who was quietly observing from his seat by the fireplace, noticed the group was fussing over Eve. He offered a small, sympathetic smile to Rita, who was pushing a steaming mug of tea towards her. "She looks like she needs it," he said softly.

"I completely agree," Rita agreed, placing a comforting hand on Eve's arm. "Just take a deep breath and tell us what's been weighing you down, Eve." Before Eve had a chance to respond, Geraint bustled through the door with a box of Emily's things, saying they were at the Archive but they clearly didn't belong there. These were personal items – a worn leather-bound journal, a tangle of dried lavender sprigs tied with faded ribbon, and a small, tarnished silver locket – that whoever was dealing with Emily's estate should have care of. He shifted the box awkwardly onto the table between Eloise and Eve, sending a puff of dust motes dancing in the afternoon light. "Just seemed to turn up," he offered, his voice quiet, almost hesitant. "Didn't quite fit in with the Archive records."

Krissy, ever dramatic, immediately launched into a playful tease. "Oh! The folklore lad finally arrived!" she exclaimed, gesturing dramatically towards Geraint with her mug. "Did you bring us any more secrets from the past?"

Eve deflected with a small smile, taking a sip of her tea. "Just some papers, I think." She didn't want to give him – or anyone – anything to latch onto. Instead, she fixed her attention on the box of Emily's belongings. Nestled amongst a stray pencil and a crumpled receipt, Eve spied a photo. It was of Louisa and Miles and – surely not, she thought, but then again – it was identical to the one Emily had given her the day before she died. Until now, she hadn't realised that had been a photo of Louisa and Miles, and why should she have? Who were they to Eve, after all. Stunned, Eve picked the photo up, turning it over in her hand, studying the detail. The grainy sepia tones captured their youth perfectly; Louisa with a mischievous glint in her eyes and Miles gazing at her with an open, almost vulnerable expression. They were standing on a windswept beach, the sea stretching out before them like a vast, grey canvas. It was a quintessential Ashcliffe-on-Sea shot – bleak but beautiful. "It's... uncanny," she murmured, more to herself than anyone else. Then, she noticed it – written on the back, barely visible beneath a smudge of what looked like saltwater, is one small difference between this photo and the one that Eve already has. "Eve's Grandparents" was scrawled in elegant cursive, almost as if Emily had just finished writing it.

Eve's fingers traced the letters, a strange warmth spreading through her. The handwriting was undeniable – instantly familiar, from her work at the Archive, where she'd spent countless hours poring over Emily's meticulous records. It was Emily's handwriting. "If Louisa and Miles were my grandparents..." she whispered, almost to herself, "who was their child?" Albert, who had been quietly observing her from his armchair, sipping Earl Grey and studying the flames in the hearth, offered a gentle prompt. "Sometimes, the people we think we know best hold the biggest surprises." A slow smile spread across Eve's face, starting at her eyes and working its way outwards. As she stared at the photo, a sudden, overwhelming recognition crashed over her – a feeling so profound it almost took her breath away. Louisa and Miles... They were her grandparents! The faded photograph, Emily's cryptic note, the feeling of connection that had been nagging at her since she received it – it all clicked.

A stunned silence fell over the group. Krissy's theatricality vanished, replaced by a quiet curiosity. Albert met her gaze gently. "Well, well," he said softly. "That's certainly something." Eve looked from face to face of the people who were closest to her in the world, her eyes wide with disbelief and a burgeoning sense of wonder. "If Louisa and Miles were my grandparents... who was their child?" she asked aloud, almost in disbelief. "Who was their child?" The stunned silence stretched on, punctuated only by the crackle of the fire, before Krissy broke it with a burst of excited energy. "Oh my gosh!" she shrieked, leaping to her feet and grabbing a scrap of paper from her bag. She began sketching furiously, her hand flying across the page, capturing the image of Louisa and Miles with an almost frantic intensity. "It's...it's like looking at a reflection! I knew it, I just knew!" Krissy looked up at Eve, her eyes wide with recognition. "They're you, aren't they? They're part of you!"

"It seems Emily knew all along," he observed, his voice calm and measured. "Or, at least, strongly suspected."

"It... it makes so much sense now," Eve said, her voice a little shaky. She turned the photo over in her hand again, examining it with fresh eyes. "Emily was my mother."

The revelation hung in the air like the sea mist, settling on each of them. Krissy continued to sketch, adding details – the curve of Louisa's smile, the way Miles's hand rested gently on hers. It wasn't just a portrait; it felt like she was capturing a memory, a secret whispered across generations. "But... how?" she asked, her voice barely above a whisper. "Louisa was married to Alexander."

"Indeed," Geraint confirmed. "A rather stoic union, if the diaries reveal anything."

"Louisa had an affair with Miles," Eloise said, wonder in her voice. "A passionate, secret affair, no doubt. With Alexander oblivious?"

"He might have been complicit," Stella remarked, "or at least not resistant to the idea." Eloise nudged Stella gently, "Don't say that about Eve's grandparents! They might not have been into the same things that... well, that a rather significant proportion of us seem to be!"

Eve felt a wave of emotions wash over her – shock, confusion, and a surprising sense of belonging. It was like a missing piece of herself had finally clicked into place. She hadn't just inherited an archive; she'd inherited a family. "Emily... she was their daughter," Eve said, the realization dawning on her. "She was my mother."

"It's beautiful, isn't it?" Rita chimed in, a touch of wistfulness in her voice. "Like a carefully guarded rose – full of thorns but exquisitely beautiful."

"The Archive... she left it for me," Eve said, turning back to the photograph. "Not just because she loved history, or because she thought I'd appreciate it. But... it's part of her." She ran her fingers over the worn leather of the box, feeling a deeper connection than ever before. "It's part of all of us." Eve looked up at Geraint, who was watching her with an expression she couldn't quite decipher – a mixture of knowing and perhaps a little bit of relief. And then it happened - a shared glance between them, fleeting but powerful. A silent acknowledgment of the secret they both now carried. Eve felt another wave of emotion – this time a touch of sadness. "She kept it hidden from me for so long," she murmured, tracing the outline of Miles's face in the photo. "Why?"

"Perhaps," Albert suggested gently, "she wanted you to discover it on your own terms."

"Or perhaps," Eloise added, her eyes twinkling, "she knew you were the one who could finally unlock its secrets." Eve looked at the photograph again, really seeing it for the first time. It wasn't just a picture of two people; it was a snapshot of a secret family, a hidden lineage. And now, suddenly, she was part of it. It felt like the beginning of something extraordinary. As she stared at the image of Louisa and Miles, bathed in the warm glow of the fireplace, she realized that her life – her family history, her identity – was about to undergo a complete transformation. "I think," she said finally, turning back to face them all, "I think I'm going to need a very strong cup of tea."

"Coming right up," Rita offered, already heading for the kettle. A comfortable silence settled over them as they refilled their mugs. Then, Geraint broke it, his gaze thoughtful. "So, you're saying your grandfather was in love with your errant grandmother, Louisa, as well as the mysterious siren of folklore fame?" he asked, a small smile playing on his lips.

Eve chuckled. "Well, maybe there's something to it."

"It certainly explains Emily's restlessness," Eloise observed, swirling her tea. "She taught me to read the sky, you know. She was a keen stargazer in her youth – I would never have got the hang of astrology without her. Let alone tarot – she said their meanings were easy to remember if you just looked hard enough... until the day you just find yourself knowing them, inside and out."

"She always said she could 'feel' the sea," Eve replied, remembering snippets of conversation with Emily. "Like it was part of her."

"Perhaps it was," Stella murmured, staring at the photograph. "A little bit of the siren, perhaps?"

A sharp voice cut through the warmth of the room. "Don't be ridiculous, Stella." Councillor Davies stood in the doorway, his face flushed with annoyance. He was holding a small, intricately carved wooden box – clearly from the Archive. "I thought I might find these," he said, gesturing to the box with an aggressive wave of his hand. "Rather personal items, wouldn't you say? Belong in Emily's private collection, not scattered about like this."

"We were just discussing her," Eve replied calmly, taking in his expression. "She had quite an interesting family history."

Davies snorted. "Indeed. A touch... complicated. Let's – let's just say certain families in Ashcliffe prefer to keep their past a little less tangled." He placed the wooden box on the table, opening it to reveal a collection of seashells – each one painted with a different scene. "Found these tucked away in her desk. Thought you might like them."

"They're beautiful," Eve said, picking up one depicting a stormy sea. "Do you know anything about them?"

"Just that they were her favourites," Davies replied curtly.

He shifted uncomfortably, glancing at Geraint who was observing him intently. "Well, I've had enough of this reminiscing. Just trying to tidy up a few loose ends." He turned to leave, then paused at the door. "By the way," he added, his voice low, "Emily mentioned in her will that she wanted you to be particularly careful with the 'Seafoam Diaries.' Said they contained... vital information." And with that, he was gone.

A ripple of anticipation went through the group. "The Seafoam Diaries?" Stella asked. "What are those?"

"No one knows," Geraint said, stepping forward. "If they ever existed at all, Emily kept them incredibly close." He looked at Eve, his eyes full of curiosity. "They're said to detail the first settlers of Ashcliffe – and their connection to the siren." Geraint let out a low whistle. "Well, well, well," he said, his eyes twinkling. "Looks like you have yourself a mystery to solve." He gestured towards the window with a thoughtful expression. "And I think it's time for another cup of tea – and perhaps a little more research. Back to the Archive?" As Eve nodded in frantic agreement, she felt a renewed sense of purpose. She wasn't just inheriting an archive, she was stepping into her family's legacy – and uncovering the secrets that had been hidden beneath the waves of Ashcliffe's past.

The door clicked shut behind Geraint and Eve, leaving a comfortable hum of speculation in its wake. Stella was the first to break the silence, swirling the remaining tea in her mug with a dramatic flourish. "Did you hear that? Emily's daughter! It' – it's like something out of one of those ancient tales."

"Seriously!" Krissy exclaimed, already pulling out her sketchbook. "Like, a secret heir! That's amazing! I need to capture this - 'Eve: The Last Lineage' – perfect for my next illustration series!"

"And the affair!" Eloise added, her eyes wide with delight. "Miles and Louisa? An almost piratical love story! It's utterly delicious." She began tapping a complex rhythm on the table with her finger. "A touch of melancholy, a dash of scandal... it's practically begging for an astrological chart!"

"It's just... Eve," Albert said quietly, his gaze thoughtful. "She was so guarded. So observant. To have been raised with this – and to have kept it from everyone for so long..."

"Well, she's a Thornton," Krissy declared, brandishing her mug like a weapon. "They're practically known for their secrets!"

"It makes so much sense now – why she loved the archive so much, why she was so close to Emily. It's like she's just discovered a piece of herself that was there all along."

"So, what do you think Geraint is up to?" Tom asked, leaning forward. "He seemed awfully knowledgeable about the folklore for someone who's clearly not local."

"And he was practically glowing when Eve left," Krissy added, with undisguised glee.

"He's definitely holding something back," Albert observed. "He's not the type to simply hand out information. He's a researcher – he wants to know."

"Maybe," Eloise said, tapping her chin thoughtfully, "he knows something about the 'Seafoam Diaries.' He probably suspects they hold the key to unlocking the secrets of the siren."

"Do you think there was a reason that Emily wanted us to be particularly careful with them?" Rita asked.

"It's got to be more than just 'careful'," Krissy said, dramatically. "It's like she knew they were important. Like they held the key to... everything!"

They fell into a comfortable murmur of speculation – theories about Geraint, about the diaries, about the significance of Miles's disappearance back in 1938. "What if he discovered something while searching for the 'key' in Louisa's Cove?" Stella said, her voice low.

"Or what if," Albert added quietly, "the key isn't a physical object at all? What if it's something... about them?"

"It is exciting," Krissy said, her voice full of enthusiasm. "Absolutely thrilling! To think, our quiet little town – and especially our lovely postwoman and archivist– is the centre of this whole thing!" She paused for a moment, then grinned. "I bet Emily knew we'd figure it out."

Eloise gasped, pointing to her tarot deck. "Look!" she exclaimed. "The Tower! Reversed... again. And... The Hermit. It's like the cards are saying – 'Dig deeper, Eve. The answers are within.'" They were just a group of friends in a quirky seaside town, but they were also part of something bigger now – guardians of a family secret, and perhaps – players in a much older story. And with the rain still falling outside, it felt like Ashcliffe-on-Sea was holding its breath, waiting to see what would be revealed next.

4

CHAPTER FOUR: SIRENS
IN THE WALLS

The rain continued its relentless assault on Ashcliffe-on-Sea – a grey, persistent flannel that seemed to seep into everything, staining the cobblestones unapologetically with dampness. It was a rain that felt ancient, as if it had witnessed countless secrets wash ashore, carrying them in on the tide. Today, it seemed particularly resonant. Inside The Saltwater Siren, a haven of faded velvet and salt-laced air, Stella was singing. She sat perched on a stool by the fireplace, her form draped in a shawl the colour of seafoam – though its once vibrant hue had been muted by unyielding rain and shadow. Her face was one of enduring beauty; weathered like driftwood smoothed by the waves, but still elegant, still possessing a certain captivating presence. Long flowing hair cascaded down her shoulders, catching the flickering light from the hearth like liquid moonlight. But it wasn't just her appearance that drew the eye – it was her voice. It carried the weight of the sea itself, layered with melancholy and a touch of something ancient and knowing.

Stella's song began slowly, a mournful solo that seemed to rise up from the floorboards and fill the small room. Her voice was rich and resonant, capable of both heartbreaking tenderness and a sudden, sharp intensity. The lyrics painted a picture of loss and longing, of a love swallowed by the sea: "The sea she sheds another tear, / for your return, my lover dear." Her fingers danced over the strings of her guitar, each note precise and deliberate. Eve found herself instinctively drawn to the music, as if pulled by an invisible current. The rain outside seemed to intensify with the song, drumming a steady rhythm against the windowpanes. Eve closed her eyes, clutching her shawl tighter around her – a simple grey wool that suddenly felt thin and inadequate against the chill. And then it hit her. A flicker, a brief impression of... lavender? Not just the scent of lavender, but Emily's lavender. The specific, slightly dusty aroma that always clung to Emily's clothes, to her hair, to the Archive itself. It was a memory, fragmented and fleeting, triggered by Stella's voice – a memory of being a little girl, curled up on Emily's lap as she read aloud from an old and weatherworn journal, all the while listening to the same haunting melody.

Krissy, who had been quietly observing Eve from her corner armchair, nudged her gently. "You alright, love? You look... pale."

"Just... a feeling," Eve murmured, opening her eyes. "Like I've heard that before." Stella's song continued to build, layering in more complex harmonies and a subtle undercurrent of urgency: "Nine months have passed and now the squall / of reddened face and lungs scream full." The lyrics suggested a birth – a child born into longing. And then, with a poignant simplicity that cut right through the music, Stella sang: "Come back to me, my love, my heart! / Echoes in the thunder start..." The words hung in the air, shimmering with a sense of desperate yearning. As Stella finished, the last note fading into the rain's steady beat, Eve felt a sudden and profound understanding wash over her. It wasn't just about Emily – it was about Louisa, too. About the secrets hidden within the lineage, within the very walls of Ashcliffe. Likely in the very walls of this place, The Saltwater Siren, which held so much of Miles's personality inside it. "That... that's 'The Siren's

Lament,'" she said, turning to Geraint, who had followed her into the room. "Emily used to play a version to me when I was little."

Geraint raised an eyebrow, a flicker of interest in his eyes. "Indeed. A rather haunting tune. And a surprisingly specific one."

The door burst open and Councillor Davies stomped into The Saltwater Siren, his face flushed with irritation. He held up another box filled with Emily's belongings – this time containing several worn diaries – "More of these! And smelling strongly of lavender, I might add. You're all wasting your time with this Archive. It's nothing but a collection of local fancies." He gestured dismissively towards Stella. "And her dreary songs." Heads turned, and Eve noticed Geraint observing the exchange – a subtle intensity in his gaze that she hadn't registered before. "He seems to know something," he murmured to her quietly, as Davies continued to grumble about the Archive's value. "I think," Eve replied, her voice barely a whisper, "that we're beginning to realize that Ashcliffe isn't just holding onto its history – it's holding onto its sirens."

"If we're going to do anything about finding out those secrets, we really do need to find Louisa's Cove. It's the logical next step." Geraint appeared confident in his words, happy to let them soak in the damp atmosphere whilst Eve considered. "You're right, let's go!" Eve said, enthusiastically.

"It feels like it's meant to be," Eve continued, her breath misting in the cool air as she and Geraint left The Saltwater Siren and began their trek towards Louisa's Cove. "Like we were always meant to find it."

Geraint nodded. "The map was remarkably specific. And Emily's mother's notes... they certainly painted a vivid picture." He scanned the darkening lane ahead, its edges blurring with rain and shadow. "It's more than just a hunch, I think. There's something compelling about it." Both Eve and Geraint were driven to reach the cove – it felt important, like they were meant to be there, as if Louisa herself was guiding them with each drop of falling rain. It wasn't simply an academic pursuit any more; it was becoming an obsession, fuelled by the fragments of memory and the lingering scent of lavender that clung to every clue.

The lanes leading away from Ashcliffe were choked with weeds and overgrown with brambles, as if nature itself was trying to reclaim what had been lost. Crumbling brick buildings leaned precariously, their windows like vacant eyes staring out at the sea. A weathered gravestone, half-buried in moss, bore an illegible name – a silent testament to lives lived and forgotten. A set of moss-covered steps led down to nowhere, disappearing into a tangle of ivy and ferns, hinting at a path long abandoned. "The rain tasted of salt and regret, washing over them as if carrying the memories of those who'd lost their way." Eve thought, pulling her shawl tighter around her. "Today feels very much like one of Albert's poems," she said, contemplating the mood that had overtaken her. "Look," Geraint said, pointing to a faded signpost half-hidden beneath a tangle of ivy. "'Thornton Estate – Keep Out.' A little dramatic, don't you think?"

"Probably," Eve replied, glancing up at the imposing silhouette of what was once the Thornton Manor – now largely collapsed into itself and overgrown with vegetation. "But it feels fitting."

The further they walked, the more oppressive the atmosphere became. The rain intensified, drumming a steady rhythm against their jackets. The wind picked up, carrying with it the mournful cry of gulls and the constant, insistent roar of the sea. "The tide is coming in quickly," Geraint observed, consulting his compass. "And fast." As they rounded the bend, the cove seemed to shrink, swallowed by the relentless advance of the sea. It wasn't just blocking them; it felt like it was actively trying to push them back, a wall of grey water churning and foaming against the rocks. The sound of the waves wasn't merely rhythmic – it felt distinctly human, as if the ocean itself were arguing with itself, thinking better of each sentence and following it up with a louder roar. "It's... intense," Eve said, her voice barely audible above the crashing waves. "Almost hostile."

Suddenly, a figure appeared on a weathered stone wall overlooking the cove. Councillor Davies was leaning against it, his face impassive, observing them with an unnervingly steady gaze. He didn't speak, offering no greeting, simply watching. His presence felt like another weight added to the growing sense of foreboding. "Well, well," he said finally, his voice dry as driftwood. "Fancy seeing you two. It's a bit far off the beaten track for a stroll, isn't it?"

"We were just finishing up at the Archive," Eve replied, trying to sound nonplussed. "Thought we'd take a little walk."

"A wise decision," Councillor Davies chuckled, a short, brittle sound. "Especially with the tide rising like that. It doesn't appreciate being disturbed." He shifted slightly on the wall, his gaze never leaving them. "I don't suppose you're looking for anything in particular?"

"Just Louisa's Cove," Geraint said simply, his eyes fixed on Davies. "We believe a key might be hidden there."

A flicker of something – amusement? – crossed Councillor Davies's face. "A key, is it? And what do you intend to unlock with that key?" He paused, letting the question hang in the air. "Perhaps the very secrets that Ashcliffe doesn't want you to find?" Before either could respond, he straightened up and continued to observe them, a silent sentinel guarding the entrance to Louisa's Cove. The tide was rising relentlessly, and with Davies watching over them, it felt as though they were no longer just seeking a hidden key – they were being watched, measured, and perhaps even tested.

"Come on," Geraint said, turning back towards the cove. "Let's not waste any more time." As they stepped onto the slippery rocks leading down to the tide line, Eve couldn't shake the feeling that they were stepping into something far older and deeper than she had anticipated – a place where the past wasn't just remembered; it was actively waiting. They finally reached Louisa's Cove – smaller and darker than either one of them had imagined. The air was thick with mist, clinging to their clothes like damp velvet, and the smell of seaweed mingled with the salty tang of the sea. It felt enclosed, intimate—as if it were a secret held close, guarding its mysteries beneath the watchful gaze of the sea. The rain hadn't let up; in fact, it intensified as they stepped onto the slick, moss-covered rocks leading down to the tide line. A palpable tension hung in the air, thicker than the mist itself. As they stood there, surveying the cove, Eve and Geraint shared a moment of recognition – a subtle shift in their gaze, a slight widening of their eyes. It was as if they'd both independently noticed something similar about the rocks – the way the grey slate blended with the darkening sea, or perhaps the peculiar angle of the sunlight filtering through the spray.

Then, for just a heartbeat, it flashed before them—a fleeting shadow that could almost be Louisa standing on the shore, her silhouette framed by the waves. Eve felt as if she could hear it, echoing throughout the cove – the mournful melody of 'The Siren's Lament.' It felt as if something of Louisa was still waiting for Miles, eternally poised to welcome him back from the sea. "Did you... did you see that?" Eve asked, turning to Geraint, a shiver running down her spine. Geraint, looking equally bewildered, said "Just a trick of the light, perhaps? But... yes. I think I did. A brief impression, like a half-remembered dream." Almost immediately, as if he felt the need to change the subject quickly, Geraint pointed towards a patch of seaweed clinging to one of the rocks. "Miles always noted in his letters something called 'Siren's Lace.'" He knelt down, examining it closely. "Remarkably similar to the description – delicate, almost translucent." Eve's eyes followed his gaze. And then she saw it – a small carving on one of the rocks, almost obscured by moss and lichen. It was a stylized wave, rendered in simple lines, with a single, outstretched hand reaching towards the water. "That's... that's a wave," she whispered, tracing its outline with her finger. "Like he wanted to reach out."

Just then, Stella appeared at the edge of the cove, seemingly having followed them. She hadn't spoken to them since they'd arrived at The Saltwater Siren, and now she simply stood there, observing them with a knowing gaze. "That song...it always finds its way back, doesn't it?"

"It does," Geraint replied, turning to her. "Do you know anything about Miles recording 'The Siren's Lament'?"

Stella nodded slowly. "Emily shared it with me, from the Archive. Last year, before I re-opened The Saltwater Siren. To be honest, I've been haunted by that tune ever since. He recorded it himself in 1938 – just before he vanished." A wave of understanding washed over Eve. The pieces were starting to fit together, forming a clearer picture of her family's tangled past. "So... he was singing it here? Before he disappeared?"

"Likely," Stella said cryptically. "This cove, Albert's always said that it holds onto things."

As the three of them turned to leave, the rain intensified, drumming against their jackets and blurring the edges of the cove. Eve saw another lavender sprig lying on the path – this one almost deliberately placed near her foot, as if offering a silent greeting. And then, carried on the wind, she heard it again – Stella's song, beginning with a hum before finding the words again – "Come back to me, my love, my heart!" A sense of unease settled over her. They were beginning to unravel something significant here, but also that they were being watched – not just by Councillor Davies, but perhaps by the cove itself, and all its secrets. As Eve flicked her eyes between her two walking companions, Geraint and Stella, she couldn't shake the feeling that they hadn't solved a mystery. That instead they had merely scratched the surface of something far more profound and perhaps, far more dangerous. The rain continued to fall, washing over them like liquid regret, carrying with it the echoes of a love lost, and a song waiting to be heard.

The rain hadn't relented; it seemed determined to cling to them as they retraced their steps from Louisa's Cove, each drop a tiny reminder of the secrets unearthed. The path leading back was narrower now, choked with slick mud and glistening pebbles, mirroring the tightening knot in Eve's stomach. Stella walked beside her, a quiet presence, her shawl billowing around her like a restless wave, while

Geraint, ever observant, scanned their surroundings with a focused intensity. "That 'Siren's Lace,'" he murmured, breaking the comfortable silence, "it's more than just a decorative plant, isn't it? It feels deliberately planted."

"Like a marker," Eve suggested, shivering slightly. "Something to guide you."

Stella nodded slowly. "Albert always says this cove holds onto things. That it remembers. He loves to tell me that the tide carries memories as well as water – sometimes bringing them back to shore, and other times dragging them out to sea."

As they rounded another bend, a thicket of gorse bushes exploded with vibrant yellow blooms, momentarily brightening the grey landscape. It was an unexpected splash of colour, almost jarring against the melancholy of the scene. "A little defiant," Eve commented, noticing how it seemed to push back against the rain and the encroaching shadows. "Perhaps," Geraint replied, his gaze fixed on a weathered stone marker half-buried in the mud – a simple arrow pointing towards the town. "Or perhaps it's simply marking the way." The lane gradually began to climb, winding its way upwards through a tangle of overgrown hedgerows. The air grew noticeably cooler, carrying with it the scent of pine and damp earth. They passed crumbling stone walls, remnants of what must have been a grand estate – silent witnesses to generations past. "Do you think there's any chance this was part of the Thornton estate?" Eve asked, pointing towards a particularly imposing ruin looming in the distance – a collapsed manor house, its silhouette stark against the darkening sky.

"It's more than possible," Geraint replied, consulting his compass again. "Likely, even. The land here has a long history. And the Thorntons were certainly influential. It's plausible they had a presence out here."

Alarmingly, a figure emerged from the mist – Councillor Davies, striding purposefully along the lane, a small black umbrella held aloft against the rain. He stopped a few feet away, his face impassive as ever.

"Still at it, I see," he said, his voice dry. "I thought you might be lost in the gorse."

"Just returning from our little stroll," Eve replied, trying to maintain her composure. "We were exploring."

"Exploring what? The secrets of Ashcliffe?" He offered a thin, sardonic smile. "Don't let the Archive consume you. Some things are best left buried."

"Like what?" Geraint challenged, stepping forward slightly.

Councillor Davies's gaze flickered towards the ruins of the manor house, then back to them. "The past," he said simply. "It tends to have a way of stirring up trouble." He turned and continued his stride, disappearing around another bend in the lane. As he did, Eve noticed something clutched tightly in his hand – a small, intricately carved lavender sprig.

"Lavender," she murmured, turning to Geraint. "Did you see that?"

"Indeed I did," he replied, his eyes narrowed. "He's been keeping at least one thing from us, it seems." The three of them quickened their pace, eager to reach the relative warmth and security of the Archive before they themselves got washed away. As they rounded the final bend, they emerged onto Ashcliffe High Street – a charming but slightly faded thoroughfare lined with quaint shops and traditional pubs. The rain hadn't stopped, but it seemed less relentless here, as if softened by the familiar sights and sounds of town. "Let's hope we can find some shelter inside," Eve said, heading towards the imposing brick building that housed the Archive.

Inside, the Archive was a welcome haven of warmth and quiet. The scent of old paper and leather filled the air – a comforting blend that immediately eased the chill from their bones. The familiar faces of Krissy, Albert, and Eloise greeted them with concerned expressions. "You look like you've been through a storm!" Krissy exclaimed, handing Eve a steaming mug of tea. "What did you find out at that gloomy cove?"

"More questions than answers," Eve replied, gratefully accepting the tea. "But it feels... significant. Like we're getting closer." As she spoke, her eyes fell upon a small table where Geraint was already meticulously scanning a photograph. He looked up as she approached. "I've been taking another look at this portrait of Miles Thornton," he said, holding up the image – a stern-faced man with piercing blue eyes and a hint of melancholy in his expression. "And I noticed something I hadn't before." He pointed to a small detail on the back of the photograph – a tiny, almost invisible inscription: 'Louisa's Cove.'

"Someone knew," Eva said, a sense of excitement building within her. "They wanted us to know." Stella said, "Well, what I know is that the rain was starting to feel a little too familiar." She looked around the Archive, taking in its cluttered shelves and overflowing boxes with a knowing smile. As they stood there, surrounded by the echoes of the past, a sense of shared purpose settled over them. They were no longer simply cataloguing documents, they were unravelling a mystery – a mystery that seemed inextricably linked to Eve's own family history as much as to the folklore of Ashcliffe itself. Eloise, her face flushed with excitement, said "I've been reading through some of Emily's notes and I think I've found something! She wrote about a specific time when the tides were particularly low at Louisa's Cove. And it was during that time that... well, that's when she said Miles left the key."

The Archive door burst open with a clatter that jerked up all of the heads of the gathered friends, and Councillor Davies strode in, his face flushed with irritation. In his hand, he held another box – this one filled with Emily's personal letters, their pages yellowed with age. He must have stopped off at Emily's cottage on the way into town, Eve realised. Did that mean he was in charge of her estate? Or did this nosy fellow just have a key and a self-imposed ability to enter whenever he please? "More clutter," he grumbled. "And still smelling of lavender. You really are wasting your time." He paused, a flicker of something – perhaps amusement – in his eyes. "But I have a feeling," he added, his voice low and deliberate, "that you're about to find out that some secrets are best left undisturbed... especially when they're tied to the sea." As Davies continued to grumble, Stella quietly placed her hand on Eve's arm. "Don't let him scare you," she whispered. "The tide is rising. And it always remembers."

5

❦

CHAPTER FIVE: LETTERS NEVER SENT

The Archive smelled, as always, of dust motes dancing in shafts of sunlight and the slightly salty tang of Ashcliffe's sea air. Even on a day like this, where the rain held back just enough to let a pale light filter through the tall windows. It was a comforting scent, familiar now – a balm against the lingering restlessness that had settled over Eve since Emily's death. She'd been at it for weeks, meticulously digitizing Emily Thornton's legacy, a slow, deliberate process of peeling back layers of history in a small-town post office archive. Today, she was tackling the final box from Miles Thornton – her grandfather, she still had to pinch herself to remember, a man shrouded in Ashcliffe mystery, having vanished during that infamous 1938 storm. The air in the Archive felt thicker today, heavier somehow, clinging to her skin like damp wool. It wasn't unpleasant, just present. Like she was sharing the space with more than just dust and paper. She'd been feeling it a lot lately – this sense that Ashcliffe itself was watching, remembering. A subtle prickle at the back of her neck when she turned, the faintest impression of movement from the corner of her eye.

Eve felt slightly drained, as if sleep hadn't fully refreshed her. The last few nights had been punctuated by fragments – a flash of grey sky, the roar of wind and waves, the scent of brine – the remnants of a dream storm, she suspected. She'd dismissed it initially as just that – a dream – but now, surrounded by Miles Thornton's things, it felt less like a random image and more like a memory trying to surface. Eve sifted through the box again – there were faded photographs of men in various tweed jackets, handwritten accounts of fishing trips, pressed flowers brittle with age, and a collection of small, polished stones. Then she spotted it: a simple, brown envelope tucked beneath a stack of invoices. It was addressed to 'Louisa Thornton' in Miles' elegant script, the ink still a deep, rich sepia. The envelope felt weighty in her hand, imbued with something more than just paper and glue. She carefully untied the faded ribbon – a pale lavender, subtly scented – that held it closed and unfolded it slowly, smoothing out the creases. Inside were two letters, tied together with the same ribbon.

Eve began to read, softly at first, her fingers tracing the loops of Miles' elegant script. "My dearest Louisa," she read aloud, "the rain here is relentless tonight, mirroring my thoughts perhaps. I long for the warmth of your smile, the sound of your laughter..." The handwriting was neat and precise, yet there was a slight rush to it, as if he were eager to get his words down before something, or someone, disturbed him. She noticed that he always started each letter with the same invitation: "Do join me for dinner at the Old Hall – if you can find us!" The paper itself felt smooth and expensive – thick stock, slightly yellowed with age. The lavender scent clinging to it was fainter now, but still present, a ghostly echo of Emily's scent – did Louisa favour lavender too, Eve wondered. She scanned the first letter, reading about Miles's thoughts on the changing tides, his observations of local wildlife, and a subtle undercurrent of longing for her company. It was filled with details – a specific type of wildflower he'd seen, the colour of the sea at sunset—as if he were trying to capture a moment in time and share it with her.

"...I find myself increasingly drawn to the sea, Louisa," Eve continued reading. "It holds both beauty and danger, just like our lives, don't you think? I fear I may be growing restless, yearning for something more than the routine of the Old Hall." Eve felt a strange pull, an unexpected connection to this man she'd only known through faded photographs and whispers. As she turned the page to the second letter, she noticed that Miles' handwriting was even more hurried, almost frantic. "Louisa, I must tell you... I saw her again last night. By the cliffs. Just for a moment – a flash of silver in the moonlight. She seemed to be beckoning..." The rain outside the Archive intensified momentarily, drumming a steady rhythm on the roof of the archive. Eve shivered, despite herself. She glanced out the window and for a brief second thought she saw someone standing by the window – perhaps it was just her imagination. The light shifted, throwing long shadows across the room, and for a moment, she felt as if the Archive itself were holding its breath, waiting.

It wasn't just the letters; it was the feeling. A sense that the town was watching her, sensing something of Miles's hidden emotions. Like she was intruding on a secret, long held and carefully guarded. The air seemed to vibrate with memory, and for a moment, Eve felt a distinct impression: that she wasn't just reading letters – she was stepping into their story. Eve continued to read, the rain outside a steady counterpoint to the rising tide of emotion within her. Miles's love for Louisa was undeniably clear, a tender and persistent current running beneath the surface of his words. But there was also something else – a sense that he was holding back, as if afraid to reveal too much. He wrote of longing, a deep ache for her presence, but also a feeling of obligation, a weight tied to his family and his position. "...Father's expectations are, as ever, heavy upon my shoulders," he wrote in the second letter. "He speaks of duty and responsibility, of securing my claim rather than Alexander's." There was a touch of melancholy in Miles's tone, as if he already knew it was a futile argument.

The letters spoke of stolen moments – a shared glance across a crowded room, a whispered conversation by the sea, a secret walk beneath the stars. Yet, they also hinted at a subtle disagreement, a difference in their perspectives on life and love. "I long to whisk you away, Louisa," Miles wrote in one, "to escape the confines of the Old Hall and lose ourselves in the wild beauty of Ashcliffe. But I fear my world is not your world." Eve noticed that he often used the phrase "waiting for the tide to reveal its secrets," a recurring motif that resonated with her in some way. It felt as if Miles believed that time – and perhaps something more – would eventually bring them together. He also pressed small, dried lavender sprigs between the pages of the letters – tiny purple emblems of his affection. As she read, Eve felt an increasingly profound connection to Louisa and Miles, no longer just names in a historical archive but people with hopes, dreams, and hidden vulnerabilities. She was experiencing their love first hand – not just through dusty photographs or faded documents, but through the intimate language of their letters. It was as if she were stepping into their story, feeling the warmth of their touch and hearing the music of their laughter.

A particular word triggered a sudden, vivid memory – a scent, really, or perhaps a taste. "Salt," Miles had written in the first letter, describing the smell of the sea at dawn. And suddenly, Eve was eight years old again, standing on the porch of Emily's cottage with her. Emily, Eve realised, must have been in her fifties – but she looked like a beacon of health and vitality, ageless and beautiful. Emily had been holding out a small, smooth seashell she'd found on the beach. She could almost feel the warmth of Emily's hand, hear her wild laughter as she told her about the creatures that lived within. It was fleeting, ephemeral – a ghost of a memory – but it was undeniably there, triggered by Miles's simple word. Eve looked down at the letters again, turning them over in her hands. Something felt off. The paper quality wasn't quite right. It was similar to the other letters in the box, certainly – creamy and thick – but subtly different. The ink was a slightly darker shade of sepia, richer perhaps, and there was a faint, almost imperceptible texture to it, like it had been mixed with something. Eve gave in to her whim, and sniffed the paper – she almost choked with the intensity of the lavender scent. "Like the ink was mixed with perfume?" Eve pondered aloud, catching her breath.

Eve examined the envelopes more closely. The ribbon tying them together was identical to the one holding the letters – a pale lavender silk, frayed at the edges. But she noticed that the ink on the address was slightly lighter, as if it had been applied later than the rest of the lettering. She pulled out another letter and compared it to the first. The handwriting in the second letter was noticeably rushed, as if Miles had been in a hurry to get his thoughts down on paper. There were even a few smudges and blots – unlike the neat, precise script she'd observed in the first. And then, she noticed it – pressed within the folds of the letter, almost hidden from view, was a tiny, perfectly formed seashell – pearlescent white with delicate pink stripes. "...I often think of you when I am by the sea, Louisa," Miles wrote in the final letter. "It is as if you are always there – a whisper on the wind, a glimmer of light on the waves." As she closed the box, Eve had the distinct impression that she wasn't just holding Miles's letters – she was holding fragments of his heart. And perhaps, she thought, she was beginning to understand why Emily had been so reluctant to discuss her family history. It seemed there were secrets lurking beneath the surface of Ashcliffe, secrets tied to the sea, to love, and to a legacy waiting to be revealed.

Feeling more than a little peckish, Eve decided to shut up the Archive for a while and visit The Chiron Cafe for lunch. Rita had taken over much of the day to day running of that place, since it's long-term tea-slinger and astrologer extraordinaire, Eloise, had begun to spend so much time at The Saltwater Siren with Stella and Albert. There was still the same rules, though – no menus, customers were served what the person behind the counter felt they most needed. The folk of Ashcliffe had long accepted Eloise's ways, and were happy to lean into similar with Rita. Having received a plate of food and a warm drink, Eve chewed thoughtfully on a corner of her sandwich – ham and pickle, Emily's favourite, according to Krissy – as she stared out at the rain-slicked beach. The salty air, thick with the promise of another storm, seemed to hum with an energy that both invigorated and unsettled her. "You're awfully quiet today," Eloise observed, tilting her head. "Lost in thought about Miles or something?"

"Just... processing," Eve mumbled, taking a large gulp of tea. "The letters. They feel so... real."

"They are real," Krissy boomed, always the pragmatist. "Dusty old love letters from a grumpy grandfather. Don't get yourself all worked up."

"It's more than that," Albert chimed in. "There's a quality to them. The paper, the ink... it feels deliberately chosen. And that scent – like someone had mixed perfume with the ink."

"Exactly!" Eve exclaimed, feeling her frustration rising. "Like it wasn't just about recording words; it was about preserving something special and distinct." They discussed it for another few minutes as Eve gratefully refuelled – a comforting blend of familiar opinions and gentle encouragement. The warmth of their friendship was a welcome anchor in the increasingly turbulent current of her research. They were, after all, the anchors that kept her from drifting too far out to sea.

Later, as Eve was carefully re-shelving the letters, Geraint appeared at the door, a worn leather satchel slung over his shoulder. "Eve," he said, a touch of urgency in his voice, "I was wondering if you might be free for a walk? The tide's turning nicely – thought we could check out Louisa's Cove properly this time, really delve for its secrets." It was an invitation Eve hadn't expected, and one that stirred something deep within her. A sudden pull towards the sea, stronger than she'd felt before. "That sounds lovely," she said, trying to sound casual. "Just... I'm a bit tired. I dreamed of such a storm last night, it really took it out of me."

Geraint paused, his gaze sharp and perceptive. "A storm, you say? Did you see anything specific?"

"Just flashes," Eve replied vaguely, clutching the side of her arm as if to ward off the lingering chill of the dream. "Grey skies, wind... the sea."

He didn't push it. "Well," he said finally, a slight smile playing on his lips, "perhaps tomorrow then?"

As she watched him head out, a prickle of unease settled over Eve. It wasn't just tiredness, there was something about the way he'd observed her – a subtle awareness that felt almost too knowing. He seemed to see more than she let on, as if he, too, sensed the secrets bubbling beneath the surface of Ashcliffe. Just then, Councillor Davies appeared in the doorway, looking even more imposing than usual. His jacket was damp, and his face held a perpetually sceptical expression. "Eve," he said, his voice clipped, "I just wanted to remind you to be careful with what you're digging up. Some things are best left buried beneath sand."

"The tide's mercy?" Eve asked, recalling his cryptic words from earlier. Davies offered a curt nod. "Precisely. Don't get too caught up in the past. It has a way of pulling you under." He fixed her with a piercing gaze before adding, almost as an afterthought, "And be careful what you unearth. Some secrets are better left undisturbed." He turned to leave, then paused at the door. "Especially those tied to the sea," he added, his voice low. "The sea remembers everything, doesn't it?"

As Councillor Davies disappeared down the hallway, a shiver ran down Eve's spine. It was as if he were echoing Miles's words from the letter – and adding a note of warning. She continued to pore over the letters, trying to decipher their meaning. The tide motif kept recurring - "waiting for the tide to reveal its secrets,", "the sea holds both beauty and danger,", "the ebb and flow of our lives.". It felt like Miles wasn't just talking about the ocean, that he was instead referring to something deeper – a hidden current that connected them all, past and present. She caught sight of Geraint standing in the doorway, watching her. He hadn't spoken, simply observed. "You seem preoccupied," he commented, his voice thoughtful.

"And you seem to pop up almost as often as Councillor Davies," Eve replied, teasing gently, "Though I certainly prefer your blend of academic logic to his cryptic tidings of doom and gloom."

"Did you notice anything interesting?" Geraint asked, side-stepping her words and instead striding confidently into the room. "In the letters? Anything at all?"

Eve hesitated. "I noticed something about the paper," she said finally. "It feels... different. Almost like it's been treated in some way."

Geraint nodded slowly. "Interesting. I examined them myself earlier. You're right to notice. The ink is unusually rich, almost iridescent in certain lights. And there's a faint watermark – a stylized seashell." He paused, his gaze meeting hers. "I believe," he said, a hint of excitement in his voice, "that they were deliberately designed to last. To hold onto their memories for generations." Geraint picked up a sprig of lavender from the pile of books in front of him. Noticing even this small movement, Eve felt a growing sense that she was caught in something much larger than herself. Something ancient, and perhaps, dangerous. The rain continued to fall, drumming a steady rhythm against the windows, as if urging her on. "Do you think," she asked Geraint, "that we're finally starting to see through the haze?" Geraint's eyes held hers for a moment, and she sensed a shared understanding – a recognition that they were both standing on the precipice of something profound. "I believe so, Eve," he said, his voice low. "I believe we are."

The rain had finally eased to a gentle drizzle by evening, leaving the air clean and salty as it drifted in through the open window of Eve's small cottage. Outside, the sea was a bruised purple under a sky slowly lightening with the promise of twilight. Her bedroom, tucked away at the back of the cottage, was a comfortable chaos – stacks of books threatened to topple from shelves overflowing with research materials, maps covered her desk in a patchwork of colours, and half-empty mugs of tea sat scattered amongst piles of digitised documents. The view from the window was quintessential Ashcliffe-on-Sea: a sliver of grey beach framed by craggy cliffs, perpetually battered by the waves.

It was a scene that had always soothed her – yet tonight, it felt imbued with an almost palpable tension. Having spent most of the day poring over Miles Thornton's letters, Eve now sank into her worn armchair with a mug of Earl Grey and a sense of profound weariness that settled over her. The scent of lavender, still lingering from the letters, mingled with the salty air to create a strangely comforting – and slightly unsettling – atmosphere. It was as if Emily had left behind more than just her archive, she'd left behind a faint residue of herself, a whisper in the wind.

Then, it began. Slowly at first, like the gentle lapping of waves against the shore. A sense of being underwater. Not drowning, not panicked – simply submerged, enveloped by a cool, dark embrace. The sounds of Ashcliffe began to fade, muffled and distorted as if heard through a thick layer of water. She was standing on a beach, but it wasn't the familiar grey expanse outside her window. This beach was wider, wilder – covered in smooth, dark stones that shifted beneath her feet. Above, the sky churned with bruised purple clouds, and the air hung heavy with the smell of salt and brine. And then she heard it: a melody, haunting and beautiful, weaving its way through the crashing waves. The Siren's Lament. It was as if the song itself was rising from the sea, pulling her in. She recognized it instantly – Stella had performed it at The Saltwater Siren earlier that day, and it had resonated deep within her. But tonight, it felt different – more urgent, more personal. It was as if the music wasn't just being played, instead it was being sung for her.

As she listened, fragments of a vision began to surface. Flashes of grey sky, punctuated by streaks of lightning. The roar of wind and waves, louder than any she'd heard in Ashcliffe – a furious, primal sound. And then, the sense of something lost beneath the seafoam: a small object, gleaming faintly in the flashes of light – perhaps a jewel, perhaps something more significant. She was looking down at the water, mesmerized, when she saw her. A woman standing just above the tide line, bathed in an ethereal silver light. Her hair flowed around her like seaweed, and her eyes held both sadness and an ancient knowing. It was Louisa Thornton – but less posed than in any of the photographs, more vibrant, almost luminous. She wore a simple white dress that billowed around her as if caught in a gentle breeze. Louisa turned towards Eve, a faint smile on her lips, and raised a hand as if to beckon her closer. "Come," she seemed to say, her voice carried on the wind. "The tide remembers everything."

Suddenly, the vision shifted. Eve was standing in the heart of the storm, feeling the full force of the waves crashing around her. Then, she saw it – a glimpse of a small boat struggling against the current, tossed about like a toy. And then, just as quickly, it was gone, swallowed by the churning sea. A sense of profound loss washed over her, a feeling that something precious had been taken from her, and from Ashcliffe itself. As Eve reached out to touch Louisa, to pull her closer, a dark shape emerged from the water – Miles Thornton, his face etched with worry. He was struggling against the waves, desperately trying to reach his lover. But then, with a final, terrifying surge, he was pulled under by the sea. The vision dissolved, and Eve was back in her armchair at home, gasping for breath. The Siren's Lament faded, leaving behind only the sound of the waves and her own racing heart. Eve sat there for a long moment, trying to piece together the fragments of the dream – or was it? She had a strange feeling that what she'd noticed glinting on the beach was none other than the small shell she'd found with Miles's letters earlier. A prickle of unease ran down her spine. The dream felt so real. So vivid.

Just then, a shadow fell across the window. She heard a hesitant knock on her cottage door, one that returned swiftly and with more gusto as it took her a few moments to collect herself before getting up. Geraint was standing in the doorway, his eyes narrowed with interest. "Asleep already?" he asked quietly. "Weirdly, I think I was," Eve replied. "I think I saw them... Louisa and Miles." Geraint stepped into the room, his gaze sweeping over the scattered books and papers on her desk. "The sea often reveals its secrets in dreams," he said, his voice thoughtful. "Especially when you're standing on the edge of something old and forgotten." He paused, then added, "Did it feel like a memory? Or perhaps... a premonition?"

"Like both," Eve replied, feeling a sudden sense that she was closer to unlocking the town's secrets than she had ever anticipated. "It felt like I was stepping into their story."

"You are part of their story now, you know, Eve," Geraint said, "and I'm wondering how that feels? To be suddenly so part of the folklore of this town, to discover a lost family... did you even know you were adopted?" He asked so matter of factly, that Eve found herself answering in the same way – as if the past was something she was on comfortable terms with. "I did. They never hid it from me, my parents – they were great friends of Emily's, she visited us often, celebrated all the key moments of our lives with us. I always thought it was kind of my parents, but now I know it was more than kindness. It was making sure that I heard the stories I needed to, experienced the love that Emily felt she could give me. Though," Eve admitted, "it does leave me with some questions. Questions that I hope the Archive can answer..." She trailed off, playing with her sleeves between her fingers idly.

"Like what?" Geraint pressed, gently.

"Well, my parents died a few years ago. My mum went first, then my dad – heartbroken, I think – followed soon after. They'd always been so deeply attuned to each other, it felt natural that they should enter death side by side." Eve said.

"So deep love has surrounded you forever?" Geraint asked. A little wistfully, Eve thought, as if his own past hadn't been quite so steadfast.

"Yes. And now it seems like the pattern of love and loss and longing runs even deeper than I realised." They looked at each other for a long moment before Eve remembered her manners and offered Geraint some tea. He accepted, gratefully, and they chatted long into the night, their laughter punctuating the weather's insistent clamouring.

PART TWO: SONGS IN THE MIST

6

CHAPTER SIX: FOLKLORE
AND FOOTPRINTS

The rain was a soft, insistent drumming against the windows of the Archive, a fitting soundtrack to the slow unravelling of Ashcliffe's past as Eve and Geraint scanned, photographed, and catalogued. It was the kind of rain that seemed to seep into everything – the brittle pages of the ancient maps, perhaps even Eve's own bones. Today, the weather mirrored the feeling in her chest: a persistent, low thrum of anticipation mixed with a touch of unease. Geraint was absorbed, his brow furrowed in concentration as he spread out a map on a large, scarred table. It wasn't a modern Ordnance Survey – this one was hand-drawn on parchment, the edges browned and brittle with age. Lines, faded but distinct, traced ancient paths along the Ashcliffe coastline – routes that looked less like roads and more like ribbons of forgotten trails.

"This," he said, his voice low and measured, "is based on folklore charts from the eighteenth century. Local legends, really, but passed down through generations. They detail not just landmarks, but... well, pathways, I suppose. Pathways tied to ancient beliefs." He tapped a delicate line with a calloused finger. "See here? This curve – it marks what they called 'The Siren's Scale' a narrow stretch of coastline known for its treacherous currents and, of course, the legend of the Siren herself." Eve leaned closer, studying the map intently. It was cluttered with symbols – stylized waves, tiny trees, and little sketches of what looked like standing stones. "So, it's not just about where she lured sailors," she said, referencing the siren myth. "It's about how they got here? Did she have paths?"

Geraint nodded, his eyes gleaming with a quiet excitement. "Precisely. The charts suggest multiple routes, all leading to certain points – particularly Louisa's Cove. And," he added, tracing another line with his finger, "this one, marked with a tiny spiral, is labelled 'The Weaver's Thread.' It connects the cove to... well, it connects the cove to Old Hall. The core of it all," Geraint continued, his voice gaining momentum fuelled by academic enthusiasm, "is this belief that Ashcliffe isn't just on the coast, it's of the coast. The land itself remembers." He gestured expansively at the map. "Let's start with Dragon's Tooth Rock. A truly unsettling tale, wouldn't you say? Locals believed a Welsh fisherman, which always appealed to me for obvious reasons, drowned in a storm centuries ago and added his tale to the stories already surrounding Dragon's Tooth Rock." Geraint rubbed his own nose. "They said if you listened carefully on a windy night, you could hear him grumbling about lost bloody catches and treacherous English tides." Geraint paused for effect. "Now it's forever hewn. Carved into the very bones of the place."

He tapped the map again, pointing to a jagged rock formation just off the coast. "Dragon's Tooth is prominent, isn't it? Almost deliberately placed. And then there's Mermaid's Pool. A beautiful name, but deceptively tricky. The tides around that pool are notoriously fickle – they shift and change without warning. It was said that if you tossed a jewel into the pool while making a wish, and it sank quickly, your wish would come true. But if it lingered on the surface, shimmering, well, it meant your wish was too greedy." Eve shifted slightly, pulling her cardigan tighter around her. "So, practical superstitions?"

"More than that," Geraint insisted. "They were connected to the land and its rhythms. The tides weren't just caused by the moon; they were influenced by something else. Something tied to the intrinsic magic of the place." He tapped a finger on Louisa's Cove again, his excitement palpable. "And then, of course, there's Louisa's Cove itself. It's the most consistently mentioned location in all these accounts – smugglers using it forays, hidden caches... and naturally, the siren."

He unfurled another section of the map, detailing a small bay tucked away on the northern coast. "The stories vary slightly, depending on who you ask. Some say she was a beautiful woman, luring sailors to their doom with her song. Others believed she was the sea – a manifestation of its power and beauty. And then there are the rituals... they'd hold them during full moons, down on the beach – offerings to appease the spirits, ensure a good harvest, to keep the worst of the storms at bay." Geraint leaned closer to Eve, lowering his voice. "They weren't just telling stories to frighten children. They were interpreting natural phenomena – a sudden squall, a high tide – as evidence of these ancient beliefs. Weaving it all together, they made sense of the world around them."

"And what about Emily?" Geraint asked, his gaze patient. "Did she tell you frightening stories about the local area when she was visiting your family?"

Eve hesitated, a familiar shyness creeping in. "She...she used to sing to me," she said, her voice barely above a whisper. "A lullaby. It felt...old." She struggled to recall the melody or lyrics – just a sense of melancholy and the smell of lavender clinging to it. It was fleeting, like trying to grasp smoke. "I can't quite remember it, but it's there, at the edges. Like looking through water that won't stop its own shifting."

Geraint nodded thoughtfully, tapping his finger on the map. "Interesting," he murmured. "The locals often said Emily had a connection to the sea – almost as if she'd been born of it." He paused, observing her carefully. "Do you remember anything else? Any specific details?" Eve closed her eyes, trying to conjure something – anything – from the depths of her memory. She pictured Emily's face, framed by rain and lavender, and suddenly a small detail surfaced: "She...she used to show me a seashell," she said, a faint smile gracing her lips. "A pearlescent one. She'd hold it up to the light and say, 'Listen closely, Eve. The tide remembers everything.'"

A warmth spread through her chest – a feeling of recognition, as if a long-dormant piece had finally clicked into place. "And she always smelled like lavender," she added, almost as an afterthought. "Like the whole town did, sometimes."

Geraint's eyes widened slightly. "That's remarkable," he said, his voice laced with excitement. "The scent of lavender was often associated with Louisa too, wasn't it? It's a key detail. Perhaps this map... perhaps it's not just charting locations, but also scents, sounds... memories." He gestured to the swirling lines on the parchment. "It seems Ashcliffe is determined to reveal itself slowly, perhaps its trying to decide if we're worthy enough to puzzle out its secrets."

"I think we've got the green light, you know. It's almost like... the Archive is helping us," she murmured to Geraint, who was meticulously photographing another set of maps. "Like it wants us to find something." Geraint, ever the pragmatic researcher, raised an eyebrow but didn't dismiss her feeling entirely. "Could be just confirmation bias, Eve. We're looking for connections and so we're seeing them." But as Eve began running her fingers along the spine of a slim volume bound in worn leather, tucked away on a lower shelf – marked simply 'Cove', she was sure there was more to it than that. This little book wanted to be found. For one thing, it wasn't in the order Emily had catalogued it: it felt deliberately hidden. Flipping through the pages, she noticed an entry dated late summer 1937: "It holds a memory, like a breath trapped in stone." The handwriting was hurried, almost frantic. Below the sentence were sketches – intricate drawings of symbols that immediately resonated with her. They resembled spirals, intertwined with stylized waves and what looked like miniature seashells. "These are the carvings!" Eve exclaimed, pointing to one of the sketches. "I saw a similar one at the cove!"

She turned the page and found Emily's notes detailing recurring motifs – seashells arranged in spirals, often near depictions of the tides. "She was obsessed with them," Eve observed, tracing the lines of another sketch. "And she noted that they appeared everywhere around Louisa's Cove." Emily wrote about feeling drawn to the cove, a sense of familiarity and recognition that surprised even her. "It holds a piece of myself," she'd written in one entry. "As if I were returning home after a long absence. It's unsettlingly familiar, yet utterly foreign." There was a passage underlined twice: 'The tide reveals, but only to those who listen.' Eve reread the entry aloud, feeling a shiver run down her spine. "'The tide reveals, but only to those who listen.'" she exclaimed. "It's like she knew...that I would be the one to find it."

Geraint leaned over her shoulder, examining the sketch of a spiral seashell with a magnifying glass. "Note the detail," he said quietly. "The spiral isn't just a simple curve, it's layered – almost as if it's designed to hold something within." He pointed to a tiny indentation in the centre of the drawing. "Almost like... a keyhole." A gust of wind rattled the windows, and for a moment, the Archive seemed to hold its breath. Eve felt a distinct shift in the atmosphere – a feeling that they were close to uncovering something significant, something deeply rooted in Ashcliffe's secrets. "I think," she said, her voice filled with a newfound certainty, "that we need to go back to Miles's letters and see if he either mentions or uses any of these symbols."

"'The tide reveals, but only to those who listen,'" Eve repeated, turning the page again and again in the slim volume. "It feels... personal. Like a message just for us." A shiver ran through Eve, this time not from the rain-damp Archive air, but from a growing sense of anticipation. "We need to see those letters again," she said decisively.

Back at her cottage, surrounded by stacks of already-digitized documents, they meticulously reviewed Miles's letters to Louisa. They'd spent the previous evening comparing them with Emily's notes, but now focused on specific phrases, searching for hidden meaning. "'The tide revealing its secrets,'" Geraint repeated, tapping a finger on the parchment. "It's not just about the sea; it's about unveiling something hidden. Something perhaps connected to Louisa." He pointed to a particularly frantic letter from late summer 1937. "Look at this – 'She was like a flash of silver in the moonlight, dancing on the waves. I felt as though I might finally grasp...something.'"

"Silver," Eve murmured, her fingers tracing the words. "Like she had silver hair? Or eyes?" Geraint nodded, pulling up a photograph of Louisa from Emily's collection. He zoomed in on a portrait, studying her features. "She did have strikingly silver-grey eyes, didn't she? And she was known for wearing silver jewellery – particularly a delicate pendant shaped like a seashell."

They continued to pore over the letters, noting Miles's consistent use of imagery related to the sea and light. He frequently described Louisa bathed in moonlight, shimmering with an ethereal glow. "He really fixated on her," Eve observed. "Obsessively."

"It suggests a deep connection, certainly," Geraint replied. "And look at this: 'I long to break free from these obligations, Louisa, to chase the horizon and find a life beyond duty.'" He highlighted another phrase. "'The tide revealing its secrets' - he feels trapped, yearning for something more." He turned to a letter written just days before his disappearance. "This one is particularly interesting," Geraint said, pointing to a large sketch tucked inside – a perfectly rendered spiral seashell, this time with tiny sequences of dots detailed neatly into the undulating spiral. "He's using the same symbol as in Emily's book."

"Maybe it's a code?" Eve suggested excitedly. "A way of communicating without being obvious?" A childhood love of crossword puzzles peeked out, surrounded by Eve's enduring Scrabble skills. "Possibly," Geraint agreed, his eyes gleaming with excitement. "Let's examine these dots more closely. They're not random. They correspond to letters in the alphabet – a simple substitution cipher." After some deciphering, they had their answer. The dots translated to: 'Look'.

"'Look? Oh!" Eve exclaimed, "Look Beneath!'" Eve exclaimed. "Like the note Emily gave me!"

Geraint nodded triumphantly. "It seems Miles was leaving clues for both Louisa and, potentially, Emily. And, through Emily, you. He wasn't just longing for a life beyond duty; he was trying to tell someone – someone who could understand – where to find something." He pointed back at the photograph of Louisa, where she was wearing a silver pendant in the shape of a seashell. He paused, a slow smile spreading across his face. "It's as if she was deliberately signalling him. A silent message whispered on the tide."

A sudden thought struck Eve. "He mentioned 'grasping something,' didn't he? Could that 'something' be the key?" She grabbed the volume of maps and turned to a sketch of Louisa's Cove – this time focusing on the spiral seashell symbol. "And if it's a key... could it be hidden within the shell?" The rain continued to fall, but now it felt less like a burden and more like a gentle encouragement. The tide, it seemed, was finally beginning to reveal its secrets.

As they pored over these details – the letters, the photographs, the ciphered seashells – Geraint noticed Eve's slight tremor, a subtle vibration in her hands like a tuning fork struck by a gentle chord. Likely caused by the rain drumming against the Archive windows and the weight of Ashcliffe's history swirling around them, he instinctively offered her his jacket. It was a well-loved number, smelling faintly of Lynx Africa and old paper, but it felt instantly comforting. Eve took it gratefully, pulling it around her shoulders. "Thank you," she murmured, her voice barely audible above the rain's rhythm. There was a brief but meaningful exchange – a shared glance, a comfortable silence as they both felt the weight of the place, the unspoken understanding that they were connected by more than just their research. It wasn't a grand gesture, just two people acknowledging the quiet intensity of the moment.

Then, he pulled out a handkerchief – a soft, linen square with a faded blue border – to wipe the rain from her cheek. Eve responded by reaching for his hand briefly, her fingers brushing against his for only a fraction of a second, before she quickly returned her attention to examining a particularly detailed map of Louisa's Cove. The contact was fleeting, almost accidental, but it sent a small jolt through both of them – a silent acknowledgement of the growing connection between them, fuelled by shared mystery and a deepening sense of place.

"You seem preoccupied," Geraint observed after a moment, his voice gentle. "Lost in the details?" Eve nodded, still slightly flushed from the brief touch of his hand. "It's just... everything feels so connected now," she said. "The letters, the symbols, Louisa herself. It's like pieces of a puzzle that have suddenly clicked into place."

"It is indeed remarkable," Geraint continued, adjusting his spectacles. "The way it's all coming together." He turned back to the photographs of Louisa, studying her face with renewed interest. "You know," Geraint said, a thoughtful expression on his face, "I've been delving into some other local legends while you were busy with the letters."

"Oh?" Eve asked, turning from her map.

"There's one that always fascinated me – 'The Seafoam Bride.'" He spread out a sepia-toned photograph of a woman standing on a rocky outcrop, gazing out at the sea. "It's a story that dates back generations: a beautiful woman who appears on stormy nights, luring sailors to their doom with her song." Geraint had connected it to the Siren legends immediately. "The locals believed she was the embodiment of the siren – both captivating and dangerous. A vision, really, a fleeting glimpse of beauty before they were dashed against the rocks."

"Do they say where she comes from?" Eve asked, intrigued.

"Often, it's said that she rises from the seafoam itself," Geraint replied. "And that on nights with a full moon and a strong tide, you can still hear her song carried on the wind."

He paused, looking at her intently. "I think Louisa might have been seen as her – the Seafoam Bride."

"So, she was the siren?" Eve mused, turning the word over in her mouth. "But a local one? Not just a mythological creature."

"Precisely," Geraint confirmed. "And if that's true... then perhaps understanding her means understanding everything. The letters, the symbols, even Miles's obsession with her. It all fits together – a tragic romance played out against the backdrop of Ashcliffe's secrets." He looked at her expectantly. "Do you think she chose to be the siren? Or was it forced upon her?"

"What I think remains to be seen," Eve said, determinedly, "but I feel that it's what Louisa thought about the whole thing that really matters." With renewed vigour, both Eve and Geraint went back to the task at hand, letting mug after mug of tea go cold as they continued to sift through documents, chasing symbols and sirens alike.

7

CHAPTER SEVEN: TRIADS AND TRIOS (PLUS ONE)

The rain continued its insistent drumming against the windows of The Saltwater Siren, a steady rhythm accompanying the melancholy notes of Stella's guitar. 'Rise Above the Siren's Snare,', a shanty that seemed to carry within it the weight of generations – or perhaps, just like tonight, the feeling of being slowly pulled under. Eve sat hunched over a small wooden table, illuminated by a single lamp, sifting through yet more of Emily's things. A tangle of lavender sprigs lay beside her, their scent still faintly clinging to the faded silk scarf she'd found tucked into one of Emily's old coats. Each object felt like a whispered secret, another piece of the puzzle that was slowly, frustratingly, coming together. "Lost again, Eve?" Stella asked softly when she'd finished performing, her voice husky from sea air and song. "The siren's got you in her grasp."

Eve nodded, pushing a stray strand of hair behind her ear. "It's just... so much. Emily left me this whole town, it feels like. And all these secrets. It's overwhelming." She picked up a small, tarnished silver locket – another of Emily's treasures – and opened it to reveal two tiny portraits: a bold Louisa and a smiling Miles Thornton.

"You look like you're about to be swallowed by it all," Eloise observed, sliding into a chair across from Eve with a dramatic flourish. "Like you've just been staring at the ghost of a particularly stubborn love."

"More like a whole family of them," Eve sighed, closing the locket and turning back to her pile of belongings.

"Oh, I know that feeling," Eloise declared, pulling out a delicate handkerchief and dabbing at her eyes theatrically. "There was this chap once. Absolute whirlwind! We met in a thunderstorm – fitting, really – and it was like being struck by lightning. Suffice to say, it didn't last. I spent twenty years wondering if 'lightning' was worth the burn." Stella strummed a chord on her guitar, adding a wistful note. "Sounds like it wasn't the siren's song to me," she murmured. "But hopefully you've seen that love is worth the risk now, eh, Eloise?" After a look of heat passed between Eloise and Stella, Stella continued, "My music... it's often just echoes of longing, you know? Like trying to catch smoke in your hands. I used to love Alanna Brooke – brilliant, fiery woman – but back in '07, she said my music was 'comfortable.' Too much so. Said I hadn't stretched myself enough."

"'Comfortable' is a brutal word," Krissy agreed, entering the fray with a mug of steaming tea. "Especially when it comes to art. It's good to be comfortable sometimes, but not if it's holding you back."

Rita followed, her own mug in hand, and added, "Exactly, Krissy! Oh my gosh, the things that we could tell Eve about love the tangled web of love..."

"We were practically fighting over him," Krissy laughed, referring to Tom. "Remember? He was so understated, we both thought the other had him!" Realising that this could get a bit too intimate for conversational purposes, Krissy attempted to change the subject. "It's brilliant what you've done for The Chiron, Rita – it feels like a whole new place."

"Well," Rita said with a blush, "thank you. I don't know if it's exactly the same place now that Eloise used to manage, but it's certainly something." She nudged Krissy before adding quietly, as if she couldn't help herself, "Tom certainly did have a way of seducing you. Didn't he, Krissy?"

Krissy smiled knowingly. "He did. And I'm glad we both realized it before it was too late."

The rain continued its steady rhythm, as if waiting for the next secret to be unveiled. Eve looked up from the locket, a new feeling stirring within her – a sense that she wasn't just piecing together Emily's past, but perhaps, her own. "It's... it's like looking at a faded photograph," Eve said quietly, turning the locket over in her hand. "I always felt a little adrift here, didn't I? Like I was watching Ashcliffe live through other people – Emily, her mother, now me. But now... now it feels like I've been waiting for this my whole life." She paused, letting the scent of lavender from the sprigs beside her mingle with the air. "Emily always hinted at something bigger, something tied to the sea, but I just thought she was eccentric. Now... now I think she was protecting me. Protecting us all." Eve traced the faces in the locket – Louisa's sharp intelligence and Miles's quiet intensity. "It's strange, isn't it? To realize that a part of you has been hidden away for so long, tucked into the pages of someone else's history." A small smile touched her lips, tinged with sadness. "I always felt a little...different. Like I didn't quite fit in. Now I think it's because I'm Louisa's granddaughter – and Miles's too! It makes sense now, all the feeling that there was something connecting me to this place."

She looked around at her friends, their faces illuminated by the lamp light. "It feels a little overwhelming, though, doesn't it? Like suddenly everyone and everything has a new layer of meaning. A siren's song woven into the everyday."

"You're not just piecing together Emily's past," Geraint had said during their nighttime chat at her cottage, over cold tea and scanned documents – and she realized he was right. "You are the past. You're part of the story, too." She closed the locket, a new resolve settling over her. "It's daunting, but... exciting. I think Emily wanted me to understand. And I will. I just hope I can find out what secrets were worth keeping for so long, and if those secrets are beautiful or dangerous."

"Eve! You won't believe this," Albert burst through the door of The Saltwater Siren, a little out of breath and clutching a thick, leather-bound book like it was a lifeline. "I've been digging – really digging – into the folklore. And... well, you're not going to believe what I found." Heads turned, and Eve immediately felt a familiar wave of anticipation. "Let me guess," Krissy said, taking a sip of her tea. "More sirens? Some pirates?"

"Better!" Albert exclaimed, placing the book on the table with a satisfying thud. "It's a collection of local legends – handwritten in the early 1900s by a certain Mr. Benjamin Applewood – yes, he seems to have been a relation of mine! And he mentions everything. The Seafoam Bride, 'The Weaver's Thread,' even details about the layout of Louisa's Cove."

"So, you've got proof?" Eve asked, her eyes widening.

"Not exactly proof," Albert admitted, running a hand through his already-dishevelled hair. "But Benjamin certainly describes a ritual – a 'Sea Blessing' performed by the women of the house to ensure a safe voyage and a bountiful catch. And it involves... lavender." He gestured vaguely at the sprigs scattered around the room.

"Lavender?" Stella repeated, intrigued. "That's odd. Very specific."

"Exactly!" Albert said excitedly. "And he also mentions a 'Key of Echoes,' hidden somewhere near the Cove – something to unlock a secret held by the tide. He even sketches it! It looks like... a seashell with a spiral inside." A hush fell over the group. Albert exclaimed, tapping excitedly on his grandfather's book. "Benjamin said it happened during a particularly heavy fog – thick enough to swallow the lighthouse. He saw someone, and she seemed... lost. Like she was searching for something or someone." He flipped through the pages, stopping at a faded sketch. "Here! Look at this. A quick drawing of Benjamin's. Just a glimpse of her, caught in the mist."

The sketch depicted a woman with long, flowing hair and an ethereal quality, standing on the cliff edge, gazing out to sea. "It's Louisa," Eve breathed, tracing the lines of the drawing with her finger. "But... how could it be?"

Albert continued, "He mentions Miles was obsessed with collecting seashells, particularly spirals. He says it was more than just a hobby – it was a ritual for him. He believed each spiral contained a fragment of the ocean's memory."

"Perhaps he thought they held secrets to Miles's disappearance." Eve said, thoughtfully.

"Precisely!" Albert replied. "And I think... I think it might be more than just a hobby. It's like he was trying to capture something – to hold onto a piece of Louisa, perhaps."

As Albert finished speaking, a combination of factors triggered a breakthrough for Eve: the scent of lavender, thick and comforting now, hanging in the air; Stella's melancholic music, weaving a spell around them; the photograph of Louisa and Miles – her grandparents – resting on the table; and finally, the worn leather-bound book itself. It all clicked into place with startling clarity. "It's... it's like looking at a faded photograph," Eve said quietly, turning the locket over in her hand. "I always felt a little adrift here, didn't I? Like I was watching Ashcliffe live through other people – Emily, her mother, now me. But now... now I think I've been waiting for this my whole life." She paused, letting the scent of lavender from the sprigs scatter around her. "Emily always hinted at something bigger, something tied to the sea, but I just thought she was eccentric. I wish I'd spent more time with her, hearing her stories for what they really were."

Eve looked around at her friends, their faces illuminated by the lamp light. "Emily wasn't just telling stories – she was one." She gestured towards Albert. "You're right. It's not just about Emily's past. I am the past. I'm part of the story, too." A slow smile spread across her face, tinged with sadness and a sudden, exhilarating understanding. "I'm Louisa's granddaughter – and Miles's too. It makes sense now, all the feeling that there was something connecting me to this place. And I think... I think Emily wanted me to understand. And I will. And I think she knew, deep down, that Miles wasn't just searching for her. He was searching for me." Outside, the rain intensified, drumming against the glass like a restless heartbeat. "It's all about the spirals," Stella murmured, strumming a single chord on her guitar. "Miles was looking for something hidden within them... just like us." Eve looked from the locket to the sketch of the 'Seafoam Bride' in Albert's book.

"It... it makes sense," Eve stammered, turning to face the circle of faces at The Siren. "Everything."

"It is a lot to take in," Stella observed quietly, nodding at the others. "A whole family history – pirates and smugglers and sirens. And now you're part of it."

"There must be other Thorntons," Eloise mused, swirling the tea in her mug. "More secrets waiting to be uncovered. Perhaps a rebellious aunt who ran off with a smuggler? A brooding uncle obsessed with collecting seaweed?"

"Or maybe," Krissy added with a grin, "a long line of siren-singers!"

A touch of fear mingled with the excitement. "It's... overwhelming," Eve admitted, feeling the weight of it all settle on her shoulders. "Like suddenly I'm tied to this place in a way I never understood before."

After a little more talk, back and forth and over and over, Eve wandered back to the Archive, the rain outside mirroring the tempest brewing within her. She ran a hand over the leather-bound cover of Emily's journal, feeling as though she were tracing not just words but also memories. Why had Emily kept it all from her? Even as an adult, hadn't she hinted at something bigger, something tied to the sea? The pirates, smugglers, and the siren – they weren't just local legends any more, they were family. A legacy of seafaring adventure, hidden secrets, and perhaps a touch of danger. Did this legacy hold a responsibility for her? To protect it? To understand it? She thought about her parents, the ones who'd died a few years back. Now, with their legacy of quiet and comfortable love set alongside whatever had happened with Emily... Eve found herself wondering, 'If Emily was my mother, then who was my father'. The question suddenly feeling urgent. Was he another Thornton, swept up in Ashcliffe's tangled history?

Looking at Emily's meticulously kept records, a sense of belonging swelled within her – a feeling that she was part of something bigger than herself, connected to generations past by the tides and the secrets they held. It wasn't just about piecing together Emily's life, it felt like she was inheriting a role, a purpose. Eve looked out at the rain-swept sea, feeling both connected and isolated. The sky was bruised with grey, and the waves crashed against the cliffs with a rhythmic intensity. The sense was that she'd only just scratched the surface of Ashcliffe's secrets - and that those secrets were ready to pull her under. Councillor Davies. He always seemed to be there – lurking in the shadows, offering cryptic warnings, guarding his own secrets. How exactly did he fit in to all of this? Was he a protector of the town's history, or just another piece of the puzzle trying to keep her contained? Eve turned back to the Archive, to Emily's legacy, to the scent of lavender and the promise – and perhaps the threat – of more to come. A smile touched her lips - a little sad, but mostly determined. "Right," she said to herself, stepping back into the rain. "Let's see what else you've got." As if in answer, a small, almost invisible indentation on the spine of one of Emily's oldest journals caught her eye. She ran her finger along it – a tiny spiral, perfectly formed. It was identical to the ones depicted within Albert's book, sketched by Benjamin Applewood, as well as having a remarkable resemblance to the ones drawn by Miles and Louisa in their letters and journals.

Just then, Councillor Davies appeared in the doorway, as if summoned by the rain itself. He was holding a single, perfect seashell – a spiralled conch, gleaming faintly in the lamplight. "A rather persistent piece of weather we're having," he observed, his voice gravelly and laced with a familiar hint of suspicion. "Almost as if the sea wants to keep its secrets."

"Did you find this?" Eve asked, holding up the shell she'd discovered in Emily's belongings. Davies nodded slowly. "Found it tucked away in Emily's desk. Thought you might appreciate it. A reminder," he added, his gaze lingering on her for a moment, "that some things are best left undisturbed."

"Like what?" Eve challenged, intrigued.

He hesitated, then placed the shell on the table, its spiral mirroring the one carved into the cover of Emily's journal. "Perhaps... like the secret to unlocking that 'Key of Echoes'."

Before Eve could press him further, a sharp knock echoed through the Archive. It was Geraint, ready to continue the digitization project, all the while looking for answers to the mysteries of Ashcliffe. Councillor Davies quickly made an exit, as he always seemed to do with Geraint was around. Just then, Albert barrelled in, looking as if he'd run all the way from The Saltwater Sire. He let out a shout of excitement. "Look at this!" He held up a page from Benjamin Applewood's book – a hand-drawn map detailing the coastline surrounding Ashcliffe. "He marks 'The Siren's Scale' with a spiral and writes: 'Where the tide whispers secrets to those who listen'."

"'The Siren's Scale'," Geraint mused. "That's where the tides are at their most treacherous. It's a narrow strip of beach, constantly battered by waves." He glanced at Eve. "And it's close to... Louisa's Cove."

"Do you think she was actually 'The Seafoam Bride'?" Eva wondered aloud.

"It certainly seems likely," Geraint replied, his gaze fixed on the map. "Consider this: The 'Sea Blessing' ritual – a way to appease the Siren and ensure safe passage for Ashcliffe's fishermen. And if Louisa was the 'Seafoam Bride,' then she would have been the one performing the blessing."

As they discussed, a memory flickered through Eve's mind – a detail Emily had mentioned almost casually: "My mother always said the sea chose its own bride."

"And what about her father?" Eloise asked. "What was Miles's role in all of this?" As if on cue, the lights in the Archive flickered and dimmed, plunging the room into semi-darkness. A gust of wind rattled the windows, carrying with it the scent of rain and – faintly – lavender. "It's like she wants us to go," Eve said softly, as if channelling the spirit of Emily. "To seek her in the waves. Let's go find out what she wants," she said. "And let's see if we can finally find out who my father was." Outside, the rain continued to fall – a constant reminder that the secrets of Ashcliffe weren't buried – they were waiting to be revealed by the tide.

8

❦

CHAPTER EIGHT: LOUISA'S COVE

The rain in Ashcliffe-on-Sea was relentless, a thick, clinging dampness. It felt like the sea itself was weeping, a constant, grey curtain drawn across the sky and blurring the horizon. The air smelled powerfully of salt and wet stone, laced with the sharp tang of seaweed and the faintest hint of lavender – Emily's enduring signature on the town, and now, increasingly, on Eve's own life. For months now, she and Geraint had been meticulously piecing together fragments of Ashcliffe's history, guided by the whispers of Emily Thornton's Archive. The journal entries, the cryptic maps, the photographs – each discovery felt like a small victory against the town's carefully culti-vated secrecy. They were convinced that Louisa's Cove held the answer to Miles Thornton's disappearance in 1938, and with it, perhaps, the key to understanding not just his fate, but her own.

Today, they were finally ready to venture there again, to properly explore the cove as revealed by the unusually low tide. It was a phe-nomenon rarely seen this late in the season – a prolonged retreat of the sea that exposed stretches of beach and rock face previously sub-merged. The tide hadn't just gone out – it had relinquished its hold, revealing a new landscape, sculpted by water and time. As they walked along the muddy path leading to the cove, the sound of the waves crashing against the cliffs intensified – a constant roar punctuated by the occasional, mournful sigh as the sea pulled back further. It felt less like entering a place and more like stepping into a memory, a slowly unfolding tableau. The grey light, filtered through the low-hanging clouds, cast long, dancing shadows that played tricks on the eye, making the weathered rocks seem to shift and change with every wave.

"It's...different," Geraint murmured, his gaze fixed on the expanse of sand before them. "Lower than I remember. More exposed."

Eve nodded, pulling her scarf tighter around her neck. "Emily said her mother loved the sea," she replied, a familiar warmth spreading through her as she remembered Emily's voice, laced with a hint of wistful longing. "That it chose its own bride." She'd had that memory – fleeting yet vivid – since they'd discovered the letters, the ones detailing Miles's passionate, complicated love for Louisa and the feeling that the tide itself held the secrets to his fate. It was a simple image, yet it resonated with an unsettling certainty.

The cove itself was dominated by a towering cliff face on one side, sculpted by centuries of wind and wave. At its base lay a small sandy beach, bordered by jagged rocks covered in patches of bright green moss. A narrow inlet, carved into the rock, offered shelter from the prevailing winds – and perhaps, Eve thought with a sudden shiver, from something else entirely. As they stepped onto the exposed sand, a sense of anticipation hung heavy in the air, like the humidity before a storm. It wasn't just the thrill of discovery, it was a feeling that they were on the cusp of something significant, something long-buried and waiting to be unearthed. "Look at this," Geraint said, pointing to a section of rock face near the inlet. The tide had revealed a dark, narrow opening, almost perfectly circular – like a doorway carved by water itself. "It's... small," Eve observed, stepping closer. "Could that have been...?" As she did, something crunched under her feet. It was subtle at first, barely perceptible when she looked down amidst the grey and brown hues of the beach, but as she bent down to examine it, she realized it was a scattering of seashells – not just any seashells. "Spiral shells," she whispered, remembering the repeated sketches they'd seen depicting them – "Look."

The rain in Ashcliffe-on-Sea intensified as they stepped fully into Louisa's Cove, transforming it from a promising reveal to a damp embrace. It wasn't merely exposed; it felt...larger, more cavernous than Eve remembered from their first visit. The tide had peeled back the layers of sand and silt, revealing a tapestry of grey rock formations – jagged teeth gnawing at the coastline, slick with seaweed and glistening with moisture. Pools of seawater, reflecting the overcast sky like scattered sapphires, collected in crevices and hollows, humming with the quiet music of dripping water. The air was thick with the scent of brine and something else – a primal, earthy fragrance that spoke of centuries spent battling wind and wave.

"Look at this," Geraint said, pointing towards the base of the cliff face where they'd previously spotted the carving. The carving was still there, though now partially submerged, as if briefly lulled back to sleep by the retreating tide. It depicted a swirling pattern – not quite a spiral, but something more fluid, like a ribbon caught in a current. It seemed to pulse with a faint energy, almost visible beneath the dampness. Eve stepped closer, her fingers instinctively reaching out to trace the outline of the carving. Geraint, pulling out a small notebook and sketching the carving, said, "There's something... deliberate about this. Not just random erosion." Suddenly, a loose pebble shifted underfoot, sending a tiny spray of wet sand upwards. As she adjusted her balance, Eve felt a slight stumble – she reached out to steady herself and instinctively grabbed for Geraint's arm. He nearly lost his footing on the slippery rock, teetering precariously close to a small drop-off before she caught him with surprising strength. "Steady!" he exclaimed, grinning as he regained his balance. "You've got reflexes like a cat."

They both laughed, momentarily distracted from the mystery of the cove. As they continued their survey, scanning the rock faces and pools for anything that might offer a clue, Eve's eye was drawn to an old, weather-beaten boulder nestled amongst a cluster of seaweed-draped rocks. It looked like it had been sitting there for centuries, silently observing the ebb and flow of the tide. "What about that one?" she asked, pointing. "It stands out like a sore thumb." Geraint followed her gaze and, with a grunt of effort, managed to shift the boulder slightly. Beneath it, partially buried in the sand and seaweed, lay an old tin lunchbox – rusted and battered by time and the elements. "Well, well," he said, his eyes widening with interest. "Fortune favours the curious." Inside, nestled amongst a tangle of damp paper and decaying fabric, was another one of Miles's journals. It was waterlogged and fragile, but the pages were legible, filled with his elegant, slightly sloping handwriting. As they carefully turned the first page, revealing a sketch of Louisa – a delicate rendering capturing her beauty and grace – it felt like holding a piece of the past in her hands.

The initial entries were familiar: observations about the weather, reflections on his life as a Thornton, and, of course, endless descriptions of Louisa. "Her eyes are the colour of the sea after a storm," he wrote in one entry, "and when she smiles... well, it's like the sun breaking through the clouds." As they turned to other pages, they discovered snippets of dialogue – Miles recounting a conversation with Louisa about the legends of the cove. "She believes," he wrote, "that the sea remembers everything. Don't forget to look beneath." Then came details of a specific ritual she'd mentioned – a ceremony performed by the women of the Thornton family on the eve of the summer solstice, held within the cove itself. "We cast lavender into the waves," he noted, "and whisper our wishes to the sea. It is said that the 'Key of Echoes' lies hidden there, waiting to be found."

"The Key of Echoes?" Geraint repeated, scribbling in his notebook. "That's intriguing." He read aloud from another entry: "Louisa says the tide reveals its secrets to those who listen closely. I believe she's right." Eve felt a thrill course through her – this was it. This was what they'd been searching for. "And did he find it?" she asked, turning the page with anticipation. The next entry was shorter, more frantic: "She heard her laughter on the wind! A flash of silver in the moonlight...the tide is pulling her back." It was followed by a hastily sketched drawing – a depiction of Louisa standing on the edge of the cove, silhouetted against the setting sun. As Eve examined the journal further, a small, dried seashell fell out from between the pages – a spiral shell, identical to those etched into the rocks and to the countless other spiral shells that seemed to permeate this mystery. Holding it up to the light, Eve felt another wave of that unsettling certainty wash over her. This wasn't just about uncovering history, this was about discovering a connection – a profound and perhaps dangerous one – to her own family's past.

"What are we going to do with this new journal of Miles's then?" Geraint asked, eyes gleaming with the joy of an academic finding an entirely new clue – one it seemed like nobody else had gotten their hands on first. "What we always do," Eve replied, "take it back to the Archive, scan it, catalogue it, and make sure it stays safe for generations to come." Geraint's look was as stormy as the weather surrounding him. "You don't want to look at it first... for, uh, personal reasons?"

"I'm the town's archivist, Geraint," Eve said sombrely, "I know what Emily would want me to do." The rain hammered down with renewed ferocity, plastering their hair to their faces and turning the slate-grey sand slick beneath their boots. The reasoned discussion now simmered with a prickly tension, fuelled by the wind and the relentless drumming of the storm. "It's like you're trying to bury it all, to pretend it didn't happen," Geraint said, his voice tight against the gale. He gestured towards the cove, encompassing its secrets. "But the past has a way of rising up." Eve shifted her weight, pulling her scarf tighter around her neck. "I'm not burying anything, Geraint. I'm uncovering it. Digitizing Emily's work – making it accessible for others to learn from. It's not about hiding; it's about understanding." She felt a familiar tightness in her chest, the weight of Emily's legacy – and now, increasingly, her own – pressing down on her.

"But you're being so careful," he pressed, his blue eyes narrowed against the rain. "Selective with what you share, almost... defensive. Like you're afraid of what you might find." He stepped closer, closing the distance between them. "Don't you feel it? This place...it remembers."

"I do," Eve replied, her voice barely audible above the wind. "That's why I want to understand it properly, not rush into conclusions based on a few faded photographs and cryptic notes."

"And what if those 'cryptic notes' are pointing towards something significant? Something that someone – perhaps someone who didn't want it remembered – wants to keep hidden?" He scanned the cove, as if searching for evidence. "You're carrying the weight of this town, Eve. And you're letting it weigh you down."

"Maybe," she conceded, a flicker of irritation in her voice. "Or maybe I just don't want to believe that everything was some grand, romantic tragedy."

The argument hung in the air for a moment, punctuated only by the crash of waves and the shriek of the wind. Then, a particularly strong gust swept across the cove, whipping rain into their faces and forcing them to shield their eyes. They instinctively huddled closer together, seeking a sliver of protection from the elements – and perhaps, something more. As they adjusted, both noticing it at almost the same time, they heard it: a low, resonant hum, just beneath the roar of the storm. It wasn't the wind, nor was it the waves. A sound. Faint, but undeniably there – like a distant choir or the murmur of voices carried on the breeze. "Did you hear that?" Eve asked, turning to Geraint. He nodded slowly, his brow furrowed in concentration. "Yes. It's... strange." He held up a hand, silencing her. "Listen." They stood for a moment longer, holding onto each other slightly for balance, straining their ears against the onslaught of sound. The hum intensified briefly, then faded again, leaving only the wind and rain.

"It felt... close," Eve whispered, shivering not just from the cold but from a sudden prickle of unease. "Like it was coming from within the rocks." As they debated whether it was simply their imaginations, playing tricks on them in the storm, a small, almost imperceptible movement caught her eye. A flash of silver – not from the rain, but from the cliff face itself. Just for a fraction of a second, illuminated by a break in the clouds, she saw a shimmer, like light reflecting off water.

She turned to Geraint, pointing. "There! Did you see that?"

He followed her gaze, his eyes widening slightly. "It was just the rain," he said quickly, but there was a hint of doubt in his voice. The rain had indeed intensified again, and as another gust buffeted them, they were forced even closer together for balance. It was in that moment – a brief, shared connection amidst the chaos – that a small spark ignited between them. His hand instinctively reached out, brushing against her arm to steady her. It was fleeting, almost unconscious, but it sent a surprising warmth through her.

Eve turned then, meeting his gaze. Geraint's eyes were dark and intense, flecked with grey from the rain and – she thought – something else. A flicker of...curiosity? Or perhaps, something deeper. There was a vulnerability there that hadn't been immediately apparent, beneath the layers of research and quiet observation. For a heartbeat, time seemed to slow down. The sounds of the storm faded into a muted background hum, and it was just them – standing on the edge of the wild, ancient cove, connected by that brief touch. Geraint didn't immediately pull away his hand, though. His fingers lingered for a moment longer than necessary, gently gripping her forearm. It wasn't a possessive grip, but one of shared awareness, of connection. "It's cold," he murmured, his voice low and slightly husky. She nodded almost without thinking, feeling the warmth of his hand against hers. "Yes," she replied, her own heart beating a little faster. "It is."

Another gust of wind ripped through the cove, tugging at their scarves and sending spray from the waves onto their faces. As they straightened up, a small smile touched his lips – a genuine, unexpected smile that seemed to chase away some of the shadows around his eyes.

"Maybe," he said, glancing towards the entrance of the cove where she'd spotted the glimmer of silver earlier, "we should look for the source of that sound." He gestured towards the narrow inlet, a hint of excitement in his voice. And as they turned to face the swirling rain and the mystery of Louisa's Cove together, it was clear that their shared pursuit of Ashcliffe's secrets had only just begun – and that something more, something decidedly electric, might be brewing beneath the surface.

The storm, which had begun as a forceful guest, tightened its grip on Louisa's Cove, transforming it into something altogether more formidable. The wind howled like a tormented spirit, whipping the rain into a blinding curtain and driving the waves higher up the beach with each crashing surge. It wasn't just a weather event any more, it felt like the cove itself was reacting to their presence, to their probing, to the questions they were asking of its ancient stones. The air thickened. The waves swelled dramatically, clawing at the base of the cliff face, sending plumes of spray that soaked them to the bone. "It's getting worse," Geraint observed, his voice barely audible above the wind. "We should head back." But Eve couldn't tear her gaze from the rock face. The intensity of the storm seemed to be sharpening everything, highlighting details she hadn't noticed before. And as if in response to that heightened focus, a brief, vivid memory flickered through her mind – not hers entirely, but overlaid onto her own experience like a superimposed image.

Eve saw, for just a fraction of a second, a woman standing on the rocks near the inlet. She was tall and slender, with long, dark hair flowing down her back. Her dress billowed around her in the wind, and she wore a simple silver necklace – shaped like a silver seashell. And then, as quickly as it appeared, the image vanished, leaving behind only a lingering feeling of melancholy and a sense of profound connection. "Did you... did you see that?" Eve asked, turning to Geraint, her heart pounding in her chest. He studied her face intently, his brow furrowed with concentration. "See what? Just the storm." But there was a subtle hesitation in his voice, as if he too had sensed something unusual. "A woman," she said, struggling to articulate the memory. "Standing on the rocks. Like... like Louisa."

As if confirming her observation, another gust of wind buffeted them, and this time, the rain seemed to thin slightly, revealing a patch of sky – just for a moment – allowing a beam of pale light to pierce through the storm clouds. And as that light touched the rock face, it revealed more of the carving: a swirling pattern, now partially unveiled from beneath years of accumulated moss and spray. It wasn't simply a wave; it was a stylized siren – a woman with long, flowing hair and fish-like scales adorning her arms, poised to lure sailors to their doom. But there was something more – a subtle detail that Eve recognized immediately: the carving of a spiral seashell nestled within the siren's hand. "It's the siren," she whispered, tracing the outline of the carving with her finger. "And look... a spiral shell." As they stood there, mesmerized by the unfolding image, a warmth spread through them – not just from the proximity to each other, but from the cove itself. A shared memory, perhaps? Or simply a resonance with its long history?

"It's like it's... telling us something," Geraint murmured, his gaze fixed on the carving. "Like it wants us to know." The storm continued its relentless assault, but it no longer felt quite so hostile. They were seeking shelter now, instinctively drawn together for comfort. Geraint unbuttoned his waterproof jacket and offered it to Eve, who gratefully accepted it, wrapping it around her shoulders. As she did, their hands brushed – a fleeting, electric touch that sent another ripple of warmth through her. "Let's find some shelter," he said, his voice softer now, the edge of professional curiosity replaced with something else. "Over there, by that cluster of rocks." They huddled together beneath the overhang of a large boulder, seeking refuge from the driving rain and the wind. The closeness was palpable – not awkward, but comfortable, as if they'd been doing it for years. Eve found herself instinctively leaning against him, drawing warmth from his presence.

"It's cold," he said again, a hint of amusement in his voice. "You're shivering."

"Only a little," she admitted, her gaze drifting to the carving on the rock face. "I think... I think this place is trying to tell us something." Geraint shifted slightly, bringing an arm around her shoulders and pulling her closer. "Maybe it just likes having company," he said, his voice low and close to her ear. "Especially in a storm like this." The touch was longer this time – a deliberate warmth against her back. She didn't pull away; she simply relaxed into it, allowing herself to be enveloped by the unexpected comfort of his presence. It wasn't just physical warmth; it was a feeling of recognition, of connection – as if she had known him for a lifetime. "I feel like I know you," she said quietly, her voice barely audible above the roar of the storm. "Even though we've only known each other for a few months."

He tilted his head up, meeting her gaze directly. "Maybe," he replied, a small smile playing on his lips. "Or maybe the sea has a way of choosing its own companions." The rain hadn't let up entirely, but it had softened to a persistent drizzle as Councillor Davies materialized at the edge of the rock formation, seemingly sculpted from the storm itself. He wasn't startled by their presence, didn't even offer an apology for his sudden arrival – just stood there, impeccably dressed in a dark coat, a hint of amusement playing on his lips. "Well, well," he said, his voice smooth as polished stone, "If it isn't the new custodians of Miss Thornton's legacy." He paused, letting the words hang in the air, laced with a subtle, knowing satisfaction. "I was beginning to think you might be lost in the Archive." Eve bristled slightly at his casualness, but Geraint stepped forward, his gaze steady. "We're making progress, Councillor," he replied, his tone measured. "We believe Louisa Thornton may have been 'The Seafoam Bride.'"

Councillor Davies chuckled, a dry, rustling sound. "A romantic notion. But the sea rarely cares for romance. It takes what it wants, and often demands payment." He turned to Eve, his eyes, surprisingly sharp behind his spectacles, assessing her. "The sea doesn't always give back what it takes."

The words hung heavy in the air, a cryptic warning that felt both ancient and immediate. Before either of them could press him for clarification, he simply nodded once – a curt acknowledgement – and was gone, swallowed by the gathering mist as quickly as he'd appeared. A flash of lightning ripped through the sky, illuminating the cove in an ethereal silver glow. For a heartbeat, everything shimmered – the jagged rocks, the glistening seaweed clinging to the shore, and Eve herself. She felt strangely exposed, vulnerable, like she was being scanned by something unseen. Geraint, ever observant, tilted his head, a dry amusement dancing in his eyes. "Well," he remarked, adjusting his waterproof jacket, "perhaps there's a new Seafoam Bride in town." She felt an odd pull, a familiar resonance. Suddenly, she noticed something she hadn't seen before – a tiny, almost invisible inscription etched into the base of the rock, just below the siren's hand. Eve knelt, brushing away the damp earth to reveal the words: "Beneath the Lace."

"'Beneath the Lace'?" Eve whispered, turning to Geraint. "What does that mean?" Another flash of lightning struck, closer this time, and for a fraction of a second, Eve saw it – not just a carving of the siren, but a faint shimmer in the air around her, like heat rising from sand. It was as if she, too, was being illuminated, revealed. And then, she felt it – a cold, slick touch on her ankle, like something wet and smooth sliding beneath her boots. She glanced down to see a single, iridescent seashell lying nestled in the mud, its spiral shell gleaming in the silver light. Before either of them could react, a low growl echoed from behind the rocks – not the sound of an animal, but something deeper, older, and undeniably watchful.

9

CHAPTER NINE:
RESONANCE

The rain hadn't entirely relinquished its grip on Ashcliffe-on-Sea when Eve finally dragged herself and Geraint back to her cottage. It wasn't the violent, howling storm of earlier that day, instead it was a persistent, almost apologetic drizzle, as if the sea itself were still wiping away its tears. The cottage, nestled just above the tide line, felt both familiar and subtly altered, imbued with the lingering energy of Louisa's Cove. It was a comfortable chaos, of course – stacks of digitized papers threatened to topple from shelves, teacups sat precariously on antique tables, and lavender sachets fought for dominance amongst the scent of beeswax polish and damp wool. But tonight, there was a deeper stillness, a quiet hum beneath the everyday clutter, as if the cottage itself were holding its breath.

The first thing Eve did was to light a fire in the hearth – a ritual she'd adopted after Emily's death, a small act of defiance against the relentless dampness and the feeling that Ashcliffe was perpetually trying to seep into her bones. The flames crackled, casting dancing shadows on the walls lined with shelves overflowing with books and curiosities, each holding a piece of the town's fragmented history. She poured herself and Geraint both a mug of Earl Grey – Emily had always favoured it – and took a long sip, letting the warmth spread through her. "It feels...charged," she said, turning to Geraint who was examining a faded map of 'The Siren's Scale,' tracing its contours with his finger. "Like something shifted while we were at the cove." Geraint nodded, his brow furrowed in concentration. "The tide certainly did. And the rain seemed to amplify it – like the sea was trying to reveal something. I particularly noticed the way that carving on the cliff face seemed brighter after the storm, almost as if it had been waiting for the water to recede."

He pointed to a small detail on the map – a fainter line branching off from 'The Siren's Scale,' leading towards the Old Hall. "And look here. This little pathway...'The Weaver's Thread' perhaps, it wasn't marked in Emily's notes, but it connects directly to the old gardens around the Hall." As they discussed the details, a strange sensation settled over Eve – not quite a memory, exactly, but more like a resonance, a vibration that seemed to hum within her bones. She felt as if she'd heard something before, seen something in Louisa's Cove, and now it was slowly bubbling up to the surface. It started subtly, a fleeting image of lavender fields stretching out towards the sea, then intensified – a snatch of melody, hauntingly beautiful and laced with both joy and sorrow.

"I keep getting this feeling," she said, her voice slightly breathless. "Like...like I'm hearing Louisa."

Geraint looked at her intently. "You've always been unusually receptive to the past, Eve. And you have that shared resemblance with Louisa – it's more than just a photograph. It's in your eyes, in the curve of your smile. It's as if...as if she left a little piece of herself within you." He gestured towards the worn leather-bound journal lying on her desk, illuminated by the flickering firelight. "Perhaps Miles's journal holds some answers. Let's start there."

Eve picked up the journal, its pages brittle and stained with seawater. A small smile played on her lips as she opened it to a random page. Her voice, at first a little hesitant, began to gain confidence as she started reading aloud, her tone deepening slightly with each sentence. "'The sea...she is both the most beautiful and the most terrifying thing I have ever known,'" Eve read, pausing for a moment to let the words hang in the air. "'A shimmering expanse of sapphire and emerald, reflecting the sky above like a shattered mirror. And yet, within that beauty lies an ancient power – a relentless strength that can swallow men whole with its briefest whim. Today, I walked along the shore, listening to her whispers, feeling the spray upon my face...and for a moment, I felt as though she was speaking directly to me.'" She continued, turning the page. "'She remembers everything,'" she read, her eyes scanning the spidery handwriting. "'The lost ships, the drowned sailors, the secrets whispered on the wind. She holds them all within her depths – treasures and tragedies alike. It is a lonely thought, to be but a small part of such an immense, knowing thing.'"

Geraint listened intently, his gaze fixed on Eve as she read. He occasionally made small observations or asked clarifying questions, feeding the momentum of her reading. "He was clearly captivated by it," he commented after a particularly evocative passage about the sea's 'hungry embrace.' "Did Emily mention anything about Miles being drawn to coastal walks?"

"Yes," Eve replied, turning another page. "'He used to spend hours down at the Old Pier, the one that's not there any more, just watching the waves." She paused. "Emily said he felt... connected to it somehow. Like it understood him better than anyone else." She continued reading, her voice now flowing smoothly. "'The tide reveals its secrets slowly, doesn't it? It pulls back the sand, exposing what was hidden beneath, and then, with a gentle surge, it carries them away again. I feel as though my life is much like that – constantly shifting, revealing glimpses of something deeper, but never quite letting me grasp hold of it completely.'"

"And," Geraint added thoughtfully, "he used the phrase 'the tide reveals its secrets' quite often, didn't he? Emily mentioned it, too, several times in her letters."

Eve nodded, a small smile gracing her lips. "It seems to have been his mantra. He wrote it after Louisa... after they spent that evening together at the cove." She turned another page and read aloud: "'Tonight, she danced with the moonlight on her skin, a flash of silver in the twilight. Her laughter echoed across the waves, as bright and fleeting as a gull's wing. I felt as though I had glimpsed something ancient and beautiful – a secret whispered by the sea itself.'" A comfortable silence settled over them for a moment, broken only by the crackling fire. Eve looked up from the journal, her eyes meeting Geraint's. She sensed a shared understanding growing between them, forged in the quiet intimacy of their discovery. "It's like... like he was trying to tell us something," she said softly. "Something about Louisa and the sea."

"Indeed," Geraint replied, his voice low. "And perhaps, something about himself." He leaned forward slightly, resting his elbows on his knees. "He was a keen observer of detail," Geraint observed, turning a page in the journal and examining a small sketch of a wave. "That's what drew him to folklore – the way it captured the spirit of a place, the stories people told themselves to make sense of the world around them." He paused, considering his words. "He was particularly fascinated by local legends. Did you know he'd spent years researching Ashcliffe's history? Before Emily, that is."

"I hadn't really thought about it," Eve admitted. "He seems to have been so busy building The Saltwater Siren into a venue, much like Stella was last year."

"More than that," Geraint smiled faintly. "He was a scholar of Welsh folklore – specifically, the traditions that had made their way to Kent over the centuries. He'd always said he felt a little bit of Cymru in Ashcliffe. It's remarkable how many stories travel across the water, you know?"

"So, what was his favourite legend?" Eve asked, leaning forward with interest. Geraint took a moment to gather his thoughts, as if carefully selecting the perfect words. "Well, he was particularly captivated by the story of Dragon's Tooth Rock. It's a relatively local tale, not widely known outside of Ashcliffe, but it held a special significance for him." He paused again, allowing Eve to anticipate. "I gave you a brief description of it before, but really it's a bit of a long one."

"Go on," she encouraged, "I'd love to hear the real version!"

"Dragon's Tooth Rock," Geraint began, his voice gaining a touch of wonder, "is a jagged outcrop of rock that juts out from the coast about a mile east of the village – you can just make it out on a clear day if you walk along the cliffs. Locals have always believed it was once the tooth of a dragon, shed during one of its battles with the sea."He described how, for centuries, Ashcliffe fishermen had told stories about the rock. "They said that when the wind blew from the north – particularly a fierce, whistling wind – you could hear the dragon's breath emanating from Dragon't Tooth Rock. It was considered both a blessing and a warning. A blessing because it meant good fortune at sea, but a warning to respect the power of the ocean."

"They'd tie little ribbons to the rock," Geraint continued, his voice filled with enthusiasm. "Red ribbons for sailors returning safely, blue ribbons for good catches... and sometimes, if they were feeling particularly generous, they'd tie white ribbons for lovers hoping for a prosperous marriage." He painted a vivid picture of the locals – their weathered faces, their thick woollens, the way they'd huddle together on the pier, listening intently to each other and the wind. "They'd listen to the wind, you see, and interpret it as the dragon speaking. A gruff voice for a storm, a softer one for calmer seas. And if you listened carefully enough," he added with a smile, "you could almost believe it."

"It sounds...magical," Eve said, captivated by his description.

"It was magical," Geraint agreed emphatically. "To the people of Ashcliffe, it wasn't just a rock. It was a living part of their history, their beliefs, their identity. And they had this wonderful tradition – every year on the winter solstice, they'd gather at the foot of Dragon's Tooth Rock and sing to the dragon, offering it gifts of seaweed and fish in thanks for its protection."

"So what specifically appealed to Miles about that legend?" Eve asked, turning to him. "Was he Welsh? Did it connect with something?" Geraint considered this for a moment, his fingers tracing patterns on the journal cover. "Absolutely it connects! His mother was Welsh, by all accounts, though she died when he was very young indeed. The imagery is firmly rooted in Cymru – the traditions of the dragons and the sea are so deeply intertwined there. But beyond that," he explained thoughtfully, "I think it was the sense of connection – to the land, to the past, to something larger than himself. It's a feeling he seemed to crave." He paused. "I get the feeling that he often felt a little... apart, in Ashcliffe, you know? Like an outsider looking in. A bit of Cymru – and that legend – helped him feel rooted, connected to the story of this place."

"I can see that," Eve said, nodding slowly. "It's like... like he was searching for a piece of himself here." She thought about her own feeling of being slightly apart, of always having felt just a little bit out of sync with Ashcliffe. "And you?" she asked, turning to him. "What drew you to folklore?"

"For me," Geraint replied, his eyes twinkling, "it's the way it reveals the hidden truths about people and places. The stories we tell ourselves shape our reality, don't they? And in a small town like Ashcliffe, those stories are often the most important thing of all."

"I can see the truth in that." Eve said, thinking of her friends – of Krissy, Albert, Stella, Eloise, Rita, and Tom, all probably clustered at The Saltwater Siren or The Chiron Cafe. "It's the way they've all lived their lives," Eve said quietly. They were a familiar tableau – Krissy meticulously arranging seashells on the counter, Albert polishing brass lamps with a handkerchief, Eloise consulting her tarot cards with an air of profound wisdom, Rita laughing heartily at something Tom had said, and Stella gesturing emphatically. What Eve usually found comforting, today she found mournfully poignant. "Content," she murmured, turning to face Geraint. "My friends, I mean. Like they've always been here, rooted in Ashcliffe."

"And you?" he asked gently, his gaze perceptive. "You've delivered mail to them all for years. You've seen their lives unfold, one letter at a time."

Eve nodded slowly, a flicker of something – sadness, perhaps – crossing her face. "I hadn't really realised what I was missing until Emily died and left her the Archive. She wasn't just an eccentric old lady, she was a huge part of my life – from my earliest childhood onwards."

Eve paused, searching for the right words. "I always thought of her as...well, as Emily. Just there. Like a constant in a world that felt like it was constantly shifting." A small smile touched her lips, tinged with nostalgia. "Like when I was about eight years old and had lost my favourite stuffed toy – a duck, I think it was. I'd been inconsolable for hours, sobbing on the front step. Then Emily just appeared, carrying a basket of lavender and a freshly baked scone. She didn't say much, just sat beside me and let me feel everything I was feeling."

"And you never really thought about it then?" Geraint asked, his voice soft.

"Never," Eve replied honestly. "I was too busy being upset! But now...now I realize she just was. She was always there to deliver a comforting word, a funny story, or sometimes, just a quiet presence. She'd always be waiting for me at the Post Office with a smile, or leave a little note tucked into my mailbag – 'Don't forget your boots!' or 'The rain will bring secrets.' It was those small things, I suppose."

She looked down at her hands, as if trying to recapture the feeling of that long-ago afternoon. "I always assumed she just liked to be helpful. But now...it feels like she was watching me, quietly observing my life, like she knew something I didn't."

"You felt a little...untethered, then?" Geraint asked, his gaze thoughtful.

"Exactly," Eve said, turning to him with a small smile. "Like I was always just passing through, delivering mail and seeing snippets of everyone else's lives – but never really part of them. Like an observer, rather than a participant. I delivered their post, yes, but they all seemed so... rooted. So sure of where they belonged." Eve gestured vaguely around the room. "It wasn't that they weren't nice people—they were lovely. But they had their routines, their families, their places in Ashcliffe. And me? I was just delivering mail."

"And you didn't realize it until now?" Geraint prompted gently.

"Not really," she admitted. "It just seemed... normal. Emily's death made me realise how much I'd taken for granted – all those small, everyday connections. It felt like a piece of myself had been missing, and suddenly, with Emily gone, it was revealed." She paused, taking a sip of her tea. "I always thought she just enjoyed the quiet life here. But now..."

"Now you suspect there's more to it than that," Geraint finished for her. "You think she deliberately kept things... hidden."

"Maybe," Eve said, a hint of excitement in her voice. "Or maybe she simply didn't realize she was hiding anything. It's funny, isn't it? I spent my whole life around her and I never really saw her. Not truly." She turned back to him, a small smile playing on her lips. "Do you think she knew – all along – that the Archive held so much more than just local history?"

Geraint nodded slowly, his eyes filled with understanding. "I believe it does. And I suspect," he added, leaning forward slightly, "that she left it to you for a reason." He paused, considering. "You have her observation, her quietness... and perhaps, a little of that same sense of being 'untethered'—a willingness to look beneath the surface."

"I've always been good at noticing things," Eve said quietly. "At seeing what others miss."

"Indeed," Geraint replied, his voice laced with a hint of anticipation. "And I think you're about to discover that Ashcliffe – and your family—has quite a few secrets waiting to be uncovered." The rain continued its steady drumming against the cottage windows, now feeling less like a persistent reminder of Ashcliffe's dampness and more like a gentle soundtrack to their conversation. A small fire crackled merrily in the hearth, casting dancing shadows that seemed to fol-low Eve's every movement. The earlier quiet had deepened, becoming richer with unspoken thoughts and shared understanding.

"There was this one time," Eve said, her voice a little lower than before, "when I was about twelve. I entered Ashcliffe's summer fete with an old apple pie recipe I'd found at the back of a notebook of Emily's. It was...it was pretty good, I thought." She allowed herself a small, wistful smile.

"And?" Geraint prompted gently.

Eve hesitated for a moment, as if trying to unearth a long-forgotten memory. "I didn't win," she said quietly. "Mr. Linden – with his ac-claimed Victoria sponge – took first place. And I just...I got so embar-rassed. I remember rushing out of the hall, hiding behind my mum's skirts. I felt like everyone was looking at me, judging me."

She looked up then, meeting Geraint's gaze for a moment. "It seems silly now, doesn't it? But at the time, it felt like such a big deal. Like I hadn't measured up." A flicker of vulnerability crossed her face – a hint of the insecurity she'd kept carefully guarded for so long.Geraint didn't say anything immediately. He simply observed her for a mo-ment, his eyes filled with a quiet empathy. Then, he reached out and gently touched her arm – a brief, reassuring gesture that sent a surpris-ing warmth through Eve. "We all have those moments," he said softly, his voice low and thoughtful. "Moments where we feel like we haven't quite lived up to our own expectations. At least you had a decent pie to eat at the end of it?"

"It's just...I always felt a bit like I was watching from the sidelines," Eve admitted, turning slightly to face him. "Like I should be doing something – more – but I never quite knew what. Emily always seemed so... involved. Always part of things." She paused, searching for the right words to express a feeling she'd carried with her for years.

"Perhaps," Geraint suggested, "that's because you were observing, noticing details that others missed. You had a quiet strength – a keen-ness of eye. And those are valuable qualities."

A shared glance passed between them – a brief but potent connection, as if they were communicating on a level beyond words. The silence stretched for a moment, filled only with the crackling fire and the rain outside."I always worried I wasn't enough," Eve confessed quietly, her gaze fixed on the flames. "That I'd just settle for a quiet life, like Emily. But now... now I think maybe it's okay to be observant, to notice things."

"It's more than okay – it's essential," Geraint replied, his voice filled with conviction. "And you have a remarkable ability to connect the dots. To see patterns where others don't." He shifted slightly, bringing himself a little closer to her. "Emily clearly recognized that in you."

"She did," Eve agreed softly. "She used to say I had 'a good eye for stories.'"

Another pause – this one felt longer, charged with unspoken emotion. The rain seemed to intensify momentarily, drumming a slightly louder rhythm against the roof. "Do you ever feel like you're waiting for something?" Eve asked suddenly, her voice barely above a whisper. "Like you're waiting for a sign or a clue? Like Emily did?" Geraint nodded slowly, his eyes searching hers. "Perhaps," he said thoughtfully. "Or perhaps 'waiting' is simply part of the journey. And maybe the clues are already there – we just need to learn how to see them." He gestured towards the window with a slight smile. "Like the rain, for example. It's been falling steadily all day, hasn't it? And now... it feels like it might be trying to tell us something."

Eve looked out at the rain, watching as it streamed down the windows in long, silvery streaks. "It does," she said quietly. "It just needs someone to listen." She turned back to face him, a small smile playing on her lips. "I think I'm starting to hear it."

A subtle shift had occurred – a loosening of the guard, a willingness to be more vulnerable. The conversation felt deeper now, richer with shared emotion and growing trust. The air in the room seemed to hum with a quiet energy – a sense that something significant was about to happen. As she looked at Geraint, she realised she wasn't just observing him any more: she was seeing him – his kindness, his intelligence, his gentle understanding. And for the first time in a long time, she felt like she belonged. Not just because of her role as postwoman, or even archivist. Not just because she was a good friend and an astute observer. No, this was different. "Thank you," Eve said quietly, her voice filled with genuine gratitude. "For listening."

The rain hadn't let up, a persistent drumming against the roof of Eve's cottage that seemed to amplify the quiet in the room. They'd been circling each other for hours now, a comfortable dance of shared theories and tentative observations about Louisa's Cove. The scent of lavender, thick with the dampness of the day, hung heavy in the air – a constant reminder of the women who had tied this place together. Now, bathed in the soft glow of a single desk lamp, the silence felt different, charged with something more than just historical intrigue. "It's...remarkable," Geraint said finally, breaking the spell, his gaze fixed on the spiral seashell Eve had been tracing patterns in with her finger. "How much of this is Emily deliberately feeding us? And how much is the Archive itself whispering?"

"I think," Eve replied, turning to face him, "it's a bit of both. She wanted to share it, but she also wanted to protect it. Like... like guarding a secret." She felt a warmth spread through her chest, a feeling that had been steadily growing since they'd met – a comforting familiarity mixed with a thrilling uncertainty. Geraint shifted slightly, the thick wool of his green jumper brushing against her arm, and the simple contact sent a shiver down her spine. "And you think she suspected... that we'd be drawn to it?"

"I do," Eve confirmed, meeting his eyes. They were a surprisingly warm shade of grey, flecked with green – like the sea just after a storm. "She always seemed to know when someone was close to uncovering something."

He nodded slowly, considering this. "It's almost as if... she wanted us to find her."

"Or perhaps," Eve said, a small smile playing on her lips, "she wanted us to find each other."

The words hung in the air, unspoken but undeniably present. The feeling of anticipation – that quiet hum of possibility – intensified. Geraint didn't immediately respond, allowing the thought to linger. He was studying Eve, really seeing her, beyond just the observant postwoman and the Archive's newest inhabitant. "You felt it too," he said quietly, his voice a little lower than usual. "When we were at the cove... that pull. Like something wanted us there."

"Like the sea really did remember," Eve echoed, remembering the vividness of their shared vision – Louisa standing on the rocks, defiant and beautiful. Geraint took a step closer, closing the distance between them. "And you," he said, his gaze lingering on her face. "You felt it too, didn't you? The connection. To Louisa... to Miles... to Ashcliffe." Before she could answer, he reached out and gently brushed a stray strand of hair from her cheek. It was a small gesture, simple and deliberate, but it sent a current through her – a warmth that spread outwards from the point of contact. He hesitated for just a moment, his hand lingering on her skin before finally drawing back. "It's been a long day," he said, offering a slight smile. "And I suspect we've only scratched the surface."

Then, with a deliberate movement, she leaned in and kissed him – softly, briefly, just a brush of lips against his. It wasn't a passionate kiss, not yet. It was more like recognition, an acknowledgement of the shared mystery, the growing connection between them. Eve straightened up then, pulling back slightly. A flicker of uncertainty crossed her face – almost imperceptible, but there. Was he cautious? Did he sense something more from her, a willingness that surprised him? Eve felt a small pang of insecurity, a tiny flutter in her chest. She'd been so focused on the past, on unravelling Ashcliffe's secrets, she hadn't really considered her future with Geraint. She certainly hadn't seen herself kissing him, not until she was there, leaning in, lips brushing against his like a promise they were both sharing. The silence returned, but it was different this time – filled with unspoken questions and possibilities. A beat stretched between them, filled with the scent of lavender and rain, and the promise of more to come. Then, he smiled again, a genuine, warm smile that reached his eyes. "Well," he said, breaking the silence. "Shall we decipher another map?"

CHAPTER TEN: THE TAMBOURINE RITUAL

The Saltwater Siren felt smaller than usual, filled with a hushed reverence. The light was muted, painting everything in shades of pewter and grey – a fitting backdrop for the quiet grief settling over the town. It wasn't a boisterous affair, no, Emily's birthday memorial was intimate, held amongst the mismatched tables and nautical décor she'd so loved. Krissy sat slumped on a stool, her usually bright eyes red-rimmed, occasionally dabbing at them with a tissue. Tom watched her quietly, his hand resting lightly on her arm in a gesture of silent comfort. Albert, as always, was observant, taking in the small details – the way the rain tracked down the windows, the faint scent of lavender clinging to the air despite it being many months since Emily had worn it.

Eloise, ever dramatic, was attempting to be comforting, offering everyone tiny cups of tea and dispensing words of wisdom – "It's just… she wouldn't want us to mourn for long!" – but her voice trembled slightly with emotion. The rain seemed to deepen its rhythm, as if joining in the quiet remembrance. It was then, amidst the grey and the damp, that a faint, familiar melody drifted from the corner – the beginning bars of a tambourine ritual, a tune Emily used to play when she wanted to evoke memories. Stella took a deep breath, her fingers dancing over the worn tambourine. It wasn't just music she was playing: it was a performance. Her shoulders relaxed slightly, and as she began "The Siren's Lament," she seemed to melt into the melody. Her eyes, usually bright and mischievous, were closed now, lost in thought. She swayed gently with the rhythm, her hands moving with a practised grace that spoke of countless nights spent captivating the patrons of The Saltwater Siren. Her face wasn't just showing sadness, it was revealing layers of memory – joy, longing, perhaps even a touch of Emily's own shrewd mischievousness.

Stella took a deep breath, her fingers dancing over the worn tambourine. It wasn't just music she was playing; it was a performance. She closed her eyes, and as she began "The Siren's Lament," she seemed to melt into the melody. Her shoulders relaxed slightly, and as she sang, "Come Back To Me, My Love, My Heart!" she didn't just sing the words; she embodied them. "The sea she sheds another tear, / for your return, my lover dear. / Nine months have passed and now the squall / of reddened face and lungs scream full." The lyrics hung in the air, heavy with longing. "She carries words across the sea," Stella sang, her voice gaining a mournful quality, "She tells me of your scuppered boat, / how no more will your laughter float." It was a heartbreaking ballad – a lament for a love lost to the sea. Eve felt it then – a distinct chill down her spine, not entirely unpleasant. As Stella sang, "Now lightning strikes this siren's heart," she caught a whiff of lavender, faint and familiar, hanging in the air like a ghost of Emily's scent. For a moment, she saw it – a flash of Emily's smile, a quick, knowing glance from across the room. It felt as though she was being watched, not with malice, but with a gentle curiosity.

Krissy, sitting closest to her, reached over and squeezed Eve's hand. "That tambourine," she whispered, her voice thick with emotion, "it's like Emily's laugh chime. It always brought such joy, you know? Like little bells ringing in the wind." The sound of the tambourine wasn't just rhythmic; it held within it the echo of Emily's warmth, her easy laughter, and a tangible connection to the past. It felt like a tiny portal opening, letting in fragments of Emily's spirit. As Stella continued, "Come back to me, my love, my heart! / Echoes in the thunder start / as I pace long and hard the floor / your footsteps never reach my door," Eve realized the song wasn't just about a lost lover – it felt tied to something deeper, something rooted in Ashcliffe itself. It was as if the sea was repeating an old story, a familiar sorrow. "As if, my love, you've longed to part... / now thunder beats for this siren's heart." The final line resonated within her. It felt... personal. Suddenly, she understood. It wasn't just a legend; it was a plea – a longing for reunion, echoing through the generations.

Stella's fingers flew across the tambourine, building to a crescendo. The sound was almost hypnotic – a swirling blend of notes and rhythms that evoked both sadness and hope. And then, just as suddenly as it had begun, it faded away, leaving a lingering resonance in the air. As Stella took a final breath, she looked up, her eyes meeting Eve's for a brief moment. There was something in her gaze – not quite a smile, but an acknowledgement, a shared understanding. It felt like Emily herself was saying, "Keep looking." And then, as if responding to the last note, a single drop of rain splashed against the windowpane – followed by another, and another - until it looked like the sea itself was weeping with them. It was then that Eve noticed, for just a second, the faint shimmer on Stella's tambourine – a hint of iridescent colour, as if it had caught a flash of silver in the moonlight.

Before Eve could make something out of the silvering of the tambourine, Eloise had sat down next to her. "There's a current of something... guarded... swirling around you," Eloise murmured, settling into the worn armchair.. Rain continued to fall, a constant, gentle reminder of Ashcliffe's damp embrace. "A feeling that secrets aren't just held, they're waiting – poised to surface." She gestured towards Eve with a delicate hand, her eyes already scanning, as if reading a map. "It's not simply intuition, you know. It's more than just sensing something is amiss. It's a wellspring of emotion that can be both beautiful and overwhelming."

Eloise laid out Eve's astrological chart – a swirling kaleidoscope of colours – on a small table. "Let's look at your foundation... Mercury in Pisces. You doesn't just think, you feel your way through life. Your intuition is a powerful guide – often subtle, oftener startlingly accurate. It's why you're so good with people, and why you picks up on the unspoken." Eloise tapped the chart thoughtfully. "And then we have Venus in Cancer – deeply connected to home and family, likely drawn to nurturing relationships. That explains your love for this town, for its history—and I suspect it's a big reason you took on Emily's archive, without ever guessing at the hidden connection between the two of you!"A pause followed as Eloise studied the placements further. "Pluto in Scorpio... now that's interesting. You're not afraid of the dark, certainly, but recently you've had to confront some intense emotions and hidden depths within yourself. There's a strength there – a resilience – forged through facing difficult truths. It suggests someone who digs beneath the surface, looking for what others hide."

Eloise diligently shifted her attention to the outer planets. "Uranus in Sagittarius... that's a key! This is where we start seeing those sudden insights – flashes of inspiration that feel like glimpses into another world. You're not just receptive, no, you're open to unexpected shifts, to being surprised by what you discover. It will be crucial as you delve deeper into these mysteries." With a slight smile playing on her lips, Eloise continued. "The Sun in Aries adds a spark – you're not afraid to pursue what you want, even if it feels a little impulsive at times. A touch of that fiery drive. And finally... Gemini Ascendant – a very telling placement. You express your dreams and intuitions through communication – the perfect placement for a postwoman and archivist! It means you're likely to piece things together by talking about them, by sharing what you discovers."

Eloise took a long, deep breath, letting the information sink in. "Saturn in Sagittarius... now that is significant. You're carrying the lessons of the past, perhaps feeling a little restricted by tradition or belief. It suggests echoes from previous lives or ancestral patterns—and someone else's secrets are intertwined with yours. It could be related to your family history, and specifically, to the long-held traditions of the Thorntons. And Neptune in Capricorn? This is where things get truly intriguing," Eloise said, leaning forward slightly. "There's an element of mystery surrounding your lineage – perhaps with some unconventional members or hidden connections. A past that isn't entirely what it seems. It suggests a blurring of boundaries between reality and illusion – a sense that not everything is as straightforward as it appears." She paused, considering Eve closely. "It's why you feel so strongly connected to Emily, to Louisa... it's in your blood. That connection goes deeper than just being a Thornton."

"The combination of those placements," Eloise explained, tracing the lines on the chart with her finger, "explains why you're so drawn to the Archive" She looked up at Eve, her gaze penetrating. "And it all connects to the sea, of course. The water element dominates – intuition, emotion... a longing for something just beyond reach. The Scorpio Pluto," Eloise emphasized, "that suggests you'll need to confront some powerful emotions, perhaps even painful ones, to uncover the full truth about her family and Ashcliffe. It's not going to be easy, but you're equipped to handle it." She glanced towards Geraint, who was listening intently. "And I suspect he has a role to play in that as well. It's no surprise you felt a presence at Louisa's Cove, Eve," Eloise concluded, her eyes twinkling. "The echoes of the past are strong there – particularly those connected to the 'Seafoam Bride'. That legend... it's more than just folklore. It speaks to something real, something deeply rooted in this place." She glanced back at Eve."So," Eloise said with a final smile, "it looks like your journey is just beginning – and it's going to be quite a ride."

As swiftly and gently as she'd arrived, Eloise got up, "Tea, anyone?" she asked. Without waiting for a response from either the wide-eyed Eve, or the rumpled Geraint, she swayed off to the bar of The Saltwater Siren. The rain continued to fall, a gentle percussion against the windows, as if echoing the quiet rhythm of remembrance. "You have a way of seeing things others miss... almost like you're tapping into something deeper," Geraint observed quietly, his gaze thoughtful as he studied Eve. "It's not just intuition; it's like you're finding your way into a current."

"Well, I do spend my days surrounded by letters and old photographs," Eve replied, self-consciously, fidgeting with the strap of her bag. "And Emily certainly had a knack for making you notice things."

"It's more than that," Geraint responded, his voice lower now. "You seem... attuned to this place. Like it holds memories waiting to be uncovered." He paused, observing her carefully. "Like you were expecting to find something here."

They fell into a comfortable silence for a moment, punctuated only by the clinking of glasses and the occasional murmur from the other guests. "It's funny," Eve said finally, "Eloise was going on about my astrological chart – it felt a bit... intense."

"She has a way of making everything intense," Geraint chuckled, a genuinely warm sound. "But I get the feeling that she's usually right." He glanced at the tarot cards spread out on the table. "The Tower reversed, The Moon... A little eccentric, a little mysterious."

"Definitely," Eve agreed, smiling slightly. "And always with that hint of something hidden." She shifted her gaze to a photograph on the mantelpiece – a faded image of Emily laughing, perched on a stool at the bar, surrounded by friends. "I always liked how she could make you feel like you belonged here."

"It's a lovely place," Geraint commented, his eyes drawn to the photo too. "A comforting sort of chaos." He noticed her lingering on Emily's face – a wistful expression in her eyes.

As they both looked at the photograph, their hands brushed slightly as they reached for it – a fleeting touch that sent a surprising little jolt through Eve. She quickly pulled her hand back, but didn't look away from the photo. "It's funny," Eve said, tilting her head slightly, "I just... I feel like she was waiting for me. Like this whole thing – finding the archive, coming here – it was all part of some plan."

"Perhaps," Geraint suggested, a hint of amusement in his voice. "Or perhaps she simply wanted to pass on a story that needed telling." He noticed something then – a subtle detail in Emily's photograph they hadn't both seen before. "Look at the lace on her dress," he said, pointing with a slender finger. "It's not just any lace – it has a tiny spiral woven into it." Eve leaned closer, examining the photo more closely. "You're right! I never noticed that before." A small smile spread across her face. "It's like she was sending us a clue."

"Or maybe," Geraint said, his voice almost a whisper as he reached out and gently brushed a stray strand of hair from her cheek – a brief, charged touch - "she knew exactly what to expect." Suddenly, a brief flashback flickered through her mind – the sound of Emily's laughter, the scent of lavender, and herself, as a very young girl, sitting on Emily's desk at the Archive. Councillor Davies had been there too, then, which seemed odd now – but at the time had seemed perfectly natural, Eve remembered. The warmth of the room seemed to shrink around Eve as he appeared now, not with a grand entrance, but with a quiet, unsettling grace. Councillor Davies had been standing near the fireplace, seemingly absorbed in observing the others, a small, almost imperceptible smile playing on his lips. Now, he moved towards her, gliding through the crowd like a shadow, and offered a polite, yet slightly unnervingly fond, smile. "Emily," he said, his voice a low rumble, "A remarkable woman... always knew how to keep things interesting." It was a simple comment, but it hung in the air, laced with a hint of something more – nostalgia, perhaps, or even a touch of regret. Then, dropping his bombshell, he continued, "Emily and I... we shared a certain understanding of Ashcliffe's secrets." He paused, allowing the words to sink in, observing her reaction carefully.

"You knew her well?" Eve asked, trying to keep the surprise from her voice.

"Well enough," Davies replied, his eyes holding hers for a moment before shifting away. "We worked together at the Archive when it was first set up – back in the eighties. I provided the muscle, you know? Moving all kinds of documents, artefacts, and equipment to the building where it's still housed today. A bit of a chaotic place, at times, but Emily kept everything running smoothly." He glanced at the spread-out astrological chart on the table, his gaze lingering on Eve's placements. "It's no surprise you felt such a strong connection to Emily. And let's just say we both felt the pull of the sea... in more ways than one."

A collective murmur rippled through the group as he spoke, and everyone turned to look at Councillor Davies with curiosity. "It's funny," he added, his eyes twinkling with a hint of amusement, "I always suspected Emily had a secret or two." He paused, then leaned in slightly, lowering his voice. "She was protecting something – or someone." Geraint glanced at Davies, then, a question in his long Welsh gaze. "The sea has a way of revealing its secrets," Davies said simply, offering another enigmatic smile. "Especially when someone's willing to listen." Councillor Davies turned, moving towards the window and gazing out at the rain-swept coastline. "You know," he murmured, almost to himself, "Emily always did love a good mystery." He paused, turning back to face them with an expression that was both knowing and slightly melancholic. "She told me once... she felt like she was waiting for someone to arrive." Then, without another word, he turned and moved towards the door, disappearing into the grey afternoon. As he stepped out into the rain, a single drop of water clung to his cheek – reflecting the light like a tiny diamond.

"He's guarding something," Geraint observed quietly, turning back to Eve. "Something big."

"It feels like...," Eve began, struggling for words, "like he's connected to Emily and my family in a way we don't yet understand." As they turned their attention back to the chart, focusing on her placement, the pieces started to fall into place. "The shared secret," Geraint murmured, pointing to a specific line in her astrological reading, "The work in the Archive in the nineteen-eighties... Could he be...?"

A gasp escaped Eve's lips. The room seemed to spin for a moment as she processed the revelation. Her father? And Emily's lover? It was all so sudden, so unexpected. "And," Eloise added excitedly, pointing to another section of the chart, "The connection between your family and Louisa's Cove is even stronger than we thought! It's like a chain linking generations – tied together by love, loss... and secrets." As if in confirmation, a faint scent of lavender drifted through the air, stronger this time, lingering just for a moment before fading away. "He's not just guarding a secret," Eve realized, her mind racing to connect all the clues. "He's protecting a legacy. It's all connected," she whispered, feeling a surge of determination. "The sea, the family... it's all waiting to be uncovered."

11

CHAPTER ELEVEN:
DIARIES FROM THE DEEP

Ashcliffe's insistent rain was threatening to break through the stoic clouds with every passing moment, within the Archive there was a weight to the air – a pull, almost like an echo of something remembered. It wasn't jarring, not exactly, but constant, a gentle tugging at the edges of Eve's awareness as she methodically scanned another box of Emily Thornton's belongings. She found herself drawn to a particularly dusty corner, tucked away behind a towering stack of maps and charts – a box labelled simply "Miscellaneous." It felt denser than the others, heavier. As she carefully lifted out a stack of yellowed letters tied with faded ribbon, a slight shift caught her eye. It wasn't dramatic, just a subtle movement – a loose panel in the wall behind a towering bookcase. It was easily missed, hidden by years of accumulated dust and shadow.

Eve knelt, brushing away the grime with the back of her hand, revealing a narrow space – dark and still – hinting at something concealed within the walls of Ashcliffe's secret repository. A shiver traced its way down her spine – not entirely unpleasant – as if she'd disturbed a long-held slumber. The pull intensified, stronger now, focused directly on that hidden recess. With a little effort, Eve managed to pry the panel loose completely, revealing a small, dusty space barely larger than herself. Sunlight struggled to penetrate the gloom, illuminating a collection of seemingly insignificant items: another diary, bound in worn leather; a few dried sea lavender sprigs, brittle with age, and a tarnished silver thimble, intricately engraved with swirling waves. Reverently, Eve opened the journal to note that it was Louisa's hand-writing inside.

A surge of surprise – quickly followed by excitement – flooded through Eve. It felt deliberate, like Emily had known exactly what she was doing. As if she'd orchestrated this little secret to be unearthed just when Eve needed it most. There was a melancholy too, a sense that she was glimpsing into Louisa's private thoughts, her last moments of reflection. The space itself seemed to hum with a quiet energy, as if holding onto the memories of those who had lingered within. But it was the diary itself that truly captivated her. It was bound in a deep indigo leather, softened and cracked with age, and embossed on the cover with a perfectly formed spiral seashell. Eve carefully lifted it out, turning it over in her hands. The shell felt smooth and cool to the touch – almost as if it had been waiting for her, patiently hidden away for decades. A small, faded ribbon tied around the spine was the same shade of lavender she'd always associated with Emily.

Opening the diary, Eve inhaled a faint scent of sea salt and laven-der, stronger than any she'd experienced in the Archive before. The first page contained Louisa's elegant script – "The tide reveals its se-crets to those who listen closely." Beneath that, a single pressed sea lavender sprig lay nestled between the pages, preserved by time and perhaps, by intention. It was as if Louisa herself had been waiting for someone to find this hidden piece of her story – and Eve felt, with a certainty that resonated deep within, that she'd just been chosen.

Eve settled into a small, dusty chair in the back of the Archive, the watery light from her desk lamp casting long shadows across the shelves. The air felt cooler now, imbued with a palpable sense of in-timacy as she opened Louisa's last diary and began to read. The first entries were simple – observations about the weather, sketches of wildflowers, reflections on Emily's growing belly. Then, gradually, the tone shifted, deepening with emotion, revealing a core of longing that resonated deeply within Eve. "The rain always seems to follow me," Louisa wrote. "As if it knows my secret. As if it longs for something wild and untamed." Eve turned the page. "And tonight...tonight I felt him again, a flicker of his presence like sunlight on the water. It's enough to drive a woman to madness, this constant yearning." The diary quickly revealed the story of Louisa's affair with Miles Thornton – a passionate, desperate dance conducted in stolen moments and whispered promises. The entries were filled with details: "He met me by the old stone bridge tonight, beneath the watchful eye of Dragon's Tooth," one entry read, "Just ten minutes – enough to feel his hand on mine, to hear him call my name. It is as if he's carved a piece of himself into my soul."

Another described a meeting by the cove: "The moon was a silver coin tossed onto the waves this evening, and Miles... Miles looked at me as if I were the only thing that mattered. We spoke of leaving, of escaping Ashcliffe and finding a small cottage by the sea - somewhere where we could simply be." The letters, tucked between the diary pages, painted an even richer picture. They began formally, polite exchanges about family affairs, but quickly blossomed into expressions of ardent affection. One, from Miles to Louisa: "My dearest Louisa, each day without you is like a wave crashing against my shore – relentless and beautiful. I find myself drawn to the sea, as if it calls for me, as if it holds your image within its depths." Another, penned in a more frantic hand: "I saw you tonight by the lighthouse, bathed in moonlight. It felt as though all of Ashcliffe was watching, holding its breath. Just ten minutes! Ten precious minutes to lose myself in your eyes."

Louisa's descriptions of her pregnancy were both joyful and fraught with anxiety. "A tiny flutter today," she wrote one day, " a promise of something new. But Alexander will never know...not yet.

I fear his disapproval, his rigid expectations." She described the constant worry of being discovered, the need to conceal her growing belly beneath layers of skirts. "I feel as if I am part sea, part woman," she wrote in one entry, "forever drawn to him, a siren caught between two worlds." She continued, "Sometimes, when the wind is just right, I can hear him calling – a low rumble like waves crashing against the cliffs. It's as though he's part of the sea itself, and he wants me to join him." Another entry described a particularly vivid dream: "I was standing on the rocks, the moonlight shimmering on the water, and Miles was reaching for me – his hand outstretched, inviting me into the waves."

The diaries revealed that they had grand plans – dreams of leaving Ashcliffe altogether, seeking out a small cottage by the coast, perhaps even near the sea. "We'll build a life where we can be ourselves," Louisa wrote, "where the only sounds are the waves and our own laughter." They spoke of naming their child after the sea – Coralia or Maris. Louisa often used the term 'the siren' to describe herself – not necessarily in a literal sense, but as if she embodied that alluring, dangerous quality, forever tempting men with her beauty and mystery. "I feel like the tide itself," she wrote in one particularly evocative entry. "Sometimes calm and serene, other times wild and untamed - always pulling at something deep within." She described her longing for Miles as a storm of its own – "a tempest that threatens to consume me." The imagery was consistently powerful: crashing waves, moonlight on the water, the scent of salt air – all reflecting her turbulent emotions. "He says he feels it too," she wrote, "this connection, this pull towards something beyond Ashcliffe. He believes we are destined for each other, that our love is written in the stars." A sketch accompanied the entry – a swirling spiral seashell, perfectly formed, with tiny dots scattered across its surface.

As Eve turned the final page, she found Louisa's last entry – dated just days before Emily was born: "I feel them coming, my little one. A new wave of love, and perhaps...a new beginning." Below that, a single pressed sea lavender sprig lay nestled between the pages, its scent faint but present. A small note scrawled in Louisa's hand read simply, "Look beneath." Eve closed the diary, feeling a profound sense of connection to this woman she had never met – a woman who had loved and lost, dreamed and yearned, all within the hidden depths of Ashcliffe's past. The rain continued to fall outside, now seeming less like a reminder of the town's dampness and more like a gentle echo of Louisa's own 'storm'.

Eve continued to pore over Louisa's diary, reading and re-reading, the rain outside now drumming a steady rhythm against the windows. As she read on, a subtle shift occurred – a feeling that she wasn't just reading about the past, but that she was being shown something. It wasn't dramatic revelation, more like a gentle unfolding, as if Louisa herself were guiding her hand across the page. Then, in an entry dated shortly after Emily was born, she found it: "I have passed down the secrets, my dear. I've kept watch, ensuring that the truth remains safe until the right time. Emily will understand, just as I did." Eve felt a prickle of excitement, a sense that she was on the verge of something significant. Eve turned the page again, and this time, Louisa revealed a revelation that almost made her drop the diary: "Alexander isn't Emily's father, it becomes more obvious by the day. It was Miles, of course – he felt it in his bones. But he kept it hidden." A sketch accompanied the entry – a simple drawing of a spiral seashell, this time with three dots arranged in a triangle around its centre. The pieces began to fall into place with astonishing clarity. Miles Thornton had vanished during the storm of 1938. He hadn't simply drowned, he'd been lured away, drawn back to Louisa by a love that defied time and circumstance. And now, it was all connected to her.

A wave of disbelief washed over Eve, followed by a surge of emotion so profound it took her breath away. Tears welled in her eyes, blurring the words on the page. It felt as if she were standing on the shores of Louisa's Cove once more, feeling the same pull, the same sense of connection to that distant woman. "She knew," Eve whispered, tracing the lines of Louisa's handwriting with a trembling finger. "Emily knew all along." Then, it hit her – the realization that Emily hadn't just left her the archive, she had deliberately orchestrated this. It wasn't random, it was a carefully laid plan, a tangible link to her family history and a way to pass on the knowledge, waiting for Eve to be ready. It felt like Emily herself was guiding her, whispering secrets across the years. Eve flipped back through the diary, searching for clues – she found this: "I planted a seed, didn't I? A small, hidden truth waiting to bloom. I felt it was time. Time for Emily to understand her lineage, to feel the pull of the sea and the longing in her heart."

The diary wasn't just a collection of words, it was a gift, a legacy. Emily had deliberately chosen this – Louisa's last diary, tucked away in its hidden corner – as the key to unlocking Eve's own past. It was as if she had known all along that her daughter needed to find it, that she needed to feel the same pull towards the sea and the mystery of their family. Eve closed her eyes for a moment, letting the feeling wash over her. She felt connected to Louisa in a way she couldn't quite articulate – a sense of shared longing, of intertwined destinies. It was as if they were two women across generations, linked by an invisible thread woven from love, loss, and secrets. "It all makes sense now," Eve breathed, her voice thick with emotion. "The scent of lavender... the seashell... it's us. It's always been us." Eve realized that Emily hadn't just protected her family's secret; she had entrusted it to her, a final act of love and connection. And as she looked out at the rain-streaked windows, she felt a sense of belonging she hadn't known was possible – a feeling of being rooted in the soil of Ashcliffe, connected to its past, and destined to play her part in its unfolding story. A small smile touched her lips. "Thank you," she whispered to Louisa, across the decades. "Thank you for letting me find you."

The scent of sea salt and lavender lingered in the air, curling around Eve like a veil, subtle but persistent. The diary sat in her lap, still warm from her touch, though the pages were cool, almost damp with time. Outside, the rain had softened, now a hush rather than a storm, as if Ashcliffe itself was listening – waiting. Eve let her fingers trail once more over the final page, over Louisa's looping signature, and the whisper of a note: Look beneath. She turned the book over in her hands, feeling its spine, its creases, and the soft impressions of age. Look beneath. Was it metaphorical? Had she already found what Louisa wanted her to see – the undeniable truth about Emily, the bloodline, the connection? Or was there more? Something physical? The question echoed, low and insistent. Eve rose slowly, moving back to the hidden alcove behind the panel. The air there was cooler, laced with something faintly mineral – stone and time. She crouched, holding the diary under the glow of her desk lamp now positioned nearby. The seashell embossed on the cover caught the light again, and as she tilted the book, something shifted. A faint rustle. A slight give.

Eve's heart quickened. Eve pressed her thumb along the back end-paper. It moved. Carefully, she peeled back the inner lining of the diary's cover – worn leather softened by years – and felt something thin, papery, tucked inside. It was a map. More a sketch, really – rendered in Louisa's delicate hand. A top-down drawing of Ashcliffe's coastline. The cliffs were mighty, the paths marked in fading ink. Several symbols dotted the margins: a star, a crescent moon, and that same spiral shell again, near a place labelled only Siren's Hollow. Eve didn't know the name, not exactly. It wasn't on any of the official coastal charts she'd studied. But the shape of the cliffs, the curve of the inlet – it looked familiar. She'd seen it from above once, standing near the lighthouse before she knew anything of Louisa or the tangled story that now wound through her veins.

The rain had stopped. Eve stood and stepped to the tall windows that overlooked the sea. Fog clung to the distant cliffs, but the tide had receded slightly, and she could just make out the darker patches of stone far below. Siren's Hollow. The name stirred something in her chest – recognition or warning, she couldn't say. She pressed the diary to her heart. Behind her, the Archive seemed quieter now, as if Louisa's voice had finally finished speaking. Or perhaps, simply, it had changed form – moved beyond paper and ink and into Eve herself. She needed air. She needed to see the sea. To feel it. Within minutes, her boots were echoing along the corridor. She pulled on her coat, the old navy one. It fit too well, the sleeves worn at the elbows, smelling faintly of lavender.

Outside, Ashcliffe shimmered with rain, the streets slick with memory. The clouds had lifted just enough to reveal a silver-gray sky, soft and bruised. Eve made her way toward the cliffs, the diary and the map wrapped in oilcloth beneath her arm. As she walked, she thought of Louisa, walking these same paths more than eighty years ago. Pregnant. In love. Afraid. Still daring to hope. That hope now lived in the very soil, in the waves, in Eve's own body. She was the proof – the end and the beginning of everything Louisa had protected. The wind picked up as she neared the lighthouse. The land curved out here, bending away from the main town. The path narrowed, overgrown with lichen and sea grass. And then she saw it. A split in the cliffs – almost invisible unless you knew what to look for. Siren's Hollow. She stood at the edge for a long moment, staring down into the cove below. The stone descended in a rough stair-step pattern, slick with moss. A narrow cave mouth yawned in the rocks near the tide line, just where Louisa had drawn the spiral on her map.

With careful steps, Eve made her way down. The wind carried the cries of seabirds and the faint rhythmic crash of waves. Here, at the base of the cliffs, the world felt older. Primal. The very rocks bore the imprint of time – scraped by water, hollowed by salt. She stepped lightly, approaching the cave. Inside, it was dark but not silent. Water lapped somewhere beyond the bend, echoing faintly. Eve lit her small pocket torch and pressed forward. The air was cool and metallic, tinged with brine and something floral – impossible, yet there all the same. Lavender. The tunnel opened slightly into a small cavern. A natural pool reflected the ceiling in broken light, and scattered along its edge were more old sprigs of dried lavender, weathered but intact. Not growing – placed. A shrine. And on the far side, half-buried in stone and sand, was another seashell – larger this time, carved from pale stone, inset into the rock itself. Three small dots surrounded it, just like the drawing.

Eve dropped to her knees, running her fingers over the indentations. It wasn't just a symbol. It was a mark of lineage. Of knowing. And this cave – this hollow – was a place of remembering. A place of initiation. Suddenly, something shifted inside her. Not pain, not fear – but a pulling sensation, low in her belly. Eve drew in a sharp breath. The realization flooded her with clarity. Louisa had written of it – of the sea calling, of Miles's presence felt in dreams and tides. Of being "part sea, part woman." Eve was feeling it now. Not metaphorically, but as truth. Her blood hummed with something ancient and wild. A connection that spanned beyond the name Thornton, beyond Ashcliffe. The sea wasn't just backdrop – it was the story. It had shaped them, called to them, claimed them. And now, it was calling Eve.

She rose to her feet slowly, gazing down at the pool. Her reflection stared back at her – pale, rain-dampened, eyes wide with understanding. Eve reached for her satchel and removed the diary. Carefully, she opened it to the final page again, running her fingers once more over the scrawled message. Look beneath. She turned the page again – nothing. Then again. Tucked between the last few sheets, another pressed flower, this one crumbling with age. Beneath it, the faintest outline of writing. Barely visible. She held it to the torchlight. "If you've found this, you've heard it too. The lullaby of waves, the longing in your chest. You carry the sea in your bones. Protect it. Remember us. When the tide rises again, be ready."

Eve's pulse thrummed in her ears. She tucked the diary back into her coat and stepped to the cave mouth. The tide had begun to return, gently now, lapping at the stones as if greeting her. The storm had passed. She turned back once, taking in the hollow, the shrine, the stone shell. Then, she climbed. Back up the worn cliff path, her fingers brushing moss and salt-worn rock. With each step, she felt steadier. Rooted. A part of something vast and unseen. By the time she reached the lighthouse again, dusk had begun to bloom. The town behind her glowed faintly, but Eve didn't look back. She stood there for a long time, wind pushing her hair into her face, diary clutched to her chest. She knew the story now. Knew her part in it. This wasn't the end, it was just the tide, turning.

CHAPTER TWELVE: STORMING THE SHEETS

The rain had been falling for hours. Not the light, sideways mist Ashcliffe was known for, but a relentless downpour that beat against Eve's cottage roof like it was trying to get in. Eve stood by the fire, clutching Louisa's diary like it might vanish if she let go. Her fingers trembled, not from the cold – she'd already changed out of her soaked clothes – but from something deeper. The heat from the fire licked her skin, but it couldn't quite reach her centre. Behind her, Geraint moved quietly. He'd removed his coat and hung it near the stove, his hair still dripping. There was something in the way he took up space that unsettled her now – not because it was unfamiliar, but because it wasn't. His presence had become a constant over these past months, a tide she'd stopped noticing until it had surrounded her entirely.

"Tea?" she asked, her voice catching.

He nodded, grateful for the pause. "Please." She turned, busying herself with the kettle. The diary sat on the table between them, its worn leather cover still damp from where she'd held it against her chest during her walk back from Siren's Hollow. The silence was heavier than it should've been. Not awkward, exactly – just full. Like the air before thunder. "You don't have to read it out loud," Geraint said gently, watching her from his seat. "Only if you want to." Eve didn't answer immediately. She poured the tea, brought his cup to him, and sat down opposite, the diary still between them. Her hands hovered over it. "She wanted me to find it," Eve said finally, almost to herself. "She hid it behind a wall panel – like she knew I'd go looking." Geraint didn't interrupt. "I keep thinking..." Eve opened the diary slowly, reverently. "If I read this to you, it stops being just hers. Or mine. It becomes... real." He nodded, understanding flickering across his features.

Eve found the page she'd marked earlier. Her voice was steady, though it didn't feel that way in her chest. "I saw him again tonight, near the cove. The wind was coming in off the sea, carrying the lavender I'd left there the night before. He didn't speak. Just looked at me the way someone might look at a ghost. Or a storm. Or both." The words filled the room. The kettle clicked off behind them, unnoticed. Eve looked up. Geraint's expression was unreadable – open, but weighted. "She loved him," Eve said. "And it nearly ruined her." There was a long pause. Then Geraint said quietly, "And yet she kept going to the sea." A shiver ran through her, though the fire crackled warmly. Eve turned the page and began to read, her voice gaining strength as she lost herself in Louisa's elegant, looping script. "The sea calls to me, Miles. It whispers your name with every wave, with every sigh of the wind. I feel tethered to it now, as if its currents run through my veins. Sometimes I think it chooses us – binds us together."

Geraint listened intently, his gaze fixed on Eve's face, which was illuminated by the flickering firelight. He noticed how her shoulders had relaxed slightly, the tension bleeding out with each turn of the page. He'd seen her wrestling with the diary for an hour already, a quiet struggle against its weight – and the secrets it held. "I long to break free,'" Eve continued, reading Louisa's words, "'to chase the sun across the water, to build a life far from Ashcliffe's expectations. But then... Then I look at you, Miles, and know that my heart is already here.'" As she read, a subtle shift occurred in Geraint. He wasn't just listening, he was seeing – seeing Louisa's yearning, her vulnerability, the fierce love that burned beneath the surface. He recognized it immediately: the same pull, the same tension between duty and desire. "It's fascinating," he murmured, breaking the silence. "She describes this feeling of being... chosen, almost. Like she was meant to be by the sea."

"Exactly!" Eve said, her eyes widening. "But what if it wasn't just romantic? What if it was something more... ancient?"

They continued reading, Louisa's words painting a vivid picture of a woman caught between two worlds: the rigid expectations of her family and the intoxicating call of the sea. She wrote of feeling like a vessel, filled with secrets, waiting to be released. "'I feel as though I carry within me the memories of all those who have loved before,'" Eve read aloud. "'The sailors lost at sea, the smugglers who sought refuge in our coves – they are all part of me now.'" Geraint nodded thoughtfully. "That connects to your research, doesn't it?" he said, gesturing towards his own bag. "Youths disappearing during storms... local legends of sirens... It's like Ashcliffe remembers everything." He pulled out a small, worn notebook and flipped through it. "I was just reading about the 'Sea Blessing' ritual. The women of the Thornton line – they were said to have a connection to the sea, a way of channelling its energy." "She wrote about it too," Eve said, turning a page. "About lavender being central to it. And... 'the Key of Echoes.'"

"The 'Key of Echoes'," Geraint repeated, a slow smile spreading across his face. "That's fascinating. It's like the whole thing was designed – not just for her, but for someone to find." He looked at Eve, and for a moment, he seemed to see something beyond the present – a lineage stretching back through generations. "Was she cursed?" Eve wondered aloud, tracing Louisa's handwriting with her finger. "Or gifted? Chosen?"

"Maybe it's not an either/or," Geraint suggested. "Perhaps it was all three. Perhaps she was chosen – to carry a certain legacy, a certain responsibility." He paused, considering his words. "It reminds me of you,

Eve. You've always had this... pull towards the past. Towards under-standing." Eve felt a warmth spread through her, a deeper connection than just shared knowledge. It was like he was seeing her, not just the woman in front of him, but the part of her that was so like Louisa Thornton, and the part that might be waiting to emerge. "Emily kept so many secrets," she said quietly. "She didn't tell me much about her family. My family, I mean."

"She protected you," Geraint replied gently. "And perhaps she was protecting the story itself. It seems like she wanted you to discover it, but on your own terms." He shifted slightly closer, and for a brief mo-ment, their shoulders brushed. "It's... overwhelming," Eve admitted, her voice barely above a whisper. "Like I'm part of something bigger than myself – something powerful. But also... frightening."

"It can be," Geraint agreed, his gaze meeting hers. "But it doesn't have to be scary. It can be beautiful. And you don't have to face it alone."

"She sacrificed so much, Emily," Eve continued, her voice gaining strength again. "To keep the secrets hidden." She paused, considering. "Do you think... do you think she wanted me to rewrite that story? To finally let it all out?" Geraint looked at her for a long moment, his eyes filled with understanding and something else – perhaps a hint of an-ticipation. "I think," he said softly, "that's exactly what she hoped."

Outside, the rain continued to fall, but inside the cottage, a dif-ferent kind of storm was brewing – a storm of shared history, whis-pered secrets, and the promise of uncovering Ashcliffe's most guarded mysteries – and perhaps, finally, discovering their own. The air shifted – a subtle thickening. It wasn't dramatic, no sudden gust or flash of lightning, just... a stillness that felt charged. Geraint and Eve made eye contact – a long, deliberate moment – a pause, a breath, the mo-ment hung, suspended between them as palpable as the dampness in the room. Eve shifted slightly on the worn armchair, feeling suddenly aware of the proximity of Geraint. It wasn't just his physical presence – it was the way he radiated warmth, a quiet confidence that seemed to draw her in. She hadn't consciously planned it, hadn't even realized she was considering it until now. It felt natural – a response to the weight of their shared knowledge, to the feeling of finally being seen. "Thank you again," she said softly, her voice a little breathy. "For... listening." It was a simple expression of gratitude, but also a subtle invitation – a way to push just a little closer without fully committing.

Geraint didn't immediately break the gaze. Instead, he tilted his head slightly, a small, almost shy movement that did something to loosen the knot in her chest. "It's easy to listen when you're surrounded by such compelling stories," he murmured, and then, slowly, deliberately, he moved closer still. His hand reached out—hesitantly at first—and brushed against hers on the open page of the diary. It was a light touch, tentative, but it sent a surprising ripple through her. She didn't pull away.

The kiss began tentatively – hesitant, as if both were unsure whether to commit. His lips were warm and soft, a little damp from the rain. But then, as if triggered by something unspoken, his pressure deepened. It wasn't a frantic, demanding kiss, but it was urgent, real – a release of all the tension that had been building between them. Eve responded instinctively, her arms moving to curl around his waist, pulling him closer. He wrapped his arms around her, drawing her into the warmth of his body. The cottage seemed to shrink around them, the firelight dancing in their eyes. It wasn't a polished, perfect kiss – her thick hair was still damp and tangled – but it was utterly genuine. They moved through the cottage then, a little clumsily at first, as if still unsure where they were going. He peeled off her woolly cardigan, his fingers brushing against hers, and she instinctively reached up to tug at the collar of his shirt, revealing the pale skin of his neck. The storm outside swelled, mirroring the rising intensity within them – a rhythmic crash of thunder punctuated by the steady drumming of rain on the roof.

It was physicality stripped bare – not about perfection or appearances, but about release, reawakening. As they kissed, she saw flashes

– images superimposed over the present: Louisa Thornton standing on the rocks, her silver hair catching the moonlight. Miles Thornton gazing at her with an intensity that mirrored his own. But these were fleeting, like memories surfacing in a dream – hers, not theirs. The scent of lavender hung heavy in the air, mingling with the damp wool and Geraint's familiar scent – a blend of woodsmoke and something subtly salty, like the sea itself. She felt as if she was submerged – adrift in a current of shared history, connected to everyone who had ever lived within Ashcliffe's boundaries. Outside, lightning flashed, illuminating the room with a brilliant white light. For a moment, it seemed as though they were suspended in time, caught between the past and the present. In the windowpane, Eve saw her own reflection superimposed on a fleeting image – Louisa, her eyes wide with both longing and a hint of something akin to sadness. "She was so strong," Eve whispered against his lips, pulling back slightly to look at him. "Despite everything."

"And you are too," Geraint replied, his voice husky. "You carry it all within you – the strength, the sorrow, the... connection." He lifted a hand and brushed a stray strand of hair from her face, his touch sending another shiver through her. Eve closed her eyes for a moment, letting herself sink into the sensation – the warmth of his body, the scent of lavender, the rhythm of his breathing. It was as if she were finally remembering something – a feeling that had been dormant within her for years. A sense of belonging. "It's... like the sea," she said softly, opening her eyes to meet his gaze. "Pulling you in, and then letting you go."

"Or maybe holding you close," he countered, a small smile playing on his lips. "And revealing its secrets—one by one." He leaned down and kissed her again, this time longer, deeper – a promise of more to come. The rain continued to fall, but inside the cottage, it no longer felt like a reminder of Ashcliffe's dampness. It was part of the storm – a beautiful, wild force that had awakened something within her, something she hadn't even known was waiting to be found. Eve wasn't sure what tomorrow would bring – perhaps more secrets, more challenges – but for now, in the warmth of his arms, surrounded by the scent of lavender and the echoes of the past, she felt a sense of peace she hadn't experienced before. She was part of something – a lineage, a legacy, a story waiting to be told. And, finally, she wasn't alone.

Geraint's fingers lingered on her cheek, calloused but careful, and Eve leaned into the touch, her breath catching in her throat. There was no mistaking the shift between them now — the awareness, the pull, the electricity humming just beneath the surface. She could feel it in the way his gaze dropped to her lips, in the steady way his chest rose and fell. The past was all around them – layered like mist over the crashing waves of emotion – but in this moment, it receded. What remained was simply this: his mouth, warm and sure against hers. Her body, already arching toward him without hesitation. He kissed her again, deeper this time, and her hands moved instinctively – sliding up beneath his shirt, feeling the heat of his skin, the firm lines of his back. He groaned softly at her touch, a sound that reverberated through her, low and needy. She tugged at the fabric, breaking the kiss only long enough to lift the shirt over his head. The firelight caught the curve of his shoulders, the pale plane of his chest, the soft scar beneath his collarbone she hadn't noticed before.

She reached out and traced it with her fingers. "What happened here?" she asked, voice husky. "Fell off a bike," he said with a lopsided smile. "Not very romantic, I'm afraid."

"It is now," she whispered, and kissed the scar. His hands tightened at her waist. Eve felt herself guided backward, her calves brushing the edge of the worn rug before her knees hit the seat of the armchair. She let herself sink down into it, breathless, heart thudding. Geraint knelt between her legs, his hands travelling up the backs of her thighs beneath the hem of her faded dress — fingers warm, patient, reverent. He didn't rush, didn't demand. He looked at her as if asking permission without speaking, and she gave it, not with words, but with the way she lifted her hips, inviting him closer.

When Geraint slipped her dress up and over her head, Eve's breath hitched. The firelight kissed her bare skin, casting shadows along her collarbone and the dip of her waist. She felt exposed, but not self-conscious — not with the way he was looking at her. Like she was something rare. Something sacred. "You're beautiful," he murmured. Not in a practised way, not as flattery. It was quiet awe. She reached for him then, drawing him into her, their mouths finding each other again – hungrier now, more sure. She fumbled with his belt, her fingers trembling, and he stilled her hands with his for a moment, then helped. The urgency was growing, yes, but so was the weight of it – the meaning behind the closeness. They were undressing not just out of want, but out of need. Connection. Understanding. Release. His trousers joined the rest of their clothes on the floor, and then he was lifting her, guiding her down onto the rug beside the fire. The wool beneath her was scratchy, grounding. Real. His body covered hers, all heat and breath and motion. His mouth found her neck, her shoulder, the curve of her breast, and she arched against him with a gasp.

Everywhere he touched her felt like discovery. She responded in kind – her hands tracing his spine, her lips brushing the sensitive spot just beneath his jaw. It was messy and uncoordinated at moments – knees bumping, a small laugh when they knocked over their mugs of tea with a thud – but it was real, alive, theirs. When he entered her, it wasn't abrupt – it was slow, careful, as if even now he wanted to be certain she was with him fully. Eve exhaled sharply, clutching at his shoulders as he moved, as her body adjusted around him. It was more than sensation – it was something elemental. Like being pulled into the sea, wave after wave, until she didn't know where her body ended and his began. They moved together in a rhythm older than words, matching breath to breath, heartbeat to heartbeat. There was a moment when their eyes met – not just a glance, but a full reckoning – and something passed between them. Not love, not yet. But the possibility of it. The bones of it. The feeling that they had stumbled onto something vast and undeniable.

Eve's climax came like a surge, a storm breaking loose inside her. She held him tightly, riding it out, hearing her own voice crying out against his neck. Geraint followed soon after, his body shuddering, his face buried in her hair as he whispered her name like a prayer. For a long time, they didn't move. Just lay there on the rug, tangled in limbs and breath, the fire flickering beside them and the rain still drumming its steady song on the roof. Eve's cheek rested against his chest, his heartbeat thudding beneath her ear. "Well," she said after a while, voice sleep-warm and drowsy. "That escalated."

He laughed, a low, contented sound, and wrapped his arms tighter around her. "I think we were halfway there the moment you opened that diary." Eve smiled, eyelids fluttering shut. The storm hadn't passed, not really. There were still secrets to uncover, truths to face. But in this moment, in this cocoon of firelight and flesh, she let herself rest – knowing that whatever came next, they'd face it together.

The warmth lingered, a comfortable echo of just moments before, but it was already beginning to fray at the edges. The scent of him – woodsmoke and sea salt – felt suddenly sharp against her skin, like a reminder of how exposed she'd been. They lay tangled on the rug, limbs intertwined, a quiet tableau illuminated by the fire, yet Eve felt utterly alone within it. Geraint shifted slightly, drawing her closer for a moment before easing back, his hand hovering near hers as if considering whether to touch her again. "You okay?" he asked, his voice low and gentle. It wasn't a question seeking reassurance, it was an observation, almost clinical in its simplicity. And that's when it hit – the sudden, sharp fracture within her calm. It started as a tightening in her chest, a familiar pressure like a held breath, then spread outwards, consuming her. "Just... just a little," she managed, pulling her knees up to her chest. The warmth of his body felt suddenly oppressive. "It was... a lot."

It was a lot. It had been everything – the slow burn of anticipation, the delicious surrender, the feeling of finally being seen and held. But now, as the initial flush faded, it felt like standing on the edge of a cliff after a gale, the wind threatening to sweep you back into the churning sea. "I just... I don't know what that is," she said, her voice gaining a little of its earlier sharpness. "All of this... all of them... It's just... so much." Eve felt it then – the weight of Ashcliffe pressing down on her, not just as history in dusty books and faded photographs, but as something tangible, something that breathed and waited. It was like being submerged again, but this time the water wasn't welcoming. It was thick with the memories of generations, each one pulling at her, demanding attention. An image flashed – vivid and unsettling – of Emily, alone in the Archive, surrounded by stacks of papers reaching to the ceiling. Emily, looking small and vulnerable, almost spectral. A tiny flicker of fear tightened Eve's chest. Was she was repeating the pattern? Becoming isolated, all the while becoming consumed by something she couldn't quite grasp?

"It's like... I'm always just on the edge," she murmured, her gaze fixed on the flames. "Always waiting for something to happen." Geraint didn't say anything, letting her unravel a little. He understood, instinctively, that sometimes the most intimate moments held the sharpest edges. "You can go," she said abruptly, pulling a woollen blanket tighter around herself. It wasn't a request; it was an order, delivered in a voice colder than the rain outside. Geraint looked momentarily surprised, but his expression didn't betray hurt. He simply nodded and carefully folded the blanket he'd been using to cover them. He moved towards the door, then paused, turning back for a moment.

"Just... let me know when you're ready," he said quietly, before stepping out into the darkness. The silence that followed was heavy with unspoken words. Eve watched him go, feeling a strange mix of relief and regret. She'd pushed him away, erected a wall between them, all while desperately wanting to hold on. Her eyes drifted to the photograph of Emily – her small, thoughtful face framed by lavender – and a fresh wave of anxiety washed over her. It wasn't just about repeating Emily's pattern; it was about inheriting her fears, her loneliness, her sense that she was destined to be caught in some ancient, swirling current. Eve pulled the blanket tighter still, burying her face in its wool. "I don't want to be like her," she whispered, a tremor in her voice. "Or like anyone." The rain intensified outside, drumming against the windows with a steady rhythm – a soundtrack to her isolation. It was beautiful, in a melancholic way, but tonight it felt less like a comforting presence and more like a constant reminder of the sea, and all its secrets – and perhaps, all its dangers.

Eve shifted slightly on the rug, trying to find a comfortable position, a sense of grounding. The room seemed to shrink around her, closing in with the weight of Ashcliffe's history, the legacy of the Thorntons, and suddenly, she felt overwhelmingly small – adrift, as if waiting for the tide to carry her out to sea. A single lavender sprig lay on the side table – a tiny, fragrant reminder of Emily, and of everything Eve was trying so desperately to escape. She reached for it, inhaling its familiar scent, and a flicker of something – perhaps hope, perhaps just stubbornness – ignited within her. She wouldn't be swallowed by the past. Not yet. She needed to go back to the Archive.

The rain had settled into a steady drum against the large, sea-facing windows, a comforting rhythm after the tempest of the past few days. The air in the Archive was thick with the scent of lavender and damp paper as Eve, decked out in her trusty headtorch and an almost palpable sense of urgency, finally tackled the last box of Emily's papers – "The Storming Sheets." These were not ordinary records, they were meticulously handwritten accounts detailing every significant event in Ashcliffe's history, dating back to the seventeenth century. Eve quickly realized these weren't just chronicle: they were coded. Each entry was subtly linked to a specific nautical chart, with symbols and abbreviations referencing locations along the coast. Eve obsessively spent hours poring over them, deciphering the clues – a broken mast represented a shipwreck, a circling gull signified smuggling, and a spiral seashell indicated a connection to the 'Seafoam Bride'. Doing this, getting lost in her work, felt much easier than getting lost in her thoughts – deciphering what exactly Geraint was becoming to her.

13

❦

CHAPTER THIRTEEN: SILENCE AFTER SONG

The rain in Ashcliffe-on-Sea hadn't stopped since Emily's death. There was a persistent dampness that seemed to cling to everything, like a memory. It seeped into the wool of Eve's coat, settled on the worn brass of the Post Office door, and clung to the back of her throat with a slight, familiar ache. This morning, it felt particularly heavy, pressing down on her as she navigated the rain-slicked streets, each delivery a small, solitary act. She'd missed her usual mug of Earl Grey, the chipped ceramic warming her hands – a simple pleasure that now seemed to require a little more effort to appreciate. Three – maybe four – had passed before she'd even registered Geraint leaning against the post box outside Mr. Linden's cottage, a worn notebook open in his hands and a frown etching itself onto his face. She'd nodded a distracted 'Good morning,' her hand already moving on to the next house, the familiar weight of the mail bag feeling heavier than usual.

It wasn't that she didn't want to acknowledge him – not entirely. It was more like... she was trying to keep the edges of things soft, to avoid any sharp angles, any potential for a deeper conversation she wasn't quite ready for. Eve had been deliberately constructing walls lately, brick by slow brick, and today, they felt particularly sturdy. The rain plastered strands of her dark hair to her forehead as she trudged past the bakery – the scent of warm bread usually a comfort – and towards Emily's cottage. It was smaller than she remembered, almost swallowed by the overgrown garden, but it held within it Emily's eccentric charm. She checked the address on the envelope: number Seven Cliffside. Another faded photograph, another cryptic note, another piece of Emily's puzzle?

The rain drummed a steady rhythm against the small panes of glass, and the air smelled faintly of lavender – always of lavender. Eve had started to notice it everywhere lately – in the scent of the rain, in the wild patches blooming along the clifftops, even, she thought, in the shadows cast by the trees. It was a constant reminder, both comforting and slightly unsettling. As she scanned the address book for her next delivery, she noticed Geraint had left his notebook on top of the postbox – a small, deliberate act that usually meant he was pondering something intensely. She picked it up, flipping through to a page filled with neat script and sketches of local landmarks. He'd been studying the coastline, charting the tides, meticulously noting the locations mentioned in Emily's journals. Next to the postbox was a small, navy blue rucksack that looked almost new. A train ticket to Cardiff peeked out of the front pocket, its date circled in pencil. Geraint was leaving. The thought hit her with the force of another raindrop, cold and unexpected. She glanced at the clock – 11:17. She'd been waiting for him, she supposed, hoping he'd linger, that they could talk. Maybe even...something more. "He said he was considering it," a voice startled her. It was Mr. Linden, clutching a damp parcel. "Said he felt like he was chasing ghosts. That the history here was beautiful, but a bit... consuming."

Eve nodded, managing a weak smile. "It is," she agreed, turning back to the notebook.

Later, as she was sorting through Emily's letters, she heard a tentative knock on the Archive's door. It was Geraint. Relief, and a flicker of something akin to disappointment, warmed her chest. He looked tired, his brow furrowed in thought. "Just wanted to say goodbye properly," he said, stepping into the cottage, shaking the rain from his coat. "And ask if you needed anything."

"No, thank you," Eve replied, her voice a little tighter than she'd intended. "I'm fine." She gestured vaguely towards that now-familiar bag by the door. "You should go. Before the storm gets worse." He tilted his head, studying her for a moment – a look of genuine confusion in his eyes. "Are you sure? You seem... distant. Like you're trying to hold something back." He paused. "Is this about us?"

Eve avoided his gaze, focusing on a faded photograph of Emily. "It's just... a lot," she murmured, not quite explaining what 'a lot' meant. "And I need... space." He seemed to accept it, for now, but there was a subtle sadness in his expression, a hint that he sensed something deeper beneath her carefully constructed facade. He picked up the train ticket, studying it briefly before saying: "Well, don't work too late. You need your sleep, you know." As the door closed behind him, and the sound of his car faded into the rain, Eve felt a shift – not just in the cottage, but within herself. The silence seemed to amplify, filled with the weight of his departure and the unspoken questions hanging between them. She glanced down at the notebook on the table, then back at the window, watching him disappear into the grey drizzle. The rain continued to fall, relentless and persistent – a fitting soundtrack to the growing feeling that she was a little bit alone in her own life. And for the first time since Emily's death, Eve wasn't sure how long she could keep it all at bay.

The rain hadn't let up when Eve finally left the Archive, and it seemed to follow her all the way to The Chiron Cafe – a small, cosy haven on Ashcliffe's main street. It was one of Emily's favourites, known for its strong coffee, comforting cakes, and the slightly eccentric collection of locals. It felt like a place where time slowed down, where you could lose yourself in a good book or a quiet conversation. But today, even The Chiron Cafe seemed subdued, as if holding its breath against the storm both outside and within. As ever, Rita made what she thought Eve needed, rather than accepting an order from the postwoman and archivist. Whilst nursing what turned out to be very hot coffee and staring out at the rain-lashed street, Krissy slid into the chair opposite Eve. Krissy didn't bother with pleasantries or small talk. "You look like you've swallowed a whole storm," Krissy observed, taking in Eve's slumped posture and the haunted look in her eyes. "And not a particularly pleasant one."

Eve grunted, stirring her coffee absently. "Just a long day."

"It's the morning still," Krissy corrected, her voice direct as always. "Since Geraint left, you've been like a statue – observing everything, but saying nothing. Honestly, it's exhausting to watch." Eve took a sip of her coffee, the heat doing little to thaw the chill that had settled around her. "I'm fine."

"You're not," Krissy insisted, leaning forward slightly. "Not really. You've always been like this, haven't you? Watching. Delivering. Never actually... participating."

"It's a job," Eve said automatically, the words sounding even to her own ears as if they'd been carefully chosen.

"It's more than a job," Krissy countered, her gaze unwavering. "It's how you see the world. You deliver letters, yes, but you don't really know the people who send them. You're always just one step removed." She paused. "Like you were with Emily. Always so attentive, so observant... but never truly letting anyone in."

Eve bristled slightly at that. "That's not fair."

"Isn't it?" Krissy pressed on. "You've built this wall around yourself, haven't you? Afraid of being known. Afraid of failing to live up to Emily's legacy – she was such a vibrant woman, and now you feel like you have to carry that on, but you're afraid of not measuring up."

"It's not just that," Eve mumbled, her gaze dropping to the rim of her mug. "It's... Louisa. And Miles. It's this feeling that everything is connected – and that if I get too involved, I'll just end up repeating their story."

"Their story was a passionate one," Krissy pointed out gently. "A little bit reckless, maybe, but full of love. And you keep thinking about it like it's some tragic curse." She gestured with her hand. "Like they were doomed from the start. Don't you think that's a little dramatic? Especially when you don't even know the whole story?"

"It's not dramatic," Eve snapped, more than a touch defensively. "It's... real. And it's scary."

"Scary is good," Krissy said with a small smile. "Means you're alive. You've been so busy trying to figure out the past that you haven't allowed yourself any chance at the present. Look at you – miles of rain, a lukewarm coffee, and a grumpy cafe."

"It's not just about the past," Eve repeated, her voice quieter now. "It's about... fear. Of being hurt. Of losing someone. Like Emily."

Krissy nodded slowly. "She wasn't always easy to know, was she? But she loved fiercely. And she let people in. She didn't hide behind observation. You need to do that same thing."

"And what if I get hurt again?" Eve asked, her voice barely a whisper.

"Then you get hurt," Krissy said simply. "But at least you'll have felt something. Like Miles and Louisa. They risked it all for each other, even when everyone told them not to. And look where it got them – a legend wrapped up in the sea."

"It got them vanished," Eve pointed out, a hint of bitterness creeping into her voice.

"Sometimes," Krissy said thoughtfully, "vanishing is just another word for being deeply loved." She took a sip of her coffee. "You've been so focused on the secrets, on the history... you've forgotten to look at the people around you. Geraint, for example. He clearly cares about you."

Eve flushed slightly. "He was just helping with the research."

"Helping and noticing," Krissy corrected. "You pushed him away before he even had a chance! You always do that – keep everyone at arm's length until they nearly break your heart."

There was a familiar rhythm to their conversations; a back-and-forth that had bound them together for years. It wasn't always easy, but it was honest. And in that honesty, Eve felt a small crack appear in the wall she'd been building around herself. "You think I should just...open up?" she asked finally, her voice tentative.

"I think you should let yourself feel," Krissy replied. "Let go of the fear a little. Let yourself be messy and vulnerable – it's what makes us human." She paused, then added with a knowing smile, "Besides, I have a feeling that's where the real adventure begins." Eve looked out at the rain-streaked window again, this time noticing the way the light caught on the droplets, creating shimmering patterns. Perhaps Krissy was right. Maybe it was time to stop observing and start living – to risk being hurt, to allow herself to be seen, and maybe, just maybe, to finally let someone in.

The rain hadn't truly eased its assault when Eve finally stepped out of The Chiron Cafe, but it felt as though a small weight had been lifted from her shoulders. Krissy's words still echoed in her mind – 'let yourself feel.' As she sorted through the mail in her postbag, a small, cream-colored envelope caught her eye. It was addressed simply to "Eve, The Archive, Ashcliffe-on-Sea." Unusual. There weren't many letters for her. Most were bills or flyers advertising local events. But this one felt different – imbued with a quiet significance that pulled at her. Inside, the letter was folded neatly with a large G as the signature. A quick glance revealed it was from Geraint. Eve was eager to know what he'd discovered. His handwriting filled the page in neat, elegant script:

Eve,

I've been at the Archive again, and I think I've found something that might resonate with you – a thread that connects everything. Emily was meticulous, of course, but she clearly wanted to keep certain things hidden. I managed to uncover a letter from Miles – one he wrote shortly before his disappearance. It's fascinating.

He talks about feeling trapped, of yearning for something beyond the obligations and expectations of his family. He describes Louisa as if she were a force of nature, a secret whispered by the sea itself. Listen to this: 'The tide remembers everything, Eve. And it will reveal its secrets in time, if only you know where to look.' It's like he was speaking directly to you.

He writes about his plans – a desperate attempt to escape with Louisa, to build a life by the sea where they could finally be themselves. He paints such a vivid picture of them, of their love and their longing. It's heartbreaking, really. Here's a snippet: 'I feel as though I am drowning in duty, Louisa, yet all I crave is to be swept away with you, to lose myself in the silver of your hair beneath the moonlight. He ends by asking her to look for 'the key' at Louisa's Cove. I've copied the whole thing out for you. I think it's significant.

Warmly,

G.

Attached to the letter was a neatly printed copy of Miles's entire letter, complete with his elegant handwriting and pressed lavender sprigs tucked into the corners. As Eve reread the passages, a strange warmth spread through her, quickly followed by a familiar pang of melancholy. The words resonated deeply within her – as if they were speaking to a part of herself she hadn't realized was still listening. "It's like he was speaking directly to you," Geraint had written. And it was. A fleeting image flashed through her mind – a flash of silver in the moonlight, a woman standing on the rocks by the sea. It was brief, almost ethereal – but undeniably Louisa. Eve had seen her before, hadn't she? In Emily's photograph. A subtle shimmer, a hint of something... else. She looked up from the letter, and for a moment, the rain seemed to intensify, as if mirroring the sudden surge of emotions within her. A shiver ran down her spine – not entirely unpleasant. It felt like a connection, a recognition, stretching back through time and generations.

She clutched the letter from Miles tighter, her fingers brushing against the pressed lavender. A memory surfaced – Emily, smelling faintly of lavender, telling her that her mother had a particular fondness for the sea and seashells. "It feels...familiar," Eve murmured to herself, her voice barely audible above the rain. "Like I've known him before." She looked out at the turbulent waves crashing against the shore, feeling as though she was standing on the edge of something vast and ancient – a secret waiting to be revealed. And for the first time since Emily's death, Eve didn't feel quite so alone. The letter from Miles had not just brought her a piece of the past; it had brought her closer to herself. And Geraint had been the one to discover it, to gently make sure Eve had the chance to read what he'd found. He was thinking of her, it seemed, even though he was no longer in Ashcliffe. What, Eve wondered in horror, have I done?

The letter from Miles trembled in Eve's hand, the words already imprinted somewhere deep inside her. She folded it carefully, almost reverently, and slipped it back into the envelope, fingers grazing the pressed lavender once more. That scent again – persistent, like memory. Like Emily. Outside, the sea roared in the distance, louder than before. It wasn't just weather any more – it was atmosphere. Omen. A presence. She sat in the window seat of the Archive, knees tucked beneath her, the envelope still in her lap. The familiar tick of the old clock Emily had insisted was "romantic in its uselessness" echoed through the dim cottage. Eve was no longer just holding a letter – she was holding a story. Their story. And somehow, her own.

As the afternoon light thinned, a memory surfaced – vivid, visceral. Emily, hair still streaked with salt after a morning swim, sat at the same table, holding up a sepia-toned photograph of Louisa. "She was thunder in silk," Emily had said, her voice rich with awe. "Refused to be erased just because she loved differently." Emily had pressed the photo into Eve's palm. "She lived the kind of truth that made people uncomfortable. But that truth — that fierce longing — it's in my blood, you know. I can feel it in the wind here." At the time, Eve had nodded politely, unsure of what Emily meant. But now... now she felt it. That fierce longing. It surged in her chest like tidewater. Eve got up and crossed to the Archive's shelves. The box of personal items Emily had kept hidden was still under lock and key. Eve retrieved it, her fingers surprisingly steady as she worked the latch. Inside: letters, old maps, a faded scarf that still held Emily's perfume. At the bottom, wrapped in oilskin, a journal with Emily's spidery handwriting. Eve skimmed it quickly, stopping at a page where Louisa's name was circled in the margin, followed by a hastily scrawled note:"The Sea Blessing. Ask Rita. Ask before it's forgotten."

Eve's breath caught. The Sea Blessing. Another flash: Eve, a teenager, standing at the back of the beach crowd, watching a small group of older villagers murmuring around a candlelit driftwood sculpture. She remembered thinking it looked like a séance or an old play, the way they whispered over tokens and seashells, then scattered them into the surf. Emily had tugged her away before she could ask questions, but now, the ritual took on a different weight. Not folklore. Not performance. A farewell. Maybe even a promise.

Eve grabbed her coat, the letter from Geraint, and the journal. The Chiron Cafe was dimly lit when she arrived back there – Rita had just begun wiping down the tables for the evening lull. The smell of lemon soap and stale coffee was oddly comforting. "Back again?" Rita asked, not unkindly.

"I need to ask you something," Eve said, slipping into the seat at the counter. "About the Sea Blessing."

Rita paused. Her hands stilled on the cloth. "Not many remember that," she said carefully.

"Emily did," Eve said. "She wrote your name next to it. Said you might know more."

Rita took a long breath and folded the cloth neatly before setting it aside. "It's not something people talk about much. Not any more. But yes... it was something we used to do. My granny used to tell me all about it, before she ever let me attend. For lovers who couldn't stay.

For stories that needed releasing." Her gaze grew distant. "The tide takes what it wants, Eve. But we used to believe that if you gave it something willingly – a memory, a vow, a hope – it might leave behind something else. Clarity. Peace."

"Did Miles and Louisa do one?" Eve asked softly.

Rita hesitated, then nodded. "They were seen down at Louisa's Cove the night before he vanished. No one admitted it aloud, but they all suspected. There was talk of tokens – pieces of their past, dropped into the sea. A necklace, a sketch, I think. Maybe even a lock of her hair." She smiled faintly. "Romantic fools. But brave. They weren't planning on running from something. They were running to it." A silence settled between them, filled only by the quiet clink of cutlery being set on a drying rack.

"Do you think," Eve began, unsure of her own voice, "that Emily wanted me to finish their story?"

Rita's eyes softened. "No, love. I think she wanted you to understand it. And then live your own."

That night, back at her cottage, Eve spread the letter, the journal, and the photograph of Louisa on the kitchen table. She turned them slowly, carefully, as though arranging puzzle pieces. And slowly, it was beginning to make sense. Louisa hadn't simply wanted to leave Ashcliffe. She had wanted freedom. To love without apology. To be unbound by the suffocating history of the town – just as Miles had. And Emily, decades later, had lived in quiet defiance of the same history. She'd created a haven in the Archive, but even she had spoken often of "what might have been." The women in Eve's lineage were seekers, dreamers, chroniclers – and sometimes, tragically, watchers. Always one step removed. Until now. Eve traced the final line of Miles's letter again: "Look for the key at Louisa's Cove." It had the feel of both a clue and a dare. And this time, Eve wouldn't ignore it.

She stood, went to the window. Rain lashed the glass, but it no longer felt oppressive – it felt cleansing. Like a hard reset. She turned to her phone, hesitating only briefly before opening her messages. Her thumbs hovered over the keyboard, then moved with quiet certainty.

Eve: I read the letter. I saw what you saw. You were right — she is a force of nature. I think... I think I'm ready to find out what she left behind. Can I meet you in Cardiff?

She hit send before she could overthink it. For a moment, nothing happened. Then the message marked Delivered. A beat passed. Two. Then a reply:

Geraint: Of course. I'll wait.

Eve let out a breath she hadn't realized she'd been holding. She turned, scanning the room, then grabbed a small canvas bag from beside the bookshelf. She packed without overthinking: a notebook, a change of clothes, Emily's journal, the envelope with Miles's letter, and her old Polaroid camera. She paused, considered, then added the scarf that still smelled like Emily – lavender and sea salt. As she zipped the bag closed, she felt something she hadn't in weeks. Direction. Eve paused at the door. Rain still sheeted down, but the clouds were breaking ever so slightly, light threading through the grey. She watched the tide pulling in and out, violent but purposeful. Eve placed a hand against the glass. For the first time since Emily's death, the silence didn't feel like absence. It felt like invitation. And she was finally, firmly, ready to say yes.

PART THREE: THE STORM OF ECHOES

14

CHAPTER FOURTEEN: FAR FROM HOME

The train hissed to a halt at Cardiff Central, spitting sunshine onto the platform. Eve stepped out, blinking against the sudden brightness, a welcome contrast to the perpetual drizzle of Ashcliffe-on-Sea. It was a good day for arriving – bright, bustling, full of the easy chatter of people heading home or off on adventures. A young girl with plaits skipped past, clutching a stuffed unicorn toy, and a man in grey tracksuit argued animatedly about football with his companion. It felt miles away from the grey, watchful quiet she'd been carrying around for weeks. Excitement fluttered in her chest, mixed with a familiar, slightly prickly apprehension – a feeling of stepping into something bigger than herself. Seeing Geraint again, after all, was both thrilling and daunting. Eve him easily enough outside the museum, a worn leather satchel slung across his shoulder. He looked exactly as she remembered: thoughtful eyes, slightly rumpled brown hair, and a smile that crinkled at the corners. "Eve! You made it," he said, offering a brief, warm hug.

The museum in Cardiff was grand, but not ostentatious. Sunlight streamed through enormous arched windows, illuminating polished marble floors and displays of meticulously arranged artifacts. It wasn't overwhelming; there was a sense of quiet reverence, as if the objects themselves were holding their breath. They headed straight for the 'Welsh Folk Art' exhibit, drawn by the promise of sailors and sea. "It's remarkable, isn't it?" Geraint murmured, his gaze sweeping over a collection of brightly painted wooden boats and intricate tapestries depicting coastal scenes. "How objects can hold memory. They aren't just things; they're vessels for the past." He gestured to a display of hand-carved bowls, their surfaces etched with swirling patterns. "Each one tells a story, if you know how to listen."

They moved deeper into the exhibit, examining tools used by fishermen, maps depicting long-forgotten routes, and delicate scrimshaw – tiny carvings made on whalebone. "It's like they absorb the emotions of those who owned them," Geraint continued, turning a small wooden sailor with outstretched arms. "The joy of a successful catch, the fear of a storm... They hold onto it all."

"Albert's always saying things like that," Eve mused, tracing the lines on a ceramic lobster pot. "That everything remembers something. That if you listen closely enough, you can hear the echoes." She'd dismissed it as sentimental ramblings back in Ashcliffe, something to do with his love story with Stella and Eloise, but now...

"Exactly!" Geraint agreed, his eyes alight with enthusiasm. "It's not just feeling; it's almost hearing – those faint reverberations of what was." He paused, a thoughtful frown on his face. "Ashcliffe was particularly full of them, you know? Like the stones themselves were whispering."

Their attention settled on a single scrimshaw – a small, intricately carved depiction of a mermaid rising from the waves. It was beautifully detailed, capturing the mermaid's flowing hair and the shimmer of her scales. "Look at this," Geraint said, pointing to the carving. "The detail... the skill. And you can almost feel the salt spray on your face." A sharp image flashed in Eve's mind: Emily, sitting at her desk in the Archive, carefully cleaning the scrimshaw with a soft cloth. She remembered the smell of lavender and dust, the quiet rustle of paper, and Emily's gentle smile. "I... I remember seeing something very similar to this in the Archive," she said, surprised by the suddenness of the memory. "Emily had it. She used to say it reminded her of sailors lost at sea." Geraint tilted his head, observing her intently. "Did she say anything else about it? About where she'd found it?"

Eve frowned, trying to grasp the feeling, the echo. "Just that... that it held secrets on its surface. And that she felt like it was waiting for someone to look beneath."

A small smile played on Geraint's lips. "Sounds familiar," he said quietly. "Like Ashcliffe itself." He glanced around the museum, as if listening for something. "It's funny, isn't it? How these little things can trigger such powerful memories. Like they're pulling at threads we didn't even know were there."

"It's... a lot," Eve said, letting the word hang in the air as they stepped out of the museum and onto the bustling streets of Cardiff. The rain from Ashcliffe seemed a distant memory; here, the sunshine felt almost aggressive, bouncing off the slate roofs and reflecting in the windows of the shops lining City Road. Cardiff rushed at them – a vibrant, chaotic tide of people and sounds. A busker strummed a lively Welsh folk tune on an acoustic guitar, competing with the chatter of students spilling out from Cardiff University, the sizzle of street food vendors grilling kebabs, and the thumping bass of music leaking from a nearby cafe. The air was thick with a medley of scents – roasted coffee beans, fragrant spices, salty sea air carried inland by a gentle breeze. It was a sensory explosion compared to Ashcliffe's muted palette.

"That's Cardiff for you," Geraint said, grinning as he navigated them through the throng, his arm brushing against hers. "A complete assault on the senses. You get used to it, eventually."

Eve took a deep breath, letting the energy of the city wash over her. It was exhilarating and slightly overwhelming – a far cry from the quiet rhythm of Ashcliffe-on-Sea. She'd imagined Cardiff would be different, but she hadn't anticipated this level of vibrancy. "It's...

intense," she admitted, adjusting to the constant flow of people. They walked for several streets, passing students laden with books and coffee cups, families browsing stalls selling handmade crafts, and groups of friends laughing over plates of paella from one of the many Spanish restaurants. The buildings were a mix of Victorian terraces and modern glass structures, reflecting Cardiff's layered history. Street food vendors lined the pavements – sizzling dumplings, fragrant curries, and sweet crepes tempting passers-by. It felt alive, breathing with a million different stories. "You'll love it here," Geraint said, gesturing to a group of musicians playing surprisingly lively grunge music near a market stall piled high with brightly coloured scarves. "It's multicultural, always something happening. And the food is amazing."

Finally, they turned onto a quieter side street and climbed the narrow steps up to Geraint's flat. It was tucked away in a brick building, its windows overflowing with trailing ivy. The flat itself was small – maybe ten by twelve – but cosy and inviting. Bookshelves crammed with books lined the walls, interspersed with maps and photographs. Mismatched furniture – a vintage armchair, a wooden desk piled high with papers, and a brightly patterned sofa – gave it a slightly cluttered, lived-in feel. Posters of Welsh bands and classic films adorned the walls, alongside some of Geraint's own research photos. "All to ourselves," Geraint announced, a mischievous glint in his eyes. "My brother's visiting family in Aberystwyth. Apparently, there's an endless supply of rugby and sheep."

"Sounds idyllic," Eve replied, stepping inside and letting the warmth of the flat envelop her.

The flat was filled with the scent of coffee and something faintly herbal – probably Geraint's attempt at brewing a calming tea. A record player sat on a small table by the sofa, and a stack of vinyl records lay waiting to be played. It felt... private. Like they'd stepped into a little corner of the city that belonged just to them. "I made some tea," Geraint said, heading towards the tiny kitchen. "Earl Grey with lavender – thought you might appreciate it."

"You know me well," Eve replied, sinking into the vintage armchair and letting out a contented sigh. It was a welcome change from the damp chill of Ashcliffe. They settled down on the sofa, mugs of tea in hand, and began to talk – about Cardiff, about their families, about everything and nothing. The city sounds filtered in through the open window – snippets of conversation, the rumble of buses, the distant chime of church bells. "It's funny," Geraint said after a while, swirling his tea. "I always felt Ashcliffe was full of echoes. Like it held onto the past really tightly."

Eve nodded in agreement. "Me too. It's like you could almost hear the voices of those who came before."

"Exactly! And I think it's because everyone is so aware of their history there. It shapes them, you know? Makes them a little... guarded." He paused, taking a sip of his tea. "But this," he gestured around the flat, "this feels different. It feels like a fresh start. All to ourselves."

"It's nice," Eve said quietly, feeling a sense of comfort settle over her. "Nice to have a bit of space."

A comfortable silence fell between them for a moment, punctuated only by the sounds of the city outside. Then, Geraint turned to her, his eyes thoughtful. "You know," he said slowly, "I was thinking about that scrimshaw... and you suddenly remembering Emily having it. It's not just coincidence, is it? It feels like... a connection." He reached out and gently touched her hand, and for the first time since arriving in Cardiff, Eve felt truly relaxed, truly present. The echoes of Ashcliffe seemed to fade away, replaced by the quiet rhythm of this new place and the growing sense that she was beginning to find her footing – not just in a new city, but in her own family history.

The sky outside Geraint's flat had shifted from gold to dusky lavender, the kind of early evening light that made everything feel suspended – like time was holding its breath. They were still on the sofa, now curled more comfortably, Eve with her legs tucked beneath her and her fingers wrapped around a second cup of tea that had long since gone lukewarm. Geraint sat angled toward her, his elbow propped on the cushion between them, fingers idly turning his mug. The conversation had mellowed into something more organic – less about catching up and more about rediscovering the way their rhythms fit. "Do you remember the night the Archive flooded?" Geraint asked, grinning crookedly.

Eve snorted. "Vividly. You made it worse, if I recall."

"I saved the sea charts!"

"You tripped over a mop bucket and took down a shelf with you!"

"Heroically," he amended, raising an eyebrow. "In my defence, the shelf was unstable."

Eve laughed, tilting her head against the back of the sofa. "I don't think the shelf was the only one! My gosh, it feels like another life."

Geraint studied her for a moment, his smile softening. "In some ways, it was."

They both grew quiet, the silence not uncomfortable, but charged – thick with the invisible threads that had been pulling tighter between them all day. A breeze rustled the ivy outside the window, and the city's hum softened to the occasional honk of traffic or distant laughter.

Geraint shifted closer, just slightly, the edge of his knee brushing hers. "It's strange," he murmured. "You being here. Feels... familiar. Like I never stopped expecting it." Eve didn't answer at first. Instead, she let her gaze drop to where their legs touched, then lifted it to meet his eyes. There was something open in his expression – unguarded, vulnerable. The quiet intimacy of the flat seemed to fold around them like a cocoon. "I missed you," she said, her voice barely above a whisper. His hand reached for hers. Not tentative. Not unsure. Warm fingers, slightly rough, closing gently around her own. "I thought about writing," he said.

"I thought about you," she replied. And then the moment tipped – slow, certain, and magnetic. Geraint leaned in and brushed his lips against hers. The kiss wasn't urgent – it was unhurried, exploratory, like reading an old book for the first time in years and rediscovering why you'd loved it. Eve responded with a soft sound in the back of her throat, her hand moving to rest lightly on his chest. His heartbeat thudded beneath her palm.

The second kiss was deeper, less careful. A quiet hunger stirred beneath the surface. His hands cupped her face, thumbs brushing along her cheekbones, and her arms slipped around his waist, drawing him in. She could feel the heat of him, the press of his body slowly leaning into hers, the scent of lavender tea and the faint, earthy tang of the city clinging to his clothes. They didn't speak as they shifted – wordless understanding moving between them as their bodies realigned. Geraint drew her up from the sofa, pulling her toward the bedroom down the narrow hallway. Their footsteps were muffled by the thick rug, and the soft thunk of the door closing behind them was almost ceremonial. The bedroom was dimly lit, still warmed by the afternoon sun. Books were piled on the bedside table, a sweater draped over a chair. It was lived-in and real, not staged or sterile. Eve stood in the middle of it for a moment, watching Geraint as he reached for her again.

Clothes came away gradually – pulled over heads, unfastened with quiet care, dropped onto the floor like they no longer mattered. There was a moment, when they were standing bare before each other, that they both paused – not out of hesitation, but reverence. They had shared this once before, but this time felt different. Weightier. More fragile and more necessary. He touched her first – just his fingertips along the curve of her shoulder, trailing down her arm as if relearning her by heart. She leaned into it, her breath catching slightly when he pressed his lips to her collarbone, tracing a slow path toward the base of her throat. Her hands slid over his back, feeling the muscle shift under skin, the heat of him anchoring her to the present.

They moved together onto the bed – soft linens catching under knees, the mattress sighing beneath them. Geraint's mouth found hers again, deeper this time, tongue flicking against hers as their hands roamed with growing urgency. His palms skimmed her hips, her back, reverent and sure, and she arched against him, feeling the electric pulse of contact. When they finally came together, it was with a slow, deliberate intensity – no frantic rush, just a steady building of sensation. His breath stuttered against her neck as he moved, and she clung to him, nails grazing down his back, her legs wrapping around his waist. Their bodies fit, and then melted, like memory and flesh colliding. The world narrowed: the rhythm of breath and heartbeat, the creak of the bed frame, the muffled moan she bit back as his hips moved with exquisite control. They whispered to each other – not words, but names, half-formed thoughts, syllables shaped from need.

There was a moment near the end, when everything slowed – the weight of him above her, his forehead pressed against hers, their breath shared in a single suspended second – and Eve felt something inside her uncoil. A knot she hadn't realized she'd been carrying for months finally released. The vulnerability didn't scare her. It felt like coming home. When they finally collapsed together, limbs tangled, skin damp and flushed, there was a silence filled not with absence, but presence.

Geraint exhaled a shaky laugh and brushed a strand of hair from her face. "Well..."

Eve smiled, eyes half-lidded. "Yeah." They lay like that for a while, her head on his chest, his fingers idly tracing circles along her back. The world outside felt distant, unimportant. Until it didn't. A sound cut through the quiet – a metallic rattle, followed by the unmistakable click of a key turning in the lock. Geraint and Eve froze. For a moment, they just stared at each other, confusion rising like a tide. "You said your brother was in Aberystwyth," Eve whispered, already reaching for the sheet.

"He is," Geraint said, low and alarmed, sitting up. Another sound – a door creaking open. A footstep. Then a muffled voice. Geraint moved swiftly, tugging on his jeans, eyes flicking toward the bedroom door. Eve wrapped the sheet around herself, heart thudding in her ears. The intimacy of a moment ago had shattered, replaced by something sharp and immediate. She looked toward him, her voice barely audible. "Who the hell has a key?" Geraint didn't answer. But his expression had shifted from confusion to something darker. "Stay here," he said. Then, barefoot and shirtless, he stepped into the hallway, the tension between what had been and what had just entered the flat pressing down like a storm front.

Eve heard the low murmur of voices from the hallway – Geraint's quick, surprised greeting, followed by a warm, chuckling reply. She scrambled into her clothes, her body still humming from before, heart now tapping with uncertainty. By the time she stepped into the living room, Geraint was already standing beside a man who could only be his brother. Llewellyn was slightly taller than Geraint, broader in the shoulders, with a streak of silver at his temples that suited him more than it should. His smile was easy, the kind that reached the eyes, and his coat still carried the damp scent of late-spring drizzle, despite the Cardiff sunshine. He looked like someone who laughed often, and meant it. "Well now," he said, eyes lighting on her. "So you're the reason Geraint's stayed out of Wales for so long, eh?"

The corner of Geraint's mouth twitched into an embarrassed grin. "Llew –"

"Oh, hush," Llewellyn said with a dismissive wave, his attention still on Eve. "I've heard exactly nothing for months, which is how I knew it was serious. Name's Llewellyn. You must be Eve." She blinked, then let out a soft laugh, the tension dissolving almost instantly. "I am. And you must be the infamous brother with the endless rugby and sheep."

Llewellyn gave a theatrical bow. "Guilty. Though this time it was mostly arguing with our little cousin about the correct way to make bara brith. She's six and terrifying."

He stepped forward and shook her hand, firm and warm, then took one sweeping look around the flat. "Well, this place is a mess. Which confirms you two are properly reunited." Eve chuckled, already feeling her shoulders relax. She liked him – his presence was calming, charming, and disarming in a way that made you feel like you'd known him for years. They settled back in the living room, the kettle boiling again like it hadn't stopped all day. Geraint disappeared into the kitchen, and Llewellyn claimed the vintage armchair, stretching his legs out with a satisfied sigh. "So," he said, turning to her. "Ashcliffe. What's it really like? Geraint paints it as a cross between Wuthering Heights and a murder mystery."

Eve smirked. "That's not entirely wrong."

"I knew it," he said, nodding. "You're from there?"

Eve hesitated. Not because she didn't want to answer – but because for once, the question didn't come with strings attached. There was no edge in his tone, no undercurrent of judgement or curiosity masked as kindness. Just genuine interest. "Born and raised," she said, leaning back against the sofa cushions. "My mum ran the bakery on the corner. My dad used to fix boats." "Sounds charming," Llewellyn said, clearly meaning it.

"It was... complicated," Eve replied. "Ashcliffe always felt like it belonged to someone else. I was just borrowing space."

"But you stayed?"

"For a while." She glanced at Geraint as he returned with three steaming mugs of tea. "Then things shifted. People changed. Or maybe I did."

Llewellyn took the tea gratefully. "Well, if you're anything like my brother here, you were probably carrying the weight of the place on your shoulders."

Eve smiled faintly. "More like swimming through it."

"Same difference," Llewellyn said, taking a sip. "Though I've always believed some towns have a kind of memory. They either keep you, or they spit you out." She didn't respond right away. Instead, she let that idea settle inside her like a stone dropped into water. It made sense. Ashcliffe had held on tightly. Sometimes too tightly. "Can I ask?" Llewellyn said gently, shifting the mood just slightly. "Did you know Emily?" Her breath caught – not painfully, but like hearing an old melody out of nowhere.

"Yes," she said. "She was a great friend to me for my whole life – her and my parents went way back, you see."

"Geraint said she was brilliant."

"She was," Eve murmured. Her eyes drifted toward the window, as a memory surfaced – small, but vivid. Emily brushing dust from a collection of nautical charts, humming under her breath, a tune that sounded like an old lullaby. She always brought lemon sweets and shared them without asking. Always kept a cardigan in the drawer, no matter the season. The quiet anchor of the Archive. "She had this way of making everything seem like it mattered," Eve said softly. "Even the smallest things. I remember once she found a pressed flower tucked into a century-old ledger and treated it like it was a diamond."

Llewellyn nodded. "People like that leave ripples."

Eve smiled, but it was a little sad. "Yeah. They do."

The room quieted for a moment – not heavy, just reflective. Outside, the sun was low, casting amber streaks across the floorboards. A nearby streetlamp flickered on with a quiet buzz, and the sounds of the city drifted in again – less chaotic now, more subdued. Evening settling over everything. "Well," Llewellyn said, standing and stretching, "I should be off. Promised Mum I'd call tonight, and if I'm late again, she'll send a guilt parcel the size of a ice-cream van." He paused before leaving, one hand on the door-frame. "It really is good to see him like this," he added, glancing between them. "Geraint's always been good at burying himself in books. Less good at... letting the past lie." Eve felt a flicker of something warm beneath her ribs.

"Neither am I," she admitted.

Llewellyn grinned. "Perfect match, then."

With a cheerful wave, he stepped into the hallway and disappeared down the stairs, the front door clicking shut behind him. Geraint came to stand beside her, his hand brushing lightly against her back.

They stood in silence, watching the fading light spill across the room. "He means well," Geraint said after a while.

"I like him," Eve replied. "He listens. Like you." A pause.

Geraint asked, "How are you doing? Really."

She leaned her head against his shoulder. "Surprisingly okay. Like... I can breathe a little easier here." They stayed there a while, not speaking, just standing in the soft hush that had returned to the flat. It wasn't that Ashcliffe had vanished. The past still lingered, just out of sight – but for the first time in weeks, it didn't feel like it was chasing her. Outside, Cardiff moved on. A siren wailed distantly, but the police kind – not the mythological kind. Someone shouted, then laughed. A dog barked once and fell silent. And inside the small, ivy-draped flat, Eve felt something she hadn't allowed herself to feel in a long time. Not resolution. Not yet. But the start of something close. And beyond it all, the echoes still waited – quiet for now, but never truly gone.

15

CHAPTER FIFTEEN: RETURN TO THE COVE

The train rattled onward, a rhythmic counterpoint to the quiet conversation between Eve and Geraint. Cardiff had been a welcome burst of colour after Ashcliffe's perpetual drizzle, but now, as they watched the grey English countryside blur past, a comfortable familiarity settled over them – a feeling of returning home, though 'home' was still proving to be a somewhat fluid concept. "It felt... right there," Eve said, her voice slightly husky from the train journey and perhaps something else. "Being somewhere new, but also feeling like you'd been there before."

"That's Cardiff in a nutshell," Geraint replied, a small smile playing on his lips. "A bit of everything, all at once. And surprisingly vibrant for a place that looks perpetually about to rain." He glanced out the window, taking in the rolling hills and distant fields. "It was good to just... be. To not have to constantly decipher what everyone else was thinking."

Eve nodded, remembering the constant pressure to piece together Emily's secrets, the feeling of being pulled in a dozen different directions. "It felt like I was wearing all of Ashcliffe's memories at once," she confessed. "Like I needed to organize them all before they swallowed me whole." The rain outside intensified as they approached Ashcliffe, transforming into a steady, insistent drumming against the train windows. It wasn't the angry, dramatic storm of previous visits; this was a quieter, more persistent rain – the kind that seeped into your bones and reminded you that you were in Kent. It felt... fitting. As the train pulled into Ashcliffe station, a tangible sense of anticipation hung in the air, a mixture of homecoming and something subtly different. The town looked smaller than Eve remembered, its grey stone buildings huddled together against the elements. The Post Office, with its familiar red door and peeling paint, seemed to beckon her back.

They stepped off the train and into a world immediately saturated with the scent of salt and damp earth. It was heavier here, richer – a smell that had always felt intrinsically linked to Ashcliffe's hidden history. As they walked towards Louisa's Cove, the rain intensified again, but this time it didn't feel cold or unwelcome. It felt... knowing. The path leading down to the cove was slick with moisture, and the waves crashed against the rocks with a renewed ferocity. The air vibrated with sound – the constant roar of the sea mixed with the soft patter of rain on stone. It wasn't just the cove that felt different this time; it was her. Eve felt it immediately – a stronger pull, a deeper resonance than she'd experienced before. It was as if the place itself were waiting for them, subtly urging them closer. "It feels... charged," Geraint said quietly, stopping to take in the view. "Like something shifted while we were gone." He noticed how the rain seemed to cling to certain spots – particularly where they'd found the carvings on the cliff face during their previous visit. A darker patch of moss gathered around the base of the carved siren, as if it had been waiting for them to return. "It's like the rain remembers," he observed, tilting his head slightly.

They moved further down the path, and the cove opened up before them – a small, sheltered crescent of sand embraced by towering cliffs. The low tide had revealed even more of the beach than they remembered, exposing a tapestry of seaweed-covered rocks and glistening pebbles. The grey light filtering through the clouds cast an ethereal glow over everything, lending the scene a touch of melancholy beauty. "It's so peaceful today," Eve murmured, letting her gaze sweep across the cove. "Despite everything."

Geraint nodded in agreement. "And familiar," he added, stepping forward and running his hand along one of the larger rocks. "Like you've been here a hundred times before." As they stood there, absorbing the atmosphere, Eve felt it again – that subtle tugging at her memory, that sense of recognition. It wasn't just about the place; it was about her. She closed her eyes for a moment, letting the sound of the waves wash over her. A fleeting image flashed through her mind: Louisa standing on the rocks, gazing out to sea, a wistful smile on her face.

"Do you... do you feel that?" she asked, turning to Geraint. "Like we're not just visiting? Like we're... returning?" He looked at her intently, his eyes reflecting the grey light and the restless sea. "I think," he said slowly, a hint of wonder in his voice, "that maybe we are." He took a step closer, reaching out to brush a strand of hair from her face. "And I have a feeling," he added softly, "that this time, it's not just the cove that remembers."

The rain continued its steady rhythm, now less like a curtain and more like a gentle hand guiding them deeper into the cove. As Eve stepped onto the slick sand, a wave of emotion washed over her – not just sadness, though there was plenty of that, but a profound sense of longing, as if she were stepping into Louisa Thornton's shoes for a fleeting moment. It tightened in her chest, a familiar ache that resonated with something deep within her own soul. It wasn't just the memory of Louisa; it felt like Louisa was remembering – remembering a life half-lived, a love cut short, a yearning for something more than duty demanded. "She was beautiful, wasn't she?" Eve murmured, almost to herself, tracing the edge of a weathered rock with her finger. It was a simple observation, but it felt laden with unspoken questions.

Geraint noticed immediately, his eyes scanning her face with quiet understanding. "More than beautiful," he replied, his voice low. "Captivating. Like she held the sea within her." He gestured to the carving of Louisa as the siren on the cliff face – a remarkably well-preserved image despite its age and exposure to the elements. "The locals believe these carvings are maintained. That's why they're so clear. As if someone, or something, wanted us to see her." He recounted a local legend he'd stumbled upon during his research – a tale passed down through generations of Ashcliffe residents. It spoke of women connected to the seafoam, 'The Seafoam Brides,' who lured sailors to their doom with their beauty and grace. But it wasn't just about seduction; it was about connection – a deep, almost spiritual link to the ocean itself. These women were said to hold secrets within them – echoes of the past, whispers of the future. "They weren't necessarily evil," Geraint explained, his gaze fixed on the carving. "Just... complicated. Drawn to the sea, shaped by it, and perhaps a little bit haunted by its vastness."

Eve felt a tightening in her chest again as she looked at the carving – at Louisa's serene expression, her slightly parted lips, as if she were about to speak a secret. It was more than just a pretty picture; it felt like a window into another time, another life. She noticed then that the scent of salt was being subtly overlaid with something sweeter – lavender. A delicate, nostalgic fragrance that hung in the air, stronger now than it had been before. "It's the lavender," she said softly, inhaling deeply. "Emily's scent. And Louisa's. And ours, I suppose."

As they moved further down towards the water's edge, the sense of presence intensified. It wasn't a dramatic, ghostly apparition – no sudden chill or blinding light. It was subtler, more pervasive – like standing in a room filled with memories waiting to be unearthed. Eve stopped abruptly, drawn to a particular stone near the tide line – a large, smooth boulder covered in patches of vibrant green moss. As she knelt down to examine it, a distinct feeling washed over Eve – as if Louisa herself was there beside her, brushing against her leg. The scent of lavender intensified, almost overwhelming, and for a moment, Eve felt like she could hear the murmur of waves and the rustle of seaweed. It wasn't just a memory; it felt real – a vivid echo of Louisa's presence. She reached out and touched the stone, feeling a strange warmth radiate through her hand. "Do you feel that?" Geraint asked, noticing her stillness. "Like... like someone was here? Just now?" Eve nodded slowly, unable to articulate what she was experiencing. It wasn't just a feeling; it was as if Louisa were offering her something – a piece of herself, a fragment of her story. "It's like... she's saying, 'You carry my strength too.'"

A wave rolled in, splashing against the rocks and soaking their feet. Eve instinctively looked out at the sea, captivated by its vastness and depth. She saw it then – not just the grey expanse of water, but a fleeting glimpse of something silver beneath the surface, as if a flash of moonlight had broken through the clouds. It was gone in an instant, but the image stayed with her – a shimmering reflection of Louisa's beauty, her longing, and perhaps, even her secret. "She wasn't just a romantic figure," Eve said, her voice gaining strength. "She was a woman caught between duty and desire, trapped by circumstance. Just like... Emily." A realization settled over her – not one of sadness, but of understanding. She'd spent so long trying to decipher Emily's secrets, to piece together the puzzle of her family history, that she hadn't truly seen her. She'd been so focused on the mystery that she'd missed the woman. "And now," she continued, turning to face Geraint, a small smile playing on her lips, "I think I'm starting to understand why." She felt it then – a sense of acceptance, not of resignation, but of recognition. The weight of the past hadn't lifted entirely, but it felt lighter now, less oppressive. She wasn't just carrying Emily's legacy, she was carrying Louisa's too – her longing, her strength, and her connection to the sea. With that in mind, she knew exactly where they needed to go next.

The rain hadn't let up when they arrived at Ashcliffe's Town Hall. It hammered against the slate roof, a steady, insistent rhythm that mirrored the nervous beat of Eve's heart. The building itself seemed to absorb the light, casting long shadows within its high-ceilinged chambers and heavy oak furniture. Councillor Davies was waiting for them in his office – a room dominated by a large mahogany desk piled high with documents and photographs. He looked older now, noticeably so. The past year hadn't been kind to him. Lines etched themselves around his eyes and mouth, hinting at a life spent wrestling with secrets. He seemed smaller too, somehow, the weight of them pressing down on him. When Eve had left for Cardiff, he'd confessed to feeling a genuine sense of loss, almost as if he'd expected her to disappear forever – something that had clearly troubled him deeply.

"Please, have a seat," he said, his voice a little raspy, a touch hesitant. "It's... good to see you again." The air in the room felt thick with unspoken questions. Eve didn't waste time on pleasantries. She took a deep breath and cut straight to the heart of it. "Are you my father?" The question hung in the air, heavy with anticipation – a single stone dropped into a still pond, sending ripples outwards. Davies didn't flinch. He simply regarded her for a moment, his eyes – a surprisingly bright blue – assessing. A small, almost imperceptible smile touched the corner of his lips. "Yes," he said quietly, as if it were the most natural thing in the world. "I am." The revelation landed with a surprising gentleness, not shattering Eve's expectations but settling into her consciousness like a familiar piece falling into place. It made sense now – the way he always seemed to be... watching. "How did you know?" she asked, trying to keep her voice steady despite the sudden rush of emotions swirling within her.

"It's hard to explain," he replied, running a hand through his thinning grey hair. "Emily and I... we had a brief affair years ago. Nothing serious, nothing lasting. Just a shared moment, really." He paused, as if searching for the right words. "When Eleanor died – my wife – I desperately wanted... to be involved in Emily's life. To know you. So, I made it my business to watch over you and Emily. It felt like the least I could do." He continued, his voice gaining a little more warmth. "It was a gentle secret, really – something we both agreed to keep.

Emily wanted to protect you, to shield you from any complications. She thought it best if you grew up without knowing." He glanced at a photograph on his desk – a faded image of a young Eve, beaming with happiness as she clutched a stuffed toy. "She was a good mother when it came down it, your Emily. A fiercely protective one."

"You kept the archives alive," Eve observed, noticing the details. "You were interested in Emily's work."

"Absolutely," he confirmed. "I admired her dedication, her passion for Ashcliffe's history. And, of course," he added with a wry smile, "knowing you were connected to it all made it even more interesting." He shared a few anecdotes – how he'd often bring Emily cups of tea when she was working late in the archives, his quiet encouragement when she'd been struggling with a particularly difficult project. "I used to tell her you had your mother's sharp eyes and your grandmother's intuition." He suspected the other councillors, particularly Bellweather and Harding, were trying to suppress certain secrets within the archives – secrets related to the Thorntons, of course. "I didn't want you to miss out on Emily's legacy," he said earnestly. "And frankly, I wasn't ready to let it all disappear."

"You wanted me to discover it," Eve realized, a slow smile spreading across her face. "It was you as much as it was Emily. All along."

"Precisely," Davies confirmed. "I knew, somehow, that you would be the one to unlock its secrets. It was my little way of keeping the family's tales alive." He leaned back in his chair, a touch of weariness entering his voice. "I didn't want to pressure Emily, though. She wanted you to find it on your own terms." He confessed that he hadn't realized just how deeply intertwined his life was with the Thorntons until recently. "It's rather... complicated," he admitted, a hint of amusement in his eyes. "I suppose I always suspected there was something special about Emily. And now... now I know why." He paused, then added quietly, "I never told her how much she meant to me – not really. Not until recently."

Eve felt a surge of empathy for him – for the years he'd spent guarding his secret, for the unspoken affection he'd held for Emily, and now, for her. She saw him then, not just as a councillor, not just as her father, but as a quiet guardian – a man who had quietly observed her life from afar, protecting her and preserving her family's history. "Thank you," she said simply, meaning more than words could express. Outside, the rain continued to fall, washing over Ashcliffe and carrying with it the secrets of generations. As they began to discuss the archives and their potential, Eve couldn't help but feel a sense of belonging she hadn't realized she was missing. She had finally found her roots, not just in the soil of Ashcliffe, but also within the heart of her family – a family whose story was far more intriguing, and far more magical, than she could have ever imagined.

The rain had softened into a gentle mist by the time they stepped outside the Town Hall. The streets of Ashcliffe glistened beneath the filtered sunlight, cobblestones dark with moisture and speckled with drifting petals from some unseen garden. The storm had passed, but the air remained charged – as if the town itself had been holding its breath and had only just now exhaled. They didn't speak as they walked, not at first. The silence between Eve and Geraint was comfortable, deep, and full of everything that didn't need to be said. When they reached the now increasingly familiar path that led back to Louisa's Cove, a soft shaft of golden light broke through the thinning clouds, spilling down the cliffs like a benediction. It struck the sea and shimmered outward in ripples, as though the horizon had opened its eyes. And then, quietly, without hesitation, Geraint reached for Eve's hand.

She let him. More than that – she returned the gesture with a gentle squeeze, grounding herself in the moment. His fingers were warm, slightly callused, familiar in a way that felt entirely new. That simple act – his hand in hers – was the kind of anchor she'd needed. Not to hold her down, but to steady her in the tide. "This feels different," he said softly, glancing toward her. "Not just Ashcliffe. Us."

She nodded. "It is." Her voice trembled, not from uncertainty, but from the overwhelming tide of knowing. "For the first time in... I don't know how long, I feel like I'm standing in my own life. Not someone else's shadow." They walked the winding path in silence again, the cove opening before them like a sacred threshold. The sea was calmer now, its breath slower, deeper, but no less powerful. The rain had rinsed everything clean, leaving behind the briny scent of promise and something softer – lavender again, yes, but mixed now with wild thyme and the lingering trace of woodsmoke.

At the cliff's edge, Geraint stopped. He turned to her, still holding her hand. "You've changed," he said. It wasn't a question. "But it's not a loss. It's like... the version of you I always felt was there, just waiting." Eve's breath caught in her throat. She looked up at him, really looked, and saw not just the man who had walked beside her through riddles and rainstorms, but the one who had believed – in Emily's cause, in Louisa's truth, and in Eve herself. "Tell me," she whispered, "what did you see in me back then? Before all this? Before you even knew?" He smiled gently, his thumb brushing her knuckles. "Someone brave enough to ask the questions no one else dared. Someone haunted, yes, but not broken. And someone who didn't realize she'd already begun rewriting her own story." She stepped closer, and when she kissed him, it wasn't with urgency or desperation. It was soft, full of salt and memory and everything they'd carried – across miles, through storms, in silence. It was a kiss layered with grief and gratitude, with questions answered and questions that no longer needed answering.

It was the kiss of two people who had seen each other – fully, deeply – and chosen not to ever turn away again. When they pulled apart, the quiet stretched again, not awkward but reverent. "I'd been waiting," Eve said.

"So had I," he replied, forehead resting against hers. "Maybe we were always meant to meet here."

The tide was rising. The cove seemed to hum, as if the cliffs themselves were resonating with some unseen vibration. Eve turned toward

the sea, her eyes narrowing slightly. And then it came. A memory –
but not a hazy flicker or a fragile echo. This one surged through her,
vivid and whole. Louisa stood on the very rocks where Eve now stood.
She was laughing – wind-tossed hair, eyes full of knowing. She turned,
and for the first time, Louisa saw her. Not as a ghost or fragment,
but as a woman reaching forward across time. She wasn't waiting for
Miles. She was waiting for Eve.

Louisa had known the truth – that her story wasn't complete, that
someone would come who could carry it, not as a burden, but as a
legacy. Louisa had looked out at the horizon not for rescue, but for
recognition. She had passed down her longing, her strength, her secrets – her truth – waiting for someone who would not flinch when
faced with all of it. Tears slipped down Eve's cheeks, though she didn't
feel sad. She felt whole. The mist curled around her ankles, whispering
its approval. The carving of Louisa, still visible through beads of water,
seemed to smile more fully now – less mournful, more assured. "I see
it now," Eve whispered. "All of it. She wasn't a ghost. She was a guide."

Geraint came to stand beside her. "And you've followed her all the
way home."

She nodded. "And now I can let her rest." They stood in silence,
letting the sea speak. The waves lapped higher against the rocks, no
longer crashing but caressing. As if even the ocean recognized the moment.

"I used to think I was just a piece of Emily's story," Eve said after
a time. "But now I know – I'm part of Louisa's too. Of all the women
who came before me. I carry them with me." Geraint smiled, his voice
quiet. "And they carry you. Every time the sea moves, every time the
wind shifts, they're reminding you that you're not alone." A soft breeze
stirred her hair. The lavender scent was fading now, replaced by the
clean, bright tang of sea air. It felt like a goodbye. But also like a beginning. "I don't need to chase ghosts any more," she said. "I don't need
every answer. I just need to live with what I know... and love what's

in front of me." She turned to him again, eyes clear, unburdened. "I choose this. I choose you."

Geraint didn't answer with words. He didn't have to. His arms came around her, and they stood there, held by the cliffs, the sea, the past, and the promise of everything yet to come. The sun broke fully through the clouds then, casting golden light across the cove. The rocks glistened. The carvings gleamed. The moss seemed greener. For a brief, impossible moment, it felt like time folded in on itself – like Louisa, Emily, and Eve were all standing in the same place, breathing the same air, touched by the same tide. And in that moment, Eve understood the final truth: that love – true, enduring, fiercely honest love – was the thread that tied every story together. Not just the romantic kind, but the kind that endures through silence, through sacrifice, through centuries of waiting. She had found it. Not in a book. Not in an archive. But here. In the cove. In herself. In him. As they turned to leave, hand in hand, the sea exhaled once more behind them, carrying their footprints into its memory.

The sky was bruising again. Out beyond the cove, the horizon darkened with the low swell of an approaching storm – thick clouds curling at the edges like ink dropped into water. But this time, the sight didn't bring dread. Only quiet anticipation. Eve stood beside Geraint at the edge of the bluff, their shoulders touching. The wind tugged gently at their coats, and the first hush of distant thunder rolled across the water like a memory returning. Ashcliffe breathed behind them – old and secretive, still holding things close to its chest. But it felt different now. Not heavy, but watchful. As if the town, like its sea, understood that some truths didn't need to be shouted. Only lived. They didn't speak. They didn't need to. Geraint turned to her, his expression soft but steady. There was salt in the air and something sweet—faint, but unmistakable. Lavender. Eve smiled before she even saw it. A single sprig, tangled delicately in the curls at the back of his head, placed there by wind or something older. A trace of Louisa, or perhaps of the place itself. Ashcliffe wasn't done with them. Not entirely.

Eve reached up and plucked the sprig gently, holding it between her fingers. "We'll never be finished with this place, will we?" she said.

"No," he replied. "But I think we're finally part of it. Not just observors."

The storm crept closer, but they stayed where they were – watching it come in, together. Unafraid. Whatever Ashcliffe still held in its depths – whatever shadows or stories might rise again – they would face it not as seekers or strangers, but as something stronger. As belonging. As the first drops of rain began to fall, they turned toward home. And the cove watched them go.

16

CHAPTER SIXTEEN: THE LAST ARCHIVE

The rain had finally eased to a gentle drizzle, a silver sheen coating the slate roofs of Ashcliffe-on-Sea as if trying to wash away the last vestiges of the storm. Inside the Archive, bathed in the warm glow of the desk lamp, Eve was immersed in the final stages of digitizing. The air smelled faintly of old paper and lavender – Emily's lingering scent – a comforting blend that had become synonymous with progress. Close-up, you could hear it: the satisfying click of the scanner as she fed in another file, followed by the whirring of the machine itself, capturing the brittle pages of Louisa Thornton's journal on her screen. Eve's fingers moved with a practiced ease, each click and swipe a small victory. She was adding the last few files – mostly faded photographs and scraps of handwritten notes – completing Emily's huge project. The one that Emily had thought would take five years had taken more like eighteen months in the capable hands of Eve. A palpable weight lifted from her shoulders with every scanned page. It wasn't just about the Archive; it felt like she was releasing something held captive for decades, perhaps centuries.

She leaned back in her chair, stretching her stiff muscles, and gazed at the screen. The digital image of Louisa's delicate handwriting swam before her eyes – a connection forged across time. A small smile touched her lips. She rotated the file slightly, examining it one last time, then clicked 'Save'. It was done. The Archive, Emily's legacy, was complete... for now. A quiet sense of accomplishment settled over her, mingled with a touch of melancholy – knowing that this digitization wouldn't truly end things, but simply change how they were experienced and accessed. The rain continued its gentle drumming against the windows as Eve settled into her usual post at the desk, the glow of the computer screen illuminating her face. It wasn't just a task; it was a ritual – documenting the completion of Emily Thornton's archive. She dipped her pen in ink, a deep indigo that seemed to echo the sea, and began:

"Entry 157. Digitization Complete. Date: October 26th."

It felt inadequate, really, to simply state the facts. It was more than just files scanned and metadata entered. As she wrote, she thought of Emily – her warmth, her eccentricity, the way she'd always seemed to know something you hadn't yet. And then, the words flowed: "The Archive is now a mirror, reflecting not just Ashcliffe's past, but also its secrets and those who have been woven into it." She paused, tapping her pen against the page. "It's strange," she murmured to herself, "to be included. To become part of the story, rather than simply observing it." A small smile touched her lips – a memory of Emily saying, "The sea remembers everything." It felt so apt now, especially after her last words. "I think," Eve wrote slowly, "that she meant it for me. That the sea... and this place... were waiting for someone to look beneath." She added: "Eve Thornton – Postwoman & Archivist. Born: 26th March 1987. Note: Feels as though a long journey has ended, but also that one has just begun. The sea remembers." She closed her notebook, a sense of quiet melancholy settling over her. It was a simple entry, perhaps, but it felt like a piece of herself had been captured – finally added to the record, alongside all those who came before.

The Archive smelled particularly potent that afternoon – a heady mix of damp paper, beeswax polish, and Emily Thornton's lingering lavender. Dust motes danced in the shafts of light filtering through the high windows, illuminating a chaotic but comforting scene: stacks of books threatening to spill onto the floor, piles of documents overflowing from wooden shelves, and maps spread across the large oak desk. Eve and Geraint were immersed in it – a pretty portrait of scholarly pursuit. "So," Geraint said, adjusting his glasses and gesturing around with a pencil, "we're still leaning towards 'Emotional Resonance and Folk Memory,' I presume?" Eve nodded, tapping a pen against her chin. "Definitely. Emily's archive is practically overflowing with it. It's not just dates and facts; there's this... feeling to it. Like the place itself remembers." She gestured around at the surrounding stacks. "I think that's what drew me to it in the first place – a sense of recognition, of having been here before."

"Methodical research," Geraint countered with a smile, "is crucial, of course. But I agree. The data is only half the story. Your intuitive grasp of the archive - your ability to feel its history – that's invaluable." He pointed to a particularly worn volume on local folklore. "We need to ground it in something concrete, though. Something beyond just 'feeling'."

"Exactly!" Eve exclaimed, leaning forward. "That's where you come in. You can sift through the records, find the corroborating evidence – the census reports, the parish registers... I can sense what might be there." She paused, considering. "It's like... Emily was deliberately leaving clues, not just for us to find, but for ourselves to discover." They continued to discuss their approach – a delightful synergy of her intuitive understanding and his meticulous research. He appreciated her openness to the intangible; she valued his grounding in historical fact. They were two halves of a puzzle, each bringing a unique perspective to their exploration of Ashcliffe's hidden past. "Perhaps," Geraint mused, "we can frame it as exploring how folk memory shapes – and is shaped by – place."

"I like that," Eve replied, scribbling notes in her own pad. "It feels... right."

The afternoon dissolved into a flurry of historical records. Armed with fresh coffee and a shared sense of purpose, Eve and Geraint had spread themselves across the archive's tables, each diving into their chosen areas. Maps were unfurled – intricate hand-drawn charts depicting Ashcliffe's coastline, overlaid with faded markings and symbols. Local histories, bound in leather and smelling faintly of mildew, lay open on the desk. "Look at this," Geraint said, pointing to a particularly detailed map from the late eighteenth century. "The 'Fisherman's Route.' It shows a direct path from Ashcliffe to... Well, it loops around to what is now called Louisa's Cove."

Eve peered closer. "And see these little symbols? Little waves with spirals inside?"

"Indeed," Geraint confirmed. "They're quite common on maps from that era. Often associated with tides and currents – but also with folklore." He flipped through the pages of a local history book. "There's even a reference here to a group called 'The Shore Watchers.' Apparently, they were tasked with observing the sea and its moods, interpreting omens, and warning the community of approaching storms."

Eve's eyes widened. "The Shore Watchers? I haven't seen anything about them before." She scanned through Emily's notes again. "Wait... she had a sketch of them – in one of her notebooks!" They spent the next hour poring over records related to The Shore Watchers, discovering they were a relatively obscure but significant part of Ashcliffe's history, particularly active during the eighteenth and early nineteenth centuries. They found references to rituals performed on the cliffs – often involving observation and... lavender.

"Interesting," Geraint said, tapping his pen against his chin. "They were known for their accuracy in predicting storms. And they were deeply connected to local folklore." He pointed to a faded photograph of a group of stern-faced men and women, dressed in period clothing. "Notice the uniforms – they're adorned with spiral seashell motifs."

"Was Louisa a Shore Watcher before she ever married into the Thorntons?" Eve asked, incredulously, holding up a portrait of Louisa.

Geraint examined the photograph carefully. "That's a fascinating question... Her gaze... it's almost like she is observing something – out at sea." He paused, considering. "It certainly feels possible. It adds another layer to the mystery. Proof, if ever I saw it, that folklore evolves with each telling."

The Saltwater Siren was unusually subdued for a Friday evening, the usual clatter of glasses and chatter replaced by a quiet anticipation. It was Emily Thornton's anniversary – one year since her sudden death, and tonight, Stella was performing "The Tide Remembers Everything," a song she'd written in honour of Emily... and of Ashcliffe's hidden past. Stella herself looked nervous, fiddling with the strap of her guitar and taking deep breaths. The air hung heavy with memory, a mixture of grief and hope. "Just breathe, Stella," Krissy offered, draping a comforting arm around her friend. "Let it carry you."

Stella nodded, adjusting the microphone. "It feels... special tonight," she whispered, glancing at the collection of Emily's belongings – a faded photograph, a lavender sprig, and Emily's favourite tambourine – arranged on a small table near the stage. "Like she's here, watching."

The room was filled with familiar faces: Krissy, Albert, Eloise, Rita, and Tom, were there with Eve and Geraint, all drawn together by their shared connection to Emily and the mysteries of Ashcliffe. A few candles flickered, casting dancing shadows across the walls adorned with nautical charts and faded photographs. As Stella began to strum a gentle chord on her guitar, a hush fell over the room – a collective holding of breath as she prepared to unveil her tribute. Stella's voice, rich and slightly melancholic, filled The Siren. "Dust motes dancing in this attic room..." she began, her fingers gliding effortlessly across the strings. It was a simple opening line, but it immediately transported you to Emily'sArchive – to the scent of old paper and the glow of the desk lamp. The melody was hauntingly beautiful, weaving together elements of folk music and something distinctly... oceanic. She sang about lost sailors and whispered secrets, about tides that remembered and stars that watched over Ashcliffe. Her voice resonated with a deep understanding of the town's history – and perhaps, its heartaches. "Wild-hearted Louisa, hair like sea foam..." she continued, her eyes closed as if seeing images from the past.

The room grew quieter with each verse. People leaned forward, captivated by Stella's performance and the evocative lyrics. A few wiped away stray tears; Mr. Linden in the corner nodded thoughtfully, a faint smile playing on his lips. The song built slowly, gaining momentum like the rising tide, carrying with it the weight of Ashcliffe's longings. Stella's voice soared as she sang, "She wears a gown of kelp and pearl..." The image was vivid – a vision of Louisa, shimmering and ethereal, caught between the land and the sea. "And in her eyes, the colour of the deep..." The lyrics were carefully layered, each phrase building upon the last to create a rich tapestry of Ashcliffe's past. "She whispers tales of longing and of grace," she sang, her voice tinged with sadness. "Of stolen kisses on the cliffside stone..." Then, "And dreams of sailing off into the unknown." The lyrics evoked specific details – a stolen kiss, a weathered stone, a yearning for adventure. It felt as though Stella wasn't just singing about Ashcliffe; she was singing of it, drawing not only upon its legends and lore, but upon its deepest truths.

"They say she rises from the foam so white..." Stella's voice held a note of both mystery and sorrow as she sang, "A siren calling, bathed in silver light." The words hung in the air, poignant and evocative – a direct reference to Ashcliffe's most enduring legend. The imagery was powerful, grounding the song in tangible details and deepening its connection to local folklore. As Stella reached the final verse, her voice full of emotion, a collective intake of breath swept through the room. It felt as though time itself had slowed down. Rita quietly wiped a tear from her eye. Councillor Davies, who'd been sitting silently throughout the song, nodded thoughtfully, a flicker of recognition in his eyes. "She left a piece of her heart beneath the waves..." Stella finished, and for a moment, everything held – silence broken only by the gentle crackle of the candles. Then, Krissy gently draped her scarf over Emily's tambourine – a small but significant gesture of remembrance.

A low murmur of appreciation rippled through the room as Stella lowered her guitar. It felt like a key had turned in something – a lock on Ashcliffe's collective memory. A sense of shared emotion hung heavy in the air, palpable and profound. Even Councillor Davies seemed moved, a subtle softening around his usually stern features. "That was... beautiful," he said quietly, almost to himself. After Stella finished, she took a moment to compose herself, her face flushed with emotion. "Thank you," she whispered, her voice slightly shaky. "It was magnificent," Albert said, his voice filled with genuine feeling. "You really captured the spirit of Emily and Ashcliffe."

"She'd have loved that," Krissy murmured. "It feels like a piece of her is back now."

"Do you think... do you think she knew?" Eve asked, turning to Geraint who was standing beside her.

Geraint gazed thoughtfully at the assembled group. "I believe she did. She had a remarkable intuition. And look," he gestured towards Councillor Davies, "even he seemed moved."

"It's just... it felt like so much history settled in that room tonight," Eva said, a little overwhelmed. "Like we'd finally unlocked something."

"Maybe," Geraint replied, stepping closer and taking her hand. "Maybe this was the beginning of understanding everything. We have a long way to go, but... with Emily's guidance, I think we're on the right track." He smiled, his eyes holding hers. "And maybe," he added softly, "we've found a little bit of ourselves along the way too."

The rain had eased to a gentle mist as Eve stepped out of The Siren, seeking refuge and a warm cup of tea with a few less mourners waiting to shake her hand. The Chiron Café, with its mismatched furniture and comforting aroma of coffee and sea air, was just what she needed. Rita, wiping down the counter with a practised hand, greeted her with a warm smile – a little guarded, perhaps, but undeniably kind. "You look like you could use one," Rita said, gesturing to a chair. "Earl Grey, strong."

"Yes please," Eve replied, gratefully accepting the steaming mug.

As she took a sip, Rita observed her thoughtfully. "You've been looking at Emily's archives like you're expecting to see something," she commented, her voice quiet. "Like you already know."

Eve hesitated for a moment. "Sometimes... it feels that way," she admitted.

Rita nodded knowingly. "Well, then you're in the right place. Let me show you something."

Rita disappeared into a small back room and returned moments later with a wooden shoebox – worn and slightly dusty, tied with a faded ribbon. It felt significant, old, radiating a quiet energy. "My grandfather used to keep things in here," Rita said, placing it on the table between them. "Things he didn't want anyone to forget." Eve carefully lifted the lid of the shoebox, releasing a faint scent of lavender and old wool. Inside lay a collection of tiny treasures – knitted booties in shades of blue and green, a worn wooden toy boat with a chipped hull, and a small seashell, smooth and pearly. She picked up one of the booties, turning it over in her fingers. "I... I've seen these before," Eve said softly, a sense of recognition washing over her. "It's like... a half-remembered dream." She reached for the wooden boat, tracing its worn edges with her thumb. "And this... I feel like I know this boat."

Rita watched her closely. "They were Louisa's," she said simply. "She used to make them for Emily." Eve felt a shiver run down her spine. It wasn't just nostalgia; there was something deeper – as if these objects held more than just childhood memories. They felt imbued with emotion, heavy with secrets. "They feel... important," she murmured, examining the seashell closely. "Like they're waiting to tell a story." Rita carefully unfolded a small, yellowed piece of paper from within the shoebox. It was a note, written in elegant script – Louisa Thornton's handwriting. "Here," she said, handing it to Eve. Eve began to read: "My dearest Miles, The tide is restless tonight, and I find my-self longing for your return. The stars seem to whisper of storms – will you be safe? Do not forget the promise we made beneath the cliffs. I wear a gown of kelp and pearl, waiting for your return."

Eve paused, her eyes widening. "'I wear a gown of kelp and pearl...'" she whispered, turning the note over in her hands. She continued reading: "Fear not for me, my love – though sometimes I feel as if I might be carried away on the next wave. Know that even here, by the sea, you are always with me. Longing to return home." A single tear traced a path down Eve's cheek. "She was so beautiful," she murmured, tracing Louisa's handwriting with her finger. "And... and so brave."

"My grandfather, Samuel – he was Ashcliffe's undertaker for over fifty years," Rita explained, joining Eve at the table. "Everyone thought of him as a quiet, respectable man. But he kept secrets."

"He didn't tell anyone," Rita continued, her voice low. "But he was the one who buried Miles after the storm. No fanfare, no ceremony – just quietly took him away in the night."

Eve stared at her, stunned. "Miles? His body?"

Rita nodded. "Samuel always said it was best that way. That keeping it simple would be easier for everyone. He protected Louisa's memory, I think – and Ashcliffe's. It wasn't a cruel thing," she hastened to add, "just... discreet."

"It's remarkable," Eve said, still processing the revelation. "To carry that secret all those years."

"He was a good man," Rita replied softly, "a quiet guardian of our town's history. And he loved Louisa very much, in his way – so did my grandmother. She was the town's midwife from Louisa's time all the way until Emily's... if you get my drift... even if it meant keeping some things hidden." She gestured to the shoebox. "My grandfather always said family is built on secrets and memories, intertwined like the roots of an old tree."

Eve picked up the small seashell again, turning it over in her hand. It was smooth and cool, radiating a subtle warmth. "It's like... he wanted us to find this," she said, looking at Rita. "He wanted us to know."

"Maybe he knew you'd come," Rita said with a knowing smile. "Ashcliffe has a way of bringing people together - of revealing its secrets in its own time." She paused. "And speaking of bringing people together... Krissy, Tom, and I were just discussing how much everyone is starting to feel the pull – like something's about to happen."

"It's funny," Eve said, a small smile playing on her lips. "I always thought I was the one feeling the pull. But maybe... maybe it's been here all along."

Rita shut up The Chiron Cafe, shooing out the few customers remaining, and telling them to "Join us at The Saltwater Siren!". Eve thought of Emily saying, "The sea always remembers." And now, looking out at the churning grey expanse of the ocean, as she walked alongside Rita, she understood. It wasn't just a poetic observation, it was a fundamental truth. The sea held all of their secrets, their loves, their losses – woven into its currents and etched onto its shores.

The rain intensified. It felt... purposeful, like a gentle push, urging her forward. She closed her eyes for a moment, feeling a strange connection to all those who had come before – the Shore Watchers, Louisa, Miles, Emily, and now herself. "It's... powerful," she murmured, opening her eyes to find Rita watching her with a thoughtful expression. "Like I've finally understood something."

"You have," Rita replied softly, offering her a small smile. "Don't try to force it. Just let it be."

Eve turned back to the sea, captivated by its restless beauty. She felt as though she could see faces in the crashing waves – glimpses of past lives, fleeting images of joy and sorrow. It was like looking into a mirror – reflecting not just her own face, but all those who had been shaped by Ashcliffe's history. Eve felt a sense of both anticipation and trepidation – a feeling that she was standing on the edge of something significant, something profound. "The tide remembers everything..." she whispered, her voice barely audible above the sound of the rain.

17

✒

CHAPTER SEVENTEEN: THE AFTERNOONERS' PICNIC

The morning in Ashcliffe-on-Sea was the kind that settled onto you whether you wanted it to or not – beautiful, undeniably, but with a touch of melancholy. It was overcast, certainly, but the grey was softened by a surprising brightness, and the sea, a shifting palette of grey-blue, stretched out to meet a sky heavy with promise. The air hung thick with the scent of salt and seaweed, mingled with the fainter aroma of woodsmoke from distant chimneys – a familiar cocktail that spoke of settled routines and enduring secrets. It was the kind of morning that suggested Ashcliffe hadn't quite shaken off its recent storms, but it was holding steady, breathing in the quiet afterglow.

Eve had received the invitation to the Afternooners' picnic with a simple card tucked into her post – a handwritten note on cream-coloured paper, signed simply "A." It felt like a casual extension of Emily's legacy – unexpected, yet perfectly fitting. The station was bustling with the usual Ashcliffe rhythm: a handful of locals catching the morning train to London, a couple of tourists snapping photos of the grey sea. It was amongst this quiet bustle that Eve spotted him

– Llewellyn, his dark hair tousled by the wind, a warm smile already spreading across his face as he greeted Eve with an enthusiastic hug. "Eve! Wonderful to see you," he said, his voice a touch deeper than Geraint's, with a warmer timbre that seemed to carry the scent of peat fires and Welsh rain. "Took me ages to find this place – felt like following a particularly stubborn sheep." The other Afternooners – Krissy, Albert, Stella, Eloise, Rita, and Tom – offered greetings, their faces etched with a comfortable familiarity. There was a touch of surprise in their eyes, a quiet acknowledgement that something had shifted since the events surrounding Emily's death.

The walk to the beach was a familiar one, a gentle incline through fields dotted with wildflowers. The group shuffled along together – Krissy chattering animatedly about her garden, Albert offering snippets of local history, and Rita quietly observing everything with a shrewd eye. "Don't let Geraint bore you with his facts again," Eloise teased, earning a small smile from Eve. "He's likeable, but sometimes he could talk to a rock."

"He just likes knowing things," Albert chuckled, glancing at Eve. "And he's quite right, isn't he? A little bit of history goes a long way."

The conversation drifted easily between them – memories of Emily, the latest gossip from the village, and a gentle ribbing about Councillor Davies's increasingly cryptic pronouncements. There was a comfortable ease to their banter, a sense that they'd known each other for years., despite Geraint's relatively recent arrival. As they neared the beach, the sound of the waves grew louder, mingling with the cheerful chatter of the group. The picnic blanket was already spread out beneath a windswept pine tree – a colourful patchwork of cushions and baskets laden with sandwiches, cakes, and lemonade – Rita and Tom's handiwork from earlier that day. The scene felt idyllic, almost jarringly so after the weight of the past few months. It was a simple celebration, a chance to reconnect and enjoy the beauty of Ashcliffe-on-Sea. And as Eve looked out at the grey expanse of the sea, she couldn't shake the feeling that even on this beautiful morning, something – perhaps just beneath the surface – was still waiting to be revealed.

The presence of Llewellyn added a whole new timbre to the group of friends. Krissy was the had the strongest visible reaction, her eyes widening slightly as she offered him a quick hug. "Well, where has Geraint been hiding you, Llewellyn? You handsome devil, get in here!" She practically vibrated with an immediate and rather obvious attraction. Rita simply raised an eyebrow and grinned. Albert, as always, was quietly observant, taking in Llewellyn's appearance – the way the wind ruffled his dark hair, the comfortable lines around his eyes, a hint of sun-kissed skin. "From Cardiff, is it?" he asked, nodding towards Llewellyn's worn leather jacket.

"Indeed," Llewellyn replied, settling onto the blanket with a relaxed grace. "Came to spend a bit of time with my rascal of a younger brother. Ashcliffe's got a good reputation for being...well, steeped in stories." He offered a wry smile. "Though I suspect it might take me longer than expected to unravel all its secrets." He launched into conversation effortlessly, turning to Tom with a quick anecdote about getting lost on the way and nearly ending up at a sheep farm – his self-deprecating humour immediately putting everyone at ease. He asked Albert about the local lighthouse, complimented Eloise's bright cardigan, and even engaged Rita in a surprisingly lively debate about the best type of seaweed for drying.

"It's funny," Llewellyn said, taking a sip of lemonade, "I feel like I've been here before, somehow. Like there's a thread connecting me to this place, though I can't quite put my finger on it... maybe it's just that Geraint won't shut up about the rain and the lack of sheep?" Krissy, who hadn't let go of his arm for a moment, chimed in, "Gosh, you have a way of drawing people in, don't you? Like, I want to tell you my whole life's story just to hear you chuckle." Llewellyn turned his attention back to the group, a hint of amusement playing around his lips. "Well, I try," he said, offering a charming smile. "It's nice to meet folks who aren't completely obsessed with local ghost stories just yet." As he continued chatting, weaving himself effortlessly into the fabric of their conversation, Albert observed him with a thoughtful expression. "He's good," he murmured to Stella. "Very good. Like a well-worn map – familiar and comforting, yet hinting at hidden paths."

Llewellyn's presence wasn't just about charm: it was about a quiet confidence, an easy warmth that seemed to radiate outwards, drawing people in and making them feel... seen. And as Eve watched him from the corner of her eye, she couldn't help but wonder what secrets he carried. Nobody was as free and easy as Llewellyn appeared to be, were they? Maybe, she thought, I'm overthinking things. He's gorgeous and warm... although clearly nothing in comparison to my Geraint – Eve blushed at that. When had he become her Geraint? When Eve returned from her thoughts, she found the rest of the group had settled down. The grey sea stretched out before them, vast and restless, meeting the sky in a hazy blue line – a constant reminder of Ashcliffe's wild, untamed spirit.

The group had settled into a comfortable rhythm of picnic preparation. Krissy, ever the enthusiastic organizer, directed operations with gusto, spreading yet more blankets across the damp sand and arranging cushions with meticulous care. Albert efficiently unpacked a wicker basket overflowing with sandwiches and cakes, while Rita quietly sorted through a cooler filled with drinks – her dry wit adding a touch of sardonic commentary to everything they did. "Right," Krissy announced suddenly, clapping her hands together, "Operation Afternooners is a go! And it's time for a little... teapot treasure hunt!"

A ripple of laughter spread through the group. "Teapot treasure hunt?" Eloise questioned, raising an eyebrow.

"Indeed!" Krissy declared, brandishing a small, handwritten card. "I've hidden five teapots around the cove – each with a clue attached! Whoever finds them all first wins... bragging rights and eternal glory!" She read out the first clue: "Find the teapot that remembers the highest tide."

"Ooh, tricky," commented Rita, scanning the shoreline. "Sounds like it's down by those rocks."

"And then there's this one," Krissy continued, pointing to a card with a slightly faded illustration. "'Find the teapot that whispers of Emily Thornton' – that's gotta be somewhere near the old lighthouse, down in Siren's Hollow!"

Llewellyn, who had been listening intently, chuckled. "Sounds like you've put a lot of thought into this."

"Of course! It's good to have a bit of fun," Krissy said, grinning mischievously. "I'm also eager to see how quickly you can find them all."

The atmosphere immediately lightened with the playful competition. The air filled with the sounds of laughter and friendly chatter as everyone scattered across the cove – searching for the hidden teapots. "I'll take the 'Emily Thornton' one!" Albert called out, heading towards the cliffs. "Always good to honour the local legends."

"Don't think you'll beat me," Krissy retorted, already sprinting towards the rocks. "I know this coastline like the back of my hand!"

General merriment settled over the group – shared jokes about past Ashcliffe incidents, nostalgic reminisces about Emily and her eccentricities, and comfortable silences punctuated by the sound of crashing waves. Eve found herself smiling easily, enjoying the warmth of the company and the simple pleasure of a sunny afternoon spent with these quirky locals. "You know," Llewellyn said, approaching her as she examined a teapot nestled amongst some seaweed, "for someone who seems to spend most of her time observing, you're awfully good at blending in."

"I've spent years as just a quiet observer," Eve replied, returning his smile. "It's taking me a minute to get fully involved in everything, it's not what I'm used to!" He winked – a small, charming gesture that made her heart skip a beat. She'd have to have a word to Geraint about the power of a well-placed wink. Suddenly, Rita yelled out from across the cove, "I've got one! The 'highest tide' teapot! It was hiding under a rock shaped like a grumpy seal!"

By the time they'd finished the hunt for teapot, the rain had ceased, leaving a glistening sheen on the sand and a feeling that something special was about to happen. As Tom raised his glass in a slightly unsteady toast, a genuine warmth spread across his face – a quiet sincerity underscored by a hint of melancholy. "To Eve," he said, his voice carrying just a touch of gravel. "May she find the Key of Echoes." His words hung in the air for a moment, heavy with unspoken meaning. Then, it was Stella's turn. She didn't simply offer a cheerful affirmation, instead she leaned forward, her eyes alight with an almost feverish intensity. "It has to be, doesn't it?" she murmured to herself, pulling out a small notebook and a pencil from her basket. As she spoke, she began sketching furiously – quick, flowing lines depicting musical notation overlaid onto a sketch of the coastline. "Think about it – Miles Thornton was obsessed with the music of the storm. He collected instruments from sailors who'd heard the siren, they said. And he believed certain intervals, particular chords... they resonated with the sea itself. Like a tuning fork. Maybe the siren wasn't just a voice – maybe her song was the key – a specific sequence that unlocks something. Like Emily always said, 'The sea chooses its own bride,' and she often chose to sing when the tide was right."

Stella pointed to a section of her sketch where she'd scribbled down musical symbols above a wave crashing against the rocks. "It's not just about finding a physical key," she explained, showing it to Eve. "It's about hearing it – feeling it in your bones." Albert added his thoughts with a thoughtful frown. "A 'literal key' does seem a bit...simplistic, doesn't it? If it's not musical, maybe it's more metaphorical. A symbol of something deeper – perhaps a connection to the land, or to their family history."

"Or maybe," Krissy chimed in, leaning forward with her hands on the blanket, "Eve is the key. Like, women in her family have always understood something about this place. It's like... she just gets it." The comment hung in the air for a moment, laced with both affection and a hint of something more. A comfortable silence settled over the group, punctuated by the cries of gulls overhead.

Geraint, who had been quietly observing, offered a wry smile. "Well, she certainly has a knack for getting lost in the details," he said, glancing at Eve. "Though I suspect her approach is slightly more intuitive than Albert's."

"He's just being practical," Eve countered with a playful roll of her eyes, returning Geraint's gaze. There was a comfortable intimacy to their banter – a shared history and a growing awareness of each other. As Eve looked at Geraint, she felt that familiar flutter in her chest, a subtle reminder of the connection they'd been building. Stella continued to elaborate on the siren legend, drawing upon local folklore. "They said," she said, her voice taking on a hushed tone, "that the siren's song could be heard even miles out to sea – a deceptive beauty that lured sailors in with promises of warmth and safety. It wasn't just about luring them onto the rocks, it was about drawing them in, promising solace and belonging."

"And," she added, sketching again, "that sometimes...women from this line were 'fused' with the sea – their spirits becoming one with its currents and mysteries." Rita, who had been quietly sipping her lemonade, offered a subtle observation that tied everything together. "It's not always about what you see, is it?" she said, her gaze drifting out to the sea. "Sometimes...it's about what you feel. About sensing things others miss."

"Exactly!" Stella exclaimed, nodding vigorously. "Like Eve – she feels the tide pulling at her, doesn't she? She just needs to learn how to listen."

The conversation flowed easily between them, weaving together threads of local lore and family history. The more they talked about the siren, the stronger the sense became that Ashcliffe was more than just a quaint coastal town – it was a place steeped in ancient magic and secrets, waiting to be uncovered. As the sun began to dip towards the horizon, casting long shadows across the beach, Llewellyn leaned forward, his eyes twinkling. "You know," he said quietly, "I'm definitely starting to believe that there's something special about this place. Something...old."

He glanced at Eve, a hint of curiosity in his gaze. "Like it remembers things." And as the last rays of sunlight faded away, leaving behind a sky painted with shades of pink and orange, it felt like Ashcliffe itself was holding its breath, waiting for Eve to unlock its secrets – one teapot, one melody, one 'key' at a time.

It was just then that Councillor Davies appeared, as if summoned by the tide itself – sudden, unexpected, yet entirely fitting with the atmosphere of Ashcliffe. One moment he was simply there, a comfortable silhouette against the grey sky, and then – without so much as an announcement – he had settled down on a blanket near them, thermos in hand and newspaper spread before him. The group was only slightly surprised – they were used to his sporadic appearances, like a particularly observant seabird – but not overly alarmed. It wasn't the first time he'd materialized out of nowhere. He simply continued reading, seemingly oblivious to their surprise, until Stella offered a gentle, "Good afternoon, Councillor."

"Just thought I'd say hello," he replied without looking up, his voice measured and polite. "It's lovely to see you enjoying the sunshine." He took a slow sip from his thermos, then folded down his newspaper with deliberate care. It was a small gesture – understated and unassuming – but it spoke volumes.

Eve found herself momentarily taken aback. She hadn't expected him, hadn't anticipated that he would join them. A little surprise mingled with a touch of guardedness settled within her – a familiar feeling sheathed in a layer of observation. She didn't immediately reject him; she simply returned his gaze, a slight lift of an eyebrow the only indication of her interest. "Hello," she said softly, keeping her tone neutral. He observed her for a moment, his grey eyes thoughtful and perhaps – Eve thought – slightly knowing. "I know you've been busy with the Archive... it must feel like a big responsibility." It wasn't a direct question, not an interrogation. It was simply an observation, delivered with genuine interest. He hadn't pressed her, hadn't offered to help or to share in her burden. "It has been," Eve admitted quietly, turning slightly towards the sea. "A lot of work, I mean. But now I've digitized everything, it feels comforting, in a way."

"Comforting?" he prompted gently. "To sift through all those old papers?"

"Yes," she said, finding herself drawn into his quiet observation. "It's like... connecting with someone who was – and is – still here."

Councillor Davies nodded slowly, as if understanding something she hadn't quite articulated. "Emily was a remarkable woman," he remarked, a hint of fondness in his voice. "Kept this town ticking over for years."

"She did," Eve agreed, her gaze fixed on the horizon. "And she left us a lot to figure out." A comfortable silence settled between them – not awkward, but filled with an unspoken awareness. He didn't try to break it, allowing her to simply be – observing her as if she were a particularly interesting exhibit in a museum.

"I was just up at the Archive myself last week," he said finally, folding his newspaper once more. "Looking through some of her correspondence. Quite fascinating."

"Did you find anything interesting?" Eve asked, a genuine curiosity prompting her to break the silence.

"A few things," he replied with a small smile. "Little snippets that paint a picture. It's amazing how much a single letter can reveal." He paused, then added quietly: "I always thought she had a rather keen eye for detail." His motivation wasn't overt, not expressed in grand pronouncements or eager offers. It was subtle – a quiet desire to be part of her world, to acknowledge her efforts, and perhaps, even to offer a little support. He seemed content simply to observe, to share in the moments, to let her know that she wasn't alone in unravelling Ashcliffe's secrets.

"Thank you," Eve said softly, turning back to him. "For stopping by."

"My pleasure," he replied, returning to his newspaper. "Just wanted to make sure you weren't getting too bogged down in all those papers."

As she watched him read, a small smile played on her lips. There was something reassuringly familiar about the Councillor – a quiet strength and an underlying sense of knowing that resonated with her own. It wasn't love, not yet, perhaps, but it felt like... a connection. A gentle thread woven into the tapestry of Ashcliffe's history, just waiting to be discovered. As the afternoon progressed, a subtle shift occurred in Ashcliffe's atmosphere – as if responding to the gathering of its residents. The grey sky deepened slightly, casting the coastline in an even more dramatic light. A fine drizzle began to fall, clinging to the heather and adding a fresh scent of salt to the air. Overhead, a lone seagull cried out, its call echoing across the cove – a plaintive sound that seemed both ancient and familiar.

Eve found herself caught between happiness and a slight sense of being overwhelmed. The company of the Afternooners was genuinely comforting – their easy banter and shared memories offering a welcome respite from her solitary work at the Archive. But with Geraint there, his quiet intensity and perceptive gaze, she felt a pull – a current of something deeper and more intriguing. It wasn't a jarring feeling, not unpleasant, but rather a gentle reminder of the complexities beneath the surface. And then, it happened – a fleeting image flashed through her mind: Louisa, standing on the rocks at Louisa's Cove, bathed in the golden light of the setting sun. It was just for a moment – a whisper of memory – but it felt incredibly vivid, as if she were actually there. Eve blinked, and the image was gone, leaving her slightly disoriented. She glanced around, half expecting someone to comment on herwardrobe, but everyone seemed absorbed in their own conversations or games.

Krissy was attempting (and failing) to teach Tom how to skip stones, while Rita patiently explained the local folklore about the

'Singing Sands' – a stretch of beach where, it was said, you could hear the voices of sailors lost at sea. – Geraint was taking notes furiously as she spoke. Albert was meticulously sorting through a collection of seashells, muttering about their geological origins. But her eyes kept drifting back to Geraint – his brow furrowed in concentration, his dark hair falling across his forehead. A small smile tugged at her lips – he looked utterly content. The rain picked up, drumming a gentle rhythm on the beach and turning the sand beneath their feet to a soft, damp powder. It didn't dampen their spirits though, instead, it seemed to deepen the sense of intimacy – as if the elements themselves were conspiring to bring them together.

As the afternoon wore on, they played games – a spirited game of charades that ended with Albert dramatically declaring himself "a very confused lobster," and a slightly chaotic attempt at building a sandcastle. With each laugh, each shared joke, Eve felt herself relaxing into the moment, letting go of some of her reserve. Finally, she found herself standing beside Geraint, watching the others. The sea stretched out before them – vast and restless, its grey surface reflecting the shifting sky. It was a beautiful scene – simple and serene – but also imbued with a sense of mystery. "It's funny," she said softly, breaking the comfortable silence. "Sometimes I feel like I've been here before."

Geraint turned to her, his eyes full of curiosity. "Do you?"

"Like... Ashcliffe knows me," she replied, gesturing towards the sea. "Even if I don't always know it myself."

He reached out and gently brushed a strand of hair from her face – a small, tender gesture that sent a warm current through her. "Perhaps," he said quietly, his gaze fixed on her. "It's just waiting for you to remember." And as the rain continued to fall, and the laughter of the Afternooners drifted across the cove, Eve realized that this was just one step on a longer journey – a path leading deeper into the secrets of Ashcliffe's past, and perhaps, into the heart of herself. The sea stretched out before them – beautiful, vast, and full of untold stories – hinting at both beauty and mystery.

18

CHAPTER EIGHTEEN: THE TIDE ALWAYS REMEMBERS

The rain continued, a persistent, cleansing drizzle that had been falling since dawn. Now it was heavier, clinging to the air with a cool dampness, but cleaner somehow, washing away the dust and grime of the day. It slicked the coastal path beneath Eve's boots – a narrow ribbon of grey-stone winding its way away from Louisa's Cove – and reflected the muted light in shifting pools. The scent was immediate, familiar: salt and the sharp tang of damp earth, overlaid with a subtle, lingering sweetness – lavender. A ghost of Emily, clinging to the air like sea foam. Eve paused, tilting her head back to take it all in. It wasn't just a pleasant smell, it felt... significant. The weight of it all settled on her then – Emily's Archive, meticulously digitized and now resting safely in the local museum, her family history unearthed and rewritten, the undeniable connection she'd always sensed to this wild, windswept place. A bittersweetness tightened around her chest – gratitude for the knowledge, the sense that she'd finally understood, but also a touch of melancholy, like watching a beloved painting fade with time.

"The Sea Remembers," Emily had said, just before she died, her voice soft and slightly breathless. It wasn't just a phrase – it felt like a promise, a key. Eve had repeated it almost as a mantra, and now, standing here on the edge of the cove, it echoed in her mind. Then she saw it – embedded in the path, half-hidden by a damp patch of moss. A spiral seashell, perfect in its symmetry, catching the light with a muted gleam. Identical to those carved into the cliff face at Louisa's Cove, and depicted repeatedly in Emily's notebooks. It wasn't just a lucky find – it felt deliberate, placed there as if a final reassurance.

The image triggered a small, fleeting memory – Emily pointing it out to her, kneeling beside her on the beach, explaining its significance. "It's a marker, Eve," she'd said, her eyes bright with that familiar spark of excitement. "A reminder that everything leaves a trace." Now, as Eve knelt to examine it more closely, brushing away the clinging earth, a shiver ran down her spine. The wind picked up momentarily, carrying with it the scent of brine and something else – something faintly floral. And without thinking, almost as if spoken aloud, she whispered: "Goodbye, Emily. Goodbye, Louisa." The sound felt strangely resonant, hanging in the air for a moment before being swallowed by the rhythmic crash of waves against the rocks. As she gazed out at the swirling grey sea, at Louisa's Cove shrouded in mist and rain, a palpable sense of presence washed over her – not threatening, but comforting, familiar. It was as if Louisa herself were watching, waiting. A single drop of rain landed on her cheek, cool and light, and for just a moment, she felt undeniably, profoundly home.

The path wound upwards now, leading her into Louisa's Cove. The rain hadn't lessened, but the light had shifted – bathing the cove in an ethereal glow as if filtering through clouds of pearl. It was darker here, more atmospheric, and the carving of the siren on the cliff face seemed clearer, almost glowing with a faint inner light. It wasn't just a depiction – it felt like a watchful eye, guarding the secrets within. As Eve approached the point where she often imagined seeing Miles Thornton standing – by himself, contemplating the sea – Eve whispered "Goodbye, Miles." This time, it was more pronounced, a genuine farewell to the man who was such a big part of the shape of Ashcliffe, to the enigma of his disappearance. A slight breeze picked up, carrying with it the faintest scent of pine and sea salt. She almost felt like she was hearing his voice on the wind, low and resonant, as if carried across the waves from a distant shore.

The path led into Siren's Hollow – a small, enclosed space dominated by ancient standing stones, covered in lichen and moss. It felt immediately colder here, imbued with an energy that prickled her skin. She continued to whisper, this time fragments of memories: Emily reading to her about pirates and smugglers, telling her of Louisa's obsession with sailors, and of the legend of the siren, snippets of conversations she'd overheard in the Archive – tales of hidden treasure and long-lost loves. A flash of colour caught Eve's eye – a patch of bright purple heather blooming amongst the grey stones. And then it came, a fragment of a memory, vivid and sudden: herself as a little girl, maybe six or seven, listening intently to Emily reading from one of Louisa's journals. She remembered the hushed tones, Emily's warm hand resting on hers, and the captivating story of the siren – a beautiful woman who lured sailors to their doom with her song. The memory sharpened, becoming clearer: Emily describing how Louisa had been captivated by the siren's beauty and mystery, drawn to her like a moth to a flame. She saw herself then, perched on Emily's lap, wide-eyed with wonder as she turned the pages of the journal. "Don't you think it's a little sad?" Emily had asked, her voice soft. "To be so beautiful, and yet so lonely?"

A deeper breath, and another memory surfaced – this time Emily was sketching in a small notebook, capturing the curve of a wave, the glint of sunlight on the water. "The sea chooses its own bride," she'd murmured to herself. The weight of knowing pressed down on Eve then – not a heavy burden, but a sense of connection, of belonging. She was carrying the echoes of generations, their loves and losses, their secrets and dreams. It wasn't just about finding answers, it was about understanding a lineage, a story woven into the fabric of Ashcliffe itself.

The path wound gently downwards again, its stone edges slick with moss and soft rain. Eve lingered by the last of the standing stones, fingers brushing over its surface as though it might hum beneath her touch. The drizzle had softened to a mist, the kind that seemed to rise as much as fall, hanging in the air like breath. The waves murmured below, tireless, patient. And then she saw him. Geraint. Her Geraint. He wasn't rushing toward her, wasn't calling her name. Instead, he moved along the coastal path with the ease of someone who had always known he would be there at just this moment. The rain had darkened his coat, clinging to his shoulders and hair, and in his hands, wrapped in a simple piece of linen, he carried something delicate. As he reached her, he unfolded the cloth to reveal a small sprig of lavender – dried, pressed, carefully preserved. Her breath caught.

He said nothing at first. He simply held it out, like a peace offering, like a memory. Eve took it gently, as though it might crumble at the touch, and held it close. A ghost of Emily passed between them. For a while, they didn't speak. They walked together, shoulder to shoulder, toward the edge of the cove. The sea pulsed before them in slow, glassy waves, the foam shining in irregular patches, silver-white against the greys and greens of the shore. The rain had slowed to a fine mist, leaving everything blurred, softened. It wasn't silence between them – more like a shared listening. The kind of quiet where words aren't needed because the air is already full. Then, softly, he said it: "Come." He didn't explain. He just nodded toward the foam, toward the ocean stretching endless and wide, and began to step down, his boots sinking slightly into the wet sand. Eve stayed where she was, watching him. He wasn't insistent. He simply waited, standing ankle-deep where the sea reached the shore and then pulled back again.

She stared at the horizon. The line where sky met water was dissolving, mist-laced and uncertain. She thought of Emily's last words. The Sea Remembers. Of Miles in his photographs with his searching eyes. She thought of the Archive, of the siren carved into the rocks at Louisa's Cove, and of the spiral shell in the path. She thought of her own breath, steady now, and how strange it was to feel so much stillness at the edge of something so vast. A step forward. Then another. Her boots touched water. The sea was warmer than she expected – not just warmer than the air, but almost strangely alive. It swirled around her feet, curling in long tendrils of foam, dancing over her ankles as if welcoming her. She looked up at Geraint. He smiled – not wide, but steady – and extended a hand. Eve took it. They walked together, slowly, deliberately, as the waves came and went. The foam grew denser the deeper they went, not receding like normal surf but clustering around their legs in iridescent whorls. The beach faded behind them in the mist, the cliffs of Ashcliffe blurring into suggestion. The world narrowed and deepened, becoming sound and light and motion. It didn't feel like walking into the ocean. It felt like stepping through a portal into somewhere else. Something else.

Eve tightened her grip on Geraint's hand. Around them, the foam shimmered, catching light from nowhere she could place. It clung not with chill but with comfort, like gauze or silk. Every step was soundless, but each seemed to carry more weight, as though they were leaving imprints not in sand, but in something older. Timeless. Then he stopped. Geraint turned to face her. The foam lapped gently at their knees now, almost reverent. His face was calm, but his eyes – those storm-grey eyes – held the flicker of something vulnerable, something fiercely human. "Eve," he said. Her name in his mouth felt like an anchor. "You've unearthed so much... for Ashcliffe, for Emily... and now, for us." She blinked, but said nothing. He went on, quietly, as if not wanting to startle whatever ancient peace surrounded them.

"You don't just belong here," he said. "You are here. You always have been. In the way you walk these cliffs, the way you listen to the stones, the way you look at the sea – as if it might speak back." Her throat tightened. He took a breath, unsteady, and reached into the pocket of his coat. From it, he drew a small object – silver, time-worn, but catching the light just so. A ring, shaped like a seashell. Not polished. Not new. The kind of thing someone might find buried at the base of a standing stone, or hidden in the pages of an old, weathered journal. He held it out. "Will you let me walk beside you?" he asked. "Not just here, not just today. Through all of it. The stories. The questions. The tides. I don't have all the answers, Eve. But I know the sea brought you back to yourself. And... I know I love the person it brought back."

Her eyes stung, salt and rain indistinguishable. She looked at the ring, then at him. The sea foamed gently at their knees, retreating and returning. Behind them, Ashcliffe waited. Ahead, only the shifting horizon. She reached for the ring. Not fast. Not theatrical. Just certain. "Yes," she whispered. It was all the sea needed to hear. They kept walking. There was no end to the sea, but the sense of movement shifted. The water deepened only slightly, never past their waists, and the foam – thicker now – clung around them like gauze spun from memory. The air shimmered. Sound grew muffled, dreamlike. Even the rhythmic crash of the waves softened, as though heard from beneath the surface of something older than time. Eve felt light. Not physically – though her body did seem to carry less weight – but in a deeper, stranger way. The burden she had carried for so long, of questions unanswered, of connections frayed and tangled, had begun to dissolve. The foam wreathed her arms and curled around her fingertips, and with it came not silence, but sensation – warmth, closeness, a sense of being deeply, profoundly held.

And then – memories. Not fragmented, not distant, but vivid, flowing as naturally as breath. She saw herself, just a few months ago, on a blanket spread across the lawn of Ashcliffe Park. The grass still dew-damp beneath them, Geraint handing her a paper-wrapped sandwich he'd claimed was "a local speciality, from The Chiron Cafe" and which turned out to be almost entirely pickled beetroot. She had laughed until her ribs ached, and he had looked at her as if the sound itself had unspooled some knot within him. Another flicker. A rainy afternoon in the Archive. She sat on the stone windowsill, pages of

Emily's notes spread around them like feathers. Geraint read aloud in a voice just above a whisper, pausing now and then to glance up at her. The room smelled of parchment and rain and his tea – spiced, with a hint of something floral. He'd brought it for her, unasked. "You looked cold," he'd said, not quite meeting her eyes.

And another. The two of them huddled under a too-small umbrella outside the butchers, laughing uncontrollably after finding a note in the Archive that read simply: "Find the bones, but beware the goat." No explanation. No context. The absurdity of it – and their shared delight in the mystery – lingered like a thread, tying them back to that moment again and again. The foam shimmered brighter for a moment, casting silver light across their faces. She turned to look at him. Geraint's hand was still in hers, his fingers interlaced with hers like roots woven into the soil. And yet... they were no longer just their own memories. She felt Miles, too – standing silently at the cliffs, his coat whipping in the wind, a letter folded tightly in his hand. Felt his yearning, his guilt. Louisa beside him, her voice fierce and wild, her eyes searching the horizon not for rescue, but for recognition. The two of them intertwined, their lives echoing against the stone of Ashcliffe and the lull of the tide. Not doomed, as the legends suggested but unfinished. Waiting.

A glimmer, a voice – Louisa's perhaps – low and sweet as the hum beneath a wave: "Even the lost things leave a wake." The sea shimmered again. Eve closed her eyes. She let it take her deeper – not into the water, but into the feeling of it. It wasn't drowning. It wasn't vanishing. It was merging. With memory. With story. With him. She understood, then. This place – Ashcliffe, the cove, the Archive, the siren carved in stone – had never asked her to solve its mysteries. Only to remember. Only to listen. Only to carry it forward. She was not here to extract answers, to carve a clear path through mystery. She was here to belong. To carry the voices of those before her not as burdens, but as echoes inside her own. Her lips parted, but she said nothing. Words felt unnecessary now. Geraint's arm wrapped gently around her waist, grounding her as the mist thickened around them. They were no longer walking, not exactly. The sea pulsed at their knees, and the horizon bled into sky. It could have been dusk. Or dawn.

The moment felt endless. And still, not empty. She leaned her head against his shoulder. He turned slightly, pressing his cheek into her hair, and they simply stood like that – joined, steady, quiet. Another memory surfaced – this one older, distant. Eve at ten, collecting shells in the shallows with Emily. She'd found a flat, heart-shaped stone and clutched it like treasure. "Some things," Emily had said, "are meant to be found. Even if you didn't know you were looking." That stone had vanished years ago. But the lesson hadn't. Now, Eve glanced down at the waves and saw a similar stone half-submerged at her feet. She didn't pick it up. Didn't need to. Just seeing it was enough – a sign, a reminder that nothing truly disappears. The tide rolled in again, brushing cool foam along her calves. She felt the salt on her lips, the dampness on her eyelashes. Somewhere distant, the faint clang of a buoy echoed – a small, rhythmic sound carried by the breeze, patient as breath. It sounded like punctuation. Like something closing. Or opening.

Geraint shifted beside her. His voice, when it came, was soft. "Do you feel it?" he asked.

Eve nodded. "I think I always did." A pause. Then: "I thought coming here would give me answers. But that wasn't what I needed. I needed... this. The remembering. The being."

"I know," he said. "That's what brought me back too. Not facts. Not the past. But the pull of it. Of you."

She smiled faintly and touched his face – thumb brushing just under his eye. "You waited."

"I would have waited forever."

The simplicity of it – no grand declarations, no melodrama – pierced her more deeply than any passionate plea. It was just truth. Quiet. Steady. Certain. They stood a little longer, the foam around them swirling like a slow dance.

Birdsong, faint but persistent, drifted from somewhere up the cliff. The rain had stopped entirely now, though droplets still clung to her lashes. She tasted them – salt and sweetness, like the memory of tears. She turned to him once more, and though she didn't speak the words aloud, she thought them clearly, as if willing them into the sea: Yes. I'll walk beside you. Wherever the story leads. The sky lightened, not dramatically, but in slow, measured hues – silver into blush, blush into pearl. The mist began to lift. Around them, the sea seemed to sigh, as though acknowledging the moment. The embrace of the tide slackened, ever so slightly, giving them room to breathe. Eve drew in a long, slow breath. The scent – brine, lavender, and distant pine – was now part of her. The sound of the waves, the heartbeat of the place, drummed quietly under her skin.

She thought of Emily. Of Louisa. Of Miles. And she thought of herself, not as an observer, not as a seeker, but as a thread in the story's weaving. A continuation. A promise kept. Geraint looked at her and, without speaking, pulled her a little closer. Their hands found each other again, not in need but in knowing. The sea foam curled around them like a signature, like a benediction. And as her eyes fluttered shut, her thoughts no longer jostled or spiralled. They settled. "The tide remembers everything..." Her hand found Geraint's again, and held it with certainty. "...and now, so do I." In the hush that followed, Eve felt something wholly, finally still. And then – quietly, somewhere beyond the mist – the first gull cried into the morning. A new day was rising with the tide.

19

CHAPTER NINETEEN: THE SEAFOAM BRIDE

The rain hadn't entirely ceased, though it was now a gentle, insistent drizzle, clinging to everything like a whispered secret. It painted Louisa's Cove in shimmering reflections – each wet rock, each smoothed pebble catching the light of the rising full moon and scattering it across the damp sand. The tide, swollen by recent storms, lapped at the edges of the beach, pulling back with a sigh that mingled with the rhythmic rush of the waves – a constant, ancient murmur. It was, in its own way, perfect. Lavender hung heavy in the air, a heady perfume mixing with the salty tang of the sea. It wasn't just the sprigs scattered around the cove – remnants from Emily's meticulously curated memorial – but a deeper scent, carried on the breeze, as if the earth itself was exhaling its memories. The stone beneath foot was cool and damp, slick in places, offering a reassuring solidity against the shifting emotions of the day. It felt as though the cove itself held its breath, poised between celebration and remembrance.

A subtle tension hung in the air, not sharp or jarring, but a delicate thread woven through the joyful preparations. A brief squall had swept across the bay just an hour ago – dark clouds gathering for a moment before dissolving into silver light. Then, for just a second, as the tide receded further than it had all morning, there was something else – a flash of pale blue beneath the surface, too quick to identify, leaving only a ripple in its wake. Geraint found Eve standing at the edge of the rocks, gazing out at the sea. She wore Emily's favourite shawl, a soft, cream-coloured wool embroidered with tiny seashells, and her face was partially hidden by a tangle of rain-dampened hair. He reached for her hand, his fingers intertwining with hers. "It feels...right here," he murmured, gesturing to the cove. "Doesn't it?"

Eve turned then, her eyes reflecting the moonlight and the sea. "Like we've finally come home," she replied softly, a hint of wistfulness in her voice. "All this way, to end up back where it all began." She glanced towards Councillor Davies, who stood patiently waiting, holding her bouquet – a riot of white roses and lavender – his face etched with a quiet dignity that belied years of carefully guarded secrets. "He looks...serious," she said, a small smile playing on her lips.

"A little bit," Geraint agreed, squeezing her hand. "But he's a good man, in his own complicated way." He paused, letting his gaze sweep across the cove, taking in the scene – the scattering of guests huddled beneath umbrellas, the musicians tuning their instruments, the scent of woodsmoke from the warming fire. "Do you still think about... Louisa?"

Eve nodded slowly. "Always. She chose this place, didn't she? This wild, beautiful corner of the world." She tilted her head back, letting the rain dampen her hair further. "And she was a Seafoam Bride... part of a legend woven into the fabric of Ashcliffe." The story had always felt almost mythical, a local lore passed down through generations. "It's more than just a story," Geraint said, his voice low. "It's in the water, in the air...in us." He gestured to the sea, its surface now reflecting the moonlight like liquid silver.

A shiver ran down Eve's spine, despite the warmth of Geraint's hand in hers. She felt it then – a subtle pull, as if the cove itself were holding its breath, waiting. A sense of something ancient and powerful, both alluring and slightly unsettling. As she looked out at the sea, she couldn't shake the feeling that tonight, with the full moon and the strong tide, the 'Seafoam Bride' might just choose to reveal herself. And for a brief moment, standing in Louisa's Cove on her wedding day, Eve wondered if she, too, was destined to be one of them – a link in a long chain of women connected to the sea, forever bound by its beauty and its secrets.

The cove itself was starting to buzz with life, guests were beginning to arrive, a colourful tapestry of Ashcliffe faces – familiar and friendly – spread beneath the striped umbrellas. Krissy, a whirlwind of pink chiffon and nervous energy, was orchestrating the final touches on the buffet table, directing Rita with enthusiastic (if slightly bossy) instructions. Eloise, ever observant, was already scanning the crowd with her tarot cards, muttering about 'energy flows' and 'potential delays.' Stella, as always, stood quietly at the edge of the gathering, a melancholic beauty radiating from within, her gaze fixed on the sea. Llewellyn, Geraint's brother, a boisterous presence in a midnight blue velvet jacket and a wide grin, was holding court near the drinks table, regaling Tom with tales of his latest fishing expeditions – punctuated by generous splashes of champagne. There was a comfortable camaraderie between the groomsmen; a subtle dance of banter and shared history that spoke volumes about their growing friendship.

As the last guests settled in, Albert shuffled forward to the makeshift podium – a large, weathered stone – and cleared his throat. "Good afternoon," he began, his voice slightly gravelly but full of warmth. "Or perhaps it's 'good evening,' considering we're being treated to this magnificent display by the moon. And the sea. Always reminding us, isn't she? Of how small – and yet, wonderfully connected – we are." He paused, taking a sip from his glass. "I've been thinking about love lately," Albert continued, his gaze sweeping across the gathering. "And loss. How often do we forget that love is simply another form of memory, isn't it? A way to keep those we've lost close." He chuckled softly. "And Ashcliffe... Ashcliffe has a remarkable knack for holding onto memories. From the smugglers who used these coves centuries ago, to Emily Thornton and her Archive – overflowing with stories waiting to be told." He glanced at Eve, a knowing smile on his face. "There are those," he added quietly, gesturing towards the sea, "who say that the 'Seafoam Brides' are always watching. Observing...waiting."

A ripple of quiet curiosity ran through the crowd. Albert continued, his speech meandering slightly now, as if lost in thought. "They were drawn to this place, you see – to the wildness, to the mystery. And perhaps... to a certain kind of longing. A yearning for something beyond themselves." Albert smiled again, a touch wistful. "It's funny, isn't it? How a simple thing - like a seashell or a sprig of lavender – can hold so much history." Albert nodded knowingly. "Let this cove be a testament to your connection, Eve and Geraint – to the sea, to Ashcliffe, and to each other. It's remarkable," Albert continued, "how even after all this time, you can still feel the echoes of the past. Like a song carried on the wind." He looked pointedly at Stella, who was gazing pensively out to sea. "And sometimes," he added with a twinkle in his eye, "the most beautiful melodies are laced with just a touch of melancholy."

As he finished, a wave crashed against the rocks, sending a spray of seawater high into the air. For a fleeting moment, as the sunlight caught the droplets, they seemed to shimmer – pale blue and iridescent, like the dress of a Seafoam Bride. A collective gasp went up from the guests. Even Councillor Davies looked momentarily startled, his expression unreadable. "Well said, Albert," Krissy declared, clapping him on the back. The rain had eased to a gentle drizzle by now, and the last of the guests were settling in as Councillor Davies approached Eve with the ring cushion. He moved with a quiet dignity, his face etched with a mixture of emotion – and perhaps, just a hint of something else. He wasn't the most demonstrative man – his expressions were often guarded, his words carefully chosen. But now, as he stood before her, bathed in the soft glow of lanterns strung across the cove, he seemed... different.

He knelt beside Eve, offering her the cushion with a gentle smile. "Eve," he said, his voice a little deeper than usual. "I believe you've inherited more than just an archive from Emily." He carefully lifted the ring cushion, revealing a simple yet exquisite silver ring – its surface smooth and cool to the touch. A tiny spiral was carved into one side – almost invisible unless you knew where to look. It was perfect. As he handed it to her, his fingers brushed against hers for a brief moment. "This belonged to Emily," he said quietly, "a reminder that even the smallest things can hold the greatest significance." He looked at her then, really looked at her, and for a fleeting second, Eve thought she saw a hint of vulnerability in his eyes – a quiet yearning for connection. "It's been... a long time coming," he murmured, almost to himself. "Protecting Ashcliffe's secrets was my duty. But it seems I also protected you from them... for a while. For perhaps too long."

Eve took the ring, turning it over in her fingers and studying the tiny spiral. "Thank you," she whispered, her voice thick with emotion. He nodded simply. "You deserve happiness, Eve. And to have found that with Geraint... well, it's a wonderful thing." He paused, then added quietly, "I cherish our friendship too." A wave of emotion washed over Eve – a mixture of joy, gratitude, and a touch of melancholy. She thought of her family – Emily, Louisa, Miles – their lives interwoven with Ashcliffe's history, their stories echoing through the generations. The 'Seafoam Brides', the pirates, the smugglers... it all seemed to converge in this moment, around her. "It's beautiful," she said, turning the ring towards the moon. "Just like Emily always knew it would be." Eve's father wasn't just giving her a ring, he was passing down a piece of Ashcliffe's history. "It's more than just a symbol," he said, his gaze fixed on the sea. "That spiral represents resilience – the ability to weather any storm. And the tide...the tide remembers everything."

Eve looked at the ring again, her heartstrings tugging. It wasn't just a seashell; it was a connection – to her family, to Ashcliffe, and perhaps, even to the 'Seafoam Bride' herself. She felt a sudden awareness of the weight of her legacy – the responsibility that came with carrying on Emily's work, with understanding the secrets of her past. But there was also a sense of peace, of belonging. She wasn't just an observer any more, she was part of something bigger than herself. "Thank you," she said again, this time with genuine warmth. "For everything."

He squeezed her hand briefly before stepping back. "Now, let the celebrations begin," he said, his voice regaining its customary reserve.

As Eve slipped the ring onto her finger, just to check – a perfect fit – she glanced at Councillor Davies. He offered her a small, almost shy smile, and for a moment, she thought she detected a hint of sadness in his eyes – as if he was giving away not just a ring, but a part of himself. Looking down at the simple silver ring, she realized it wasn't just about love or family; it felt like a key – unlocking a deeper understanding of her place within Ashcliffe's story, and perhaps... within the legend of the 'Seafoam Bride'." The rain began to fall again, softer this time, as if blessing their union. And in that moment, surrounded by the warmth of her friends and family, bathed in the light of the full moon and the shimmer of the sea, Eve knew she was finally home – ready to embrace whatever mysteries Ashcliffe held in store.

The cove held its breath as Stella stepped forward, bathed in the warm glow of lanterns and the silvery light of the full moon. Rain had ceased entirely now, leaving a glistening sheen on the wet sand and rocks – a perfect stage for the wedding to unfold. Rita and Tom, beaming with pride, presented the cake – a masterpiece adorned with intricately carved seashells and delicate sprigs of lavender – a beautiful testament to local traditions and a clear nod to Ashcliffe's maritime heritage. As Stella began to play "The Siren's Lament," a haunting melody that seemed to rise from the depths of the sea itself, a palpable shift occurred in the atmosphere. The music was melancholic yet beautiful, filled with longing and a touch of sorrow – perfectly capturing the spirit of the cove. And then, it happened.

During Stella's performance, Eve felt the weight of the seafoam beneath her feet, the pull of the tide within her soul. It was as though the past was reaching out to claim her, welcoming her into its fold. As Stella reached a particularly poignant crescendo, the rain fell soft and gentle, like tears. And then, everyone noticed – a subtle shift in the light, a shimmer in the air. The sea seemed to be responding to the music, its waves growing slightly larger, moving with a rhythmic grace. Albert stepped forward, his face illuminated by the lantern light. He gestured towards the gathering guests. "This isn't just a wedding," he announced, his voice carrying across the cove. "It's a continuation of an ancient 'Sea Blessing' ritual – one that has been performed in Ashcliffe for generations to ensure the happiness and prosperity of the couple and this town." He paused for effect. "It was originally intended for sailors returning from long voyages, but over time, it evolved – incorporating elements tied directly to the 'Seafoam Brides' – women chosen for their connection to the sea, women who held a special place in the hearts of Ashcliffe."

"The ritual," he continued, "is designed to bind Eve and Geraint to this land, to the sea, and to each other – ensuring that their love will endure through thick and thin, just as those 'Seafoam Brides' did before them." He gestured towards a small bowl filled with dried lavender. "As you know," he said, his gaze fixed on Eve, "lavender has always been significant in Ashcliffe – a symbol of remembrance, protection, and love." Then, during the ceremony – as Geraint slipped the swirled silver ring onto her finger – Albert instructed that a small bowl of lavender be tossed into the waves. "This," he explained, his voice filled with quiet reverence, "represents Eve's acceptance of her family's legacy – and of her place within Ashcliffe's story." As the bowl was lifted, a hush fell over the gathering. Geraint handed it to Eve, who took a deep breath and tossed the lavender into the sea. As it floated towards the waves, it seemed to dissolve almost immediately, leaving behind a faint shimmer – as if a tiny piece of its magic had been absorbed by the ocean itself.

"And now," Albert declared with a warm smile, "let us witness the joining of two hearts and the continuation of an ancient tradition."

The music swelled again, and Geraint led Eve towards the altar – a simple stone circle adorned with seashells and wildflowers. As they exchanged vows, looking out at the sea and the faces of their loved ones, Eve felt a profound sense of connection – not just to Geraint, but to her family, to Ashcliffe, and to the generations who had come before. During the exchange of rings, she turned to face the sea, feeling an undeniable pull towards its vastness. She closed her eyes for a moment, and in that instant, she knew – with absolute certainty – that she was home.

As the final notes of "The Siren's Lament" faded away, the rain began to fall again – this time with a gentle rhythm, as if blessing their union and celebrating the beginning of their new life together in the heart of the sea. And for a brief moment, everyone felt it – a sense that something ancient and powerful had been awakened in Ashcliffe that evening – a promise of love, legacy, and perhaps... a glimpse into the future. The full moon reached its peak, bathing the cove in an almost blinding silver light. It seemed to pulse with a gentle energy, intensifying the feeling of magic that hung heavy in the air. As if on cue, a particularly strong tide rushed in – a wave of cool water that surged up the beach, swallowing the sand and rocks in its wake. The waves crashed against the cliffs with renewed vigour, as if celebrating the union taking place before them.

During a brief lull in Stella's haunting performance of "The Siren's Lament," Eve saw her. Not as a fleeting glimpse or a ghostly apparition – but as a vibrant, almost ethereal figure standing on the rocks – Louisa Thornton herself. She was radiant, bathed in moonlight, with long flowing hair that seemed to dance in the wind and eyes that held both sadness and an undeniable warmth. It wasn't a startling revelation; it felt... inevitable. As if she had been waiting her entire life to see her grandmother. Eve stared, transfixed, as Louisa simply stood there – observing her, smiling gently. It was as though time itself had paused for that single moment. There was no speech, no greeting – just a profound sense of recognition and acceptance. Then, she communicated –

not through words, but through images and feelings. Eve saw flashes of Louisa's life: her laughter echoing across the cove, her yearning for adventure, her love for Miles, their secret meetings by the sea. She felt Louisa's longing to escape Ashcliffe, her desire for a life filled with passion and freedom. She heard a wave whisper, "You are home."

It wasn't just Louisa she saw, Eve also saw glimpses of herself – not as she was now, but as a Seafoam Bride too. Not luring sailors to their doom, but choosing them – men drawn to the wildness of the sea, just as she was. A wave of understanding washed over Eve – it wasn't about seduction or tragedy: it was about connection. A reciprocal exchange of love and longing that spanned generations. Geraint noticed Eve's trance-like state immediately. He'd been watching her intently throughout the song, a concerned furrow in his brow. As she remained fixed on the sea, her gaze intense and unwavering, he instinctively reached out and gently took her hand. His touch was warm and reassuring – grounding her back to the present moment. "Everything alright?" he murmured, his voice soft with concern. Eve nodded slowly, unable to speak. She felt a strange sense of peace now – as if a long-held burden had been lifted from her shoulders.

The last image she saw was Louisa extending her hand towards her, a silent invitation to join her in that timeless realm. As the vision dissolved completely, leaving only the sound of the waves and Stella's continuing song, Eve turned to Geraint, a genuine smile gracing her face. "She...she said I'm home," she whispered.

Geraint squeezed her hand tightly. "I told you," he said simply, his eyes filled with warmth. "You were always meant to be here." He tilted his head slightly, observing the small bowl of lavender that still rested on the sand near the altar. "It wasn't about sacrifice," he murmured. "It was about choice." A wave of emotion washed over Eve – a mixture of joy, gratitude, and a profound sense of belonging. She finally understood her family's legacy, her connection to Ashcliffe, and her place within its story.

Councillor Davies stepped forward, his gaze sweeping across the gathering. "Well done, my dear," he said quietly to Eve. "You've truly earned your place amongst the Seafoam Brides." He offered her a small, enigmatic smile – as if sharing a secret known only to them. As they embraced, bathed in the light of the full moon and surrounded by the sounds of the sea, Eve knew that she wasn't just marrying Geraint – she was joining a lineage of strong, independent women, bound together by love, loss, and the enduring magic of Ashcliffe. And as she looked out at the ocean – vast, wild, and endlessly beautiful – she felt ready to embrace whatever mysteries lay ahead. The rain had ceased completely now, leaving behind a glistening sheen on the sand and a cool, salty breeze in its wake. The cove was bathed in the soft glow of moonlight, casting long shadows across the beach. Eve and Geraint stood hand-in-hand, their figures silhouetted against the sea – two souls united by love, history, and a shared connection to Ashcliffe's secrets.

They watched as the waves rolled in, each one carrying with it whispers of the past – echoes of sailors, lovers, and 'Seafoam Brides'. The tide continued its steady rhythm, a constant reminder of the ebb and flow of time and memory. "It feels... right," Eve murmured, turning to Geraint and offering him a shy smile. "Like everything is finally falling into place."

He squeezed her hand reassuringly. "It always did, Eve," he said, his voice filled with warmth. "You just needed to find your way back to it."

She gazed out at the sea, lost in thought. "I used to think I had to solve everything – uncover all the secrets, understand every detail," she said softly. "But now... now I realize it's not about knowing. It's about accepting." She paused, taking a deep breath of the salty air. "About trusting in the mystery – and in the people we share our lives with."

Turning back to face him, she added quietly, "And knowing that sometimes, the greatest adventures are found not by seeking answers, but by simply letting go."

Geraint stepped closer, gently tucking a strand of hair behind her ear. "Like the sea," he said, his eyes sparkling in the moonlight. "It doesn't question its currents. It just flows." A comfortable silence fell between them for a moment – broken only by the sound of the waves and the distant cry of a seagull. Then, Eve turned back to the sea, her gaze filled with a newfound sense of peace and wonder. "I think," she said softly, "that Louisa was right. It is about being connected – to our family, to this place... and to something much larger than ourselves." She looked up at the full moon, now hanging high in the sky – a silvery orb presiding over the cove. "And I think," she continued, a hint of a smile playing on her lips, "that maybe, just maybe, we were destined to be 'Seafoam Brides' after all."

Taking another step forward, Geraint leaned down and kissed her forehead. "Then let's embrace it," he whispered. "Let's let the sea decide."

As they stood there together, hand-in-hand, watching the waves roll in – carrying with them the secrets of Ashcliffe and the promise of a future filled with love and adventure – Eve felt a sense of hopefulness wash over her. It was as if the very air around them shimmered with magic. She turned back to Geraint, her eyes reflecting the moonlight and the sea – and for a brief moment, she thought she saw a hint of something else in his – a knowing smile, a shared secret. "You know," she said, turning back to the ocean, "I think... as the tide remembers everything, so too will we."